HONEST DECEPTIONS

HONEST DECEPTIONS

a novel by

HANNAH HESS

Caravel Books
an imprint of Pleasure Boat Studio
New York

ISBN 978-1-929355-86-0
Library of Congress Control Number: 2013938023

Design by Susan Ramundo
Cover by Herb Stern, with Laura Tolkow

Pleasure Boat Studio books are available through the following:
SPD (Small Press Distribution) Tel. 800-869-7553, Fax 510-524-0852
Partners/West Tel. 425-227-8486, Fax 425-204-2448
Baker & Taylor Tel. 800-775-1100, Fax 800-775-7480
Ingram Tel. 615-793-5000, Fax 615-287-5429
Amazon.com and bn.com

and through
PLEASURE BOAT STUDIO: A LITERARY PRESS
www.pleasureboatstudio.com
201 West 89th Street
New York, NY 10024

Contact Jack Estes
Fax: 413-677-0085
Email: pleasboat@nyc.rr.com

To my sister, Liz Stern,
and to my granddaughters
Allie, Jenny, Sophia, Stephie, Zoe

Hannover, Germany, August 1939

Martin took a last look around the empty apartment. The crates, with their furnishings, had left for New York. The sun streamed through the curtainless windows. A ball of dust sat in a corner, and he stooped to pick it up, putting it, absently, into his trouser pocket. The light spaces on the walls were ghosts of the pictures that had, until recently, hung there. He shook off the memories of the seven years he and Claire had nested here, picked up his medical bag, checked to make sure the passports were safely stowed. He closed the door on the memories, locked it, and went downstairs.

He rang the super's bell, and, wordlessly, handed the keys to Herr Julke, who took them gingerly, as though to avoid contamination with Jewish germs. Without a word he gave the Nazi salute and slammed the door. Martin shrugged. There was one man he wouldn't miss. While Herr Julke had, when they'd first moved into the apartment, been obsequious, and couldn't do enough for Herr Doktor and his family, since January 30, 1933, when Hitler had become Chancellor, everything had changed. Repairs remained undone, garbage stayed uncollected. Herr Julke had hinted broadly that this was not the neighborhood for Dreksjuden and while he had, grudgingly, continued to take their rent money, he had grinned only when Martin had told him they were leaving.

Outside in the warm air Martin took a deep breath and squared his shoulders. He started down the street toward Willie's house. Willie and Martin had been friends since university days, and while Willie had been saddened when Martin told him of their emigration, he had understood. Claire and the children were with Willie, and the four of them would stay until they left for Hamburg in the morning.

Martin, Claire, Willie, and his wife, Eva, sat in the Meinhoff dining room. The dining table was covered by a white linen cloth. The sideboard and vitrine, as well as the chairs on which they sat, were a rich mahogany, the seats upholstered in a dark maroon brocade. On the sideboard stood a silver coffee and tea service, with sugar and creamer. Behind the glass of the vitrine were Meissen figurines—dancers and shepherds—as well as demitasse cups and saucers. The windows were covered with heavy silk drapes in a dark champagne color. On the walls were portraits of men in three piece suits, their watch chains prominent on their protruding bellies. Each patriarch boasted a dueling scar. Clearly Willie's family had gone to University for generations.

The remains of a farewell dinner had been cleared by Suze, the Meinhoff maid, and only their wine glasses and the crumbs of a *ruhrkuchen* remained. The children had been tucked into their beds. Peter was sharing a room with little Willy, who, at almost two, was a golden-haired smiling angel. While, unlike Peter, he did not yet talk or walk, he was an exceptionally good-natured child. Nine-month-old Margot was in a crib in the room Martin and Claire had been sharing since their furniture had gone into the crates.

"This has been wonderful," Claire said, taking a sip of the dessert wine. "I don't know what we'd have done without you."

"You'd do the same for us," Willie said. He lit a cigarette and inhaled deeply, accenting the dueling scar that merely heightened his blond good looks. His blue eyes looked sincerely at Martin. "I hate this," he said. "I wish we could go, too."

"It will pass," Eva said. She was small, plump, like a sparrow. She patted Claire's hand. "When this is over you can come back."

"Never," Claire said. "I don't go where I'm not wanted."

"But ... you'll be wanted again, you'll see," Eva protested. "Hitler doesn't speak for all of us."

"I know not for you, personally," Claire persisted. "But for enough of you. But let's not spoil our last evening together. You've been wonderful friends."

"Our only friends," Martin said.

"That can't be true," Eva demurred.

"It is true. Our only Christian friends. Heinrich wanted to buy my equipment, what's left of it, but I haven't heard a word from him since I told him you were taking it over, Willie."

"Yeah, well, Heinrich. He was always an opportunist."

"But surely," Eva said, "what about Helmut? Julius? Oskar? You were all such good friends."

"Nothing," Martin said. "I suppose I understand. They have their positions, their families. But that's why I'm so grateful to you both . . ."

"Don't," Willie said. "I'm embarrassed. Let's talk about something else. Is your position . . ."

"Mama," a voice wailed from somewhere back in the apartment.

"That's Peter," Claire said, rising.

"Suze will take care of it," Eva said.

Claire shook her head. "No, I'll go. He doesn't usually wake."

She came back a few minutes later, holding her son. His cheeks were flushed, his blond hair pasted wetly to his forehead.

"He's burning up, Martin."

Martin stood, put his hand to the boy's forehead. "Does something hurt?"

The boy buried his head in his mother's neck.

Martin felt his neck. "Swollen glands," he said. "Open your mouth and say 'Aaah,' Peter."

The boy shook his head and buried it deeper. Claire sat down, and placed him on her lap with his back against her breasts.

"Be a good boy, sweetie. Open your mouth and say 'Aaah' for Daddy."

Martin tilted the boy's head back. "Aaah," he said.

Martin shook his head. "Flaming red. Let me get my bag."

When he returned he took out his stethoscope, and put it against Peter's chest, then turned him gently and listened to his back.

"A big cough for Daddy," he said. Peter coughed.

Martin shook his head. He took off the stethoscope and extended it to Willie.

"Listen. What do you think."

Willie listened, said, "Cough, Peter," and listened again. He handed the scope back to Martin.

"Congested," he said. "And he feels very hot."

"Let's give him some aspirin. And a cool bath. Try to get the fever down."

They spent a sleepless night. They had moved Margot's crib into little Williyd. He tossed and whimpered, his breathing rapid and shallow. By morning, when they took his temperature, it was almost 42.

"He can't travel," Martin said.

"But our boat . . . our exit passes. If we don't go . . ."

"You take the baby. I'll stay here with Peter, and when he's well we'll follow."

"Let's all go. I don't want to leave without you."

"They'd never let us take him like this. And if you and Margot go now it'll be easier for me to get passage for Peter and me. You know how hard it is to get four places now, with everyone wanting to leave."

"We should have gone years ago," she said bitterly.

"I wanted to," he reminded her. "But that's pointless now. This is the best way. In a week he'll be good as new, won't you, Petey? Then we'll follow. And this way," he said, flashing the grin she loved, "you'll have the house all ready for us, and dinner on the table. What should Mama cook for us when we get to New York, Peter?"

"Ice cream," he said, perking up for a moment.

Claire fought back tears. "Ice cream it is, sweetie."

CHAPTER 1

New York City, May 1963

Margot looked around the empty apartment. She dropped her keys, along with her new medical diploma in its burgundy leather case, onto the shelf next to the front door. The dust motes danced in the sun streaming through the living room windows. Through the glass doors she could see the room where she and her mother had spent so many evenings, reading and listening to the classical music her mother had loved. When Margot had gone off to college she had tried, with her summer earnings, to buy her mother a turntable and records.

"I'll never get the hang of it," Claire had said. "The radio is fine."

She had been among the last to get a television, had saved, instead, for a washing machine so she didn't have to put their clothes where other people's dirty clothes had been. Her friends had thought her strange—who needed a washing machine when there were perfectly good ones in the basement? But Claire had never cared what people thought. TV she could do without. The washing machine had held pride of place in the kitchen.

Margot kicked off her heels, picked them up, and walked down the long hallway past what had been her mother's bedroom and into her own. She took off the shirtwaist dress she'd worn under her cap and gown, and hung it in the closet. The graduation had been bittersweet. While she was proud of the M.D. next to her name, proud that it was with honors, she'd had no family to share it with. John, her boyfriend, had said, "You can share my parents. Hell, you can *have* my parents," but it wasn't the same. Claire's death, in January, had left her without a family, if you didn't count aunts and uncles and cousins. They were family, she supposed, but they all had their own lives, their own concerns. She had no one, anymore, for whom she was central.

She put on a pair of gym shorts and a tee shirt, then went back into the kitchen and poured herself a glass of grapefruit juice. She sat down at the kitchen table and went through the mail. Mainly junk: a couple of graduation cards, stiff with canned senti- ment, from her aunts and uncles; some letters still addressed to her mother. These she opened before tossing them into the junk pile. She knew she needed to go through her mother's things, decide what to keep and what to throw out. Once she started her intern- ship she knew she'd have no time—but it could wait 'til tomorrow. She was meeting John and his parents for a celebratory dinner in … she looked at her watch … a little less than two hours. She needed a nap and a shower.

Two hours later, napped and showered and suitably dressed in a teal blue silk suit Claire had sewed for her before she'd gotten too sick, she sat at a table at Downey's Steak House, facing John's parents. Dr. Watt was on his second glass of top-of- the-line scotch. His shiny, florid face under carefully cut blond hair hinted that he had had some fortification at the hotel earlier. His wife, every one of her honey-colored hairs obediently in place, sipped a Gibson. Dr. Watt wore a navy blazer with buttons that screamed eighteen carat, gray slacks with a sharp crease, an excruciatingly starched shirt, a Yale tie, and black tassel loafers shined to a gloss even brighter than his face. His wife was elegant in a silk Castleberry knit in a shade slightly lighter than her hair. Her makeup was artfully applied, her face so smooth that Margot was sure she'd had the best plastic surgeon money could buy. John sat next to her, handsome in his blazer and chinos. His shirt, though, was light blue, and his tie had been loosened.

"Would you like a drink?" Dr. Watt asked after she'd been seated.

"Just some iced tea for now," she said. "Maybe I'll have some wine with dinner."

"We can't toast you with iced tea," Dr. Watt said. "Have something. Champagne?"

"Yes, let's, darling," Mrs. Watt said, exposing perfect white teeth in what could have passed for a smile. A waiter was summoned.

"Let's have a bottle of the best champagne you have," Dr. Watt commanded. "These two … ," he pointed his chin at John and Margot, "have just graduated from midical school. The young lady with honors."

The waiter bowed, not quite from the waist, and went off.

"Would have been nice if you'd gotten honors, too," Dr. Watt said to his son.

"Yes, Dad. But you know what they say at med school?"

"No, son, what do they say at med school … these days?" His teeth, also perfectly white and even, were not quite clenched.

"What do they call the person who graduates last in his class at Columbia med?"

"What?"

"*Doctor*," John said with a grin.

The waiter returned with the bottle, flourishing the label at Dr. Watt, and, therefore, sparing him the necessity of a retort.

After the cork was popped, the bubbly tasted and found satisfactory, the waiter poured into four flutes before stepping back with another bow.

"To the new doctors," Dr. Watt said. "May you make the profession proud."

They drank. Margot squeezed John's hand under the table.

"So," Dr. Watt said, "John tells me you're doing your internship in pediatrics. A good field for a woman."

"If she doesn't have children of her own," objected Mrs. Watt. "Imagine, being called out in the middle of the night, away from your own husband." She shook her head at the thought. Nary a hair moved.

"Yes," John said. "I suggested dermatology. No one calls in the middle of the night with an itch emergency."

"Or opthalmology," Dr. Watt said.

"Actually, I wanted surgery, but they gave the spots to two guys."

"Surgery's no specialty for a woman," Dr. Watt pronounced.

"Apparently that's what the Sinai people thought too," she said. "I had better grades, better recommendations, but . . ."

"Yeah, but they had something you don't have," John said. Margot gave him a look. He wasn't going to say "penis" in front of his mother, was he?

"Pull," John continued. "They're both *sons of.* How do you think I got my orthopedics internship? Yes, Father, I'm duly grateful. I know Yale would never have taken me otherwise."

"Why don't we order," Mrs. Watt chirped brightly.

When they returned to her apartment John pulled her to him.

"God, I'm going to miss you," he said.

"We have almost two months," she said.

"I have to go back with my parents. Father laid down the law."

"The law?"

"He won't pay my rent if I stay down here. He wants me home until I start at the hospital. Says his partner's away and he needs my help."

"You could stay here. I have an extra bedroom."

"I wouldn't need an extra bedroom."

They had moved into the living room, settled onto the oversized velour couch. They kicked off their shoes, and lay next to each other. She wriggled out of her jacket, tossed it onto the armchair halfway across the room. He got up, took off his blazer and tie, and placed them neatly on the chair. He came back to the couch and put his arms around her, letting his hand slip under her blouse, and around to cup her breast. She moved closer to him, put her hands under his shirt. She felt him hardening against her. His hand moved under her skirt, stroked her thigh, moved past the garter belt and under the panties. His mouth found her breast, hot through the silk blouse and bra. His finger moved into her. He took her hand, put it on his erection, his other fingers making slow circles inside, around and around and . . . . God, she wanted him.

"Take it out," he said.

She unzipped him, felt the tight curls on his belly. His penis, fully erect, sprang out.

"Let me," he groaned.

"No, I can't."

His fingers continued their circling. She moved closer into him. He took her hand, guided it on him, up and down, up and down, until he shuddered and came. His hand still inside her, he continued his stroking until she too climaxed. Then they lay next to each other, legs intertwined.

"God, I want you," he said.

"I want you too, John."

"Then why not?"

"I can't afford to get pregnant."

"I have condoms."

"And I promised my mother I wouldn't, 'til I'm married."

He said nothing. Slowly he unbuttoned her blouse, took off her bra. She took off his shirt. He stood, took off his slacks and briefs, then unzipped her skirt, pulled off her garter belt and panties, and rolled her stockings down and off. He kissed her leg up and up, and buried his head in her hair.

"You're beautiful," he said. She held his head against her, stroking his hair.

"You could stay," she said. "Just . . . not all the way."

After a while they moved into her bed, and much later they slept.

In the morning she fixed breakfast before he went to meet his parents at the hotel.

"I'll come down weekends," he said before he left. "Or you can come up to our place."

When he was gone she straightened up the living room, picking up her clothes from where they'd dropped. She shook her head at herself. Technically she was still a virgin, she supposed.

Did it matter? Yes, she'd promised her mother.

CHAPTER 2

Hannover, August 31, 1939

The apartment was unnaturally quiet. Eva had put little Willy to bed hours ago, and had herself retired to their bedroom. Peter, still fretful with his fever, had been harder to pacify. Martin sat by his bedside, stroking his blond hair until the boy finally fell asleep. Now he sat in the living room with Willie. A balloon of cognac was in Willie's hand; a cigarette lay in the ashtray on the table next to his armchair, the smoke curling into the light of the floor lamp behind Willie's chair. Martin's cognac sat untasted on the table next to the sofa where he sat. The tables were dark mahogany, shiny with polish, their surfaces inlaid in a dark brown leather. Both were covered by hand-crocheted doilies. The coffee table in front of the sofa, a companion to the end tables, was also protected by a doily, and covered with medical journals, as well as a copy of the morning's *Tageblatt*. Its headline screamed about some Polish perfidy. A photo of Hitler at a rally, adoring crowds with raised arms below the balcony on which he stood, took up half a page under the headline.

"You can't open a paper without seeing that clown." Willie sighed, picking up his glass and inhaling before taking a sip. "Ah, Martin, we should all have left years ago."

Martin said nothing. His deep brown eyes behind his glasses opened more widely.

"Have you been able to get passage?" Willie asked his friend.

"Not yet. There's a possibility for next Tuesday. Peter should be well again by then. And I have a definite reservation for September 12th, the Tuesday after that. Can you put up with us that long?"

"As long as you need. I wish you didn't have to go at all."

"Life isn't possible for us here anymore, Willie. You know that."

"Of course I do. I just mean I wish it weren't that way, that you didn't have to go. You're my best friend."

"You've been more than a friend, Willie. A brother couldn't have done more."

"I wish I could do more. I wish I could change this whole lunacy. I used to think it would pass, but now . . . I think we're in for some bad years. You're lucky to be getting out."

"I'm glad Claire and the baby are out. And I'll be glad to be gone too. But I'll miss you, Willie."

"When it's all over maybe you'll come back. Or we'll come to America. And we'll be your guests, Martin."

Martin lifted his glass. "To our reunion in America." He took a sip.

Soon afterwards they finished their cognac and went to bed.

In the morning the radio crowed the news that German forces had invaded Poland by air, land, and sea. The announcers spoke of the cowardly Poles, of the brave German soldiers. Military music played. Nazi flags flew from all the windows. In the streets neighbors smiled and *Heil Hitler*ed and congratulated each other on the return of the territories that had been perfidiously taken from the Fatherland. The radio spoke of long lines at army centers, of patriotic Germans signing up to help restore Germany to the glory stolen from it by its enemies.

Eva shook her head as she listened. She was in the kitchen, feeding lunch to the two little boys. Peter, for the first time in a week, was without fever, and he chattered happily as he spooned soft boiled egg into his mouth and hair. Little Willy, in a high chair next to Peter, gnawed on a piece of zweiback.

"I'm so glad he's better," she said to Martin, who sat at the table drinking a cup of coffee. "I hate to see them sick."

"It's a wonder Willy didn't catch it. Try telling two-year-olds about germs."

"He's a tough one," she said. "He's only had one cold in his whole life. Funny . . ."

"What?" he asked.

"That he's so healthy physically . . ." She paused, waited for Martin to say something. When he didn't, she continued, ". . . and yet . . ." Again she paused.

"And yet?"

"Willie's never said a word to you?"

"About what?"

"And you've never noticed . . . that he's . . . slow?"

"Children develop at different rates, Eva."

"Yes, I know that, and Willie knows that, Martin. But, look at the two of them."

"I have, I do."

"And you don't see it? He doesn't talk, not even 'Mama' and 'Papa.' He doesn't walk. He didn't sit up until he was ten months old. Peter says whole sentences. Yes, I know. I was a children's nurse before we married, and I know children develop at different rates. Some talk early. Some walk early. But there are normal ranges, and he's just not in any of them. He's a warm and wonderful child, always happy. But he's not normal."

"What does Willie say?"

"He doesn't talk about it. But he worries, I know him. I thought maybe he'd talked to you."

"Not a word. Not ever."

"And now this," she said, pointing to the radio. "Where will it all end?"

"I don't know. I imagine England and France will do something now."

"They didn't when the Fuehrer"—she sneered at the name—"marched into Czechoslovakia."

"But England and France have a treaty with Poland."

"Then we'll have war."

They heard a key in the lock. Willie strode into the kitchen, his medical bag still in his hand. He took off his hat, and placed it on top of the bag on a chair near the door.

"I closed the office. No one was coming in. They're all too busy celebrating. When I told Grete I was closing up, she asked whether I was going to enlist. Hah! They've all gone completely crazy. They think this is some kind of picnic?"

Little Willy held his arms up. Willie scooped him out of his high chair, gave him a kiss on top of his blond curls, then set him back in his chair. He wiped zweiback crumbs off his suit jacket, tousled Peter's hair, went to the sink to wash his hands and then sat down next to Martin.

"I'll have a cup of coffee, Eva," he said.

"I was just making lunch."

"I'll have some coffee anyway. So . . . we're in it now. Doesn't anyone remember the last war?"

"I don't, really. I was just a child," Eva said. "I remember we didn't have much to eat, but that's all."

"Well, I was old enough. And it wasn't a picnic. And this won't be either. We're in for some bad times." He looked at Martin. "I hope the ships will still sail."

"America isn't going to war, even if England and France do."

"If you can get that ship next Tuesday . . . I wouldn't wait."

"Don't worry. I won't."

"Maybe I'll go to the Lloyd office this afternoon," Willie said. "I think you should stay indoors today."

"I wasn't planning on going out."

"We may have to offer someone a little something."

"Whatever you have to do, Willie. I have some money still."

"Of course Germans are incorruptible, but still . . ."

"What if the ships aren't sailing anymore?" Eva worried.

"Then you're stuck with me," Martin said.

After lunch Martin put Peter down for a nap, and Eva settled Willy in with his favorite teddy bear. Willie left, and Martin and

Eva sat in the kitchen. They had turned the radio off, tired of the jingoistic speeches and military music, but they spoke little, each busy with his or her own thoughts. When first Willy and then Peter awakened, Martin played with them. By the time Willie returned it was already getting dark. He passed the kitchen, went into the bedroom, and changed out of his suit. When he came back into the kitchen he shook his head sadly.

"They've canceled all sailings," he said.

"To everywhere?" Martin asked.

"For the next week. And there was a sign saying that Jewish tickets were no longer valid."

"How can that be?" Eva asked. "If they have tickets . . ."

"They can do whatever they want," Martin said. "We have no rights anymore."

"Things may be better tomorrow," Willie said.

"And why would you think that?"

"Well . . . they can't be worse, can they?"

"They're business people," Eva said. "They'll come to their senses. In a week, two, they'll realize they need the business, and the ships will sail again."

"I think maybe I should move somewhere else. I don't want to make things difficult for you."

"Don't even think of it," Eva said. "You're safe here, and you're not going anywhere 'til we can put you on that ship to America."

After the boys were asleep, they listened to the radio. The bulletins proclaimed unresisted forward movement, glorious German advances. Hitler ranted. Others warned of traitors and saboteurs who would be harshly dealt with. The Jews, in particular, were warned to beware. This time the German Volk would not be betrayed.

"I'm going to bed," Eva said at ten. Willie kissed her on the cheek, then turned off the radio and put a platter on the gramophone.

"A little Shubert," he said, "to remind us that not all Germans are barbarians."

He went to the sideboard, got out the bottle of cognac and two glasses. He poured a generous shot into each glass, handed one to Martin. He warmed his glass in the palms of his hands before taking an appreciative sip.

"Ah, if only one could shut out the world." He sat in his armchair, stretched his legs in front of him. "Eva told me she spoke to you about Willy?"

Martin nodded.

"You must have noticed. But you've never said a word."

"Children develop at . . ."

"Yes, yes, I know. But we both know that's not what it is. We're doctors. He'll never be normal."

"There are schools."

"There **were** schools. This is the Third Reich."

Martin said nothing.

"You know what they do with idiots in the Third Reich."

"He's not an idiot."

"He's not going to be a member of the Master Race, Martin. It's too late for fooling ourselves. What's his future going to be? If we're lucky, they'll just sterilize him. If we're not lucky . . ."

On the gramophone the hauntingly beautiful voice of Joseph Schmidt sang *Der Erl König*.

"He's young. By the time he's ready for school this might all be over."

"I hope you're right. Certainly he's not in immediate danger. Luckily he's not mongoloid. He doesn't **look** different, and as you say, by the time he has to go to school maybe we'll be living in a sane society again."

"One can only hope."

"I've talked it over with Eva."

"What?"

"If you . . . now that the war has started. Things are going to get worse for the Jews. You know you're welcome here as long as you can stay. But if things change, if they make you leave . . ."

"I said I'd go. I don't want to make things difficult for you, Willie. You know that."

"No. That's not what I"m saying. We don't want you to leave. Only, only, if they make you leave . . ."—he paused, then rushed ahead—"take Willy instead of Peter. They're the same age. They're both blond. Peter isn't circumcised. Let us keep Peter, and you take Willy."

"What?"

"That way, Peter will be safe. And when this is all over, you can come back and get him."

Martin shook his head.

"Why not?" Willie asked. "What I hear, they're not treating the Jews very well in the collection centers. And there's talk of shipping them to the east, for their 'safety.' They did it after Krystallnacht. Now that the war's started . . ."

"What if I can still get on a ship?"

"Then of course you'll take Peter. I'm just thinking worst case. As long as you can stay here nothing changes. It's only in the event that they come for you . . ."

In the background Schmidt sang.

"And Eva is agreeable?"

"She . . . she understands Willy is doomed if the Nazis stay in power. And what kind of life would Peter have if you get sent to a camp? This way at least Peter will be safe. We'll take care of him; you know we will. And when it's over you'll come back, and then you and Peter can join Claire and the baby in America."

"I don't have to answer you right now, do I?"

"Of course not. Nothing may happen anyway. This is only in case."

He took a slug of cognac. Martin closed his eyes, listened to Schmidt singing 'Die Forelle.'

"Just think about it."

Martin finished his cognac. He took the glass into the kitchen and rinsed it. When he came back into the living room Willie was sitting in his chair, his head in his hands. The gramophone record had finished, and was spinning continuously. He went to the player, carefully lifted the record and replaced it in its sleeve. He shut off the player.

"We've let Suze go," Willie said.

"Suze? Why?"

"She was making noises. Said she wasn't comfortable working where there were Jews."

"I told you we should find another place."

"No. That's not why I'm telling you. I just wanted you to know, it'll be safe. Suze won't be here. Peter will be safe."

"And what did Suze say when you told her she was fired?"

"She said she was joining the *Lebensborn* movement."

"What in the world is that?"

"She's going to make Aryan babies for the Fatherland."

Martin smiled. "Well, lots of luck. If they're all as intelligent as she is, the Fatherland may be in a lot of trouble."

"One can only hope. But seriously, Martin. Think about it. It probably won't be necessary, but in times like this one has to be prepared."

"And you're willing to give up your son?"

"If it comes to that, Martin, we'd lose him anyway. What did they teach us in medical school? Triage? Save the ones you can save. If we can save Peter . . . ."

They went to bed soon afterward. Martin did not sleep. He spent long hours looking down at his sleeping son.

CHAPTER 3

Wolfenbüttel, May 1963

"A letter for one of us, Papa," Willy Meinhoff said as he came into the office. "From America."

"From America?" his father asked. "Who in America would write to us?"

"A secret admirer? It's addressed to Dr. Willibald Meinhoff. It doesn't say the elder or the younger. The postmark is from New York, but the return address is from a medical center."

"Maybe they want to offer you a job," his father said. "Maybe they heard of your stellar academic record."

"I graduated, didn't I?"

"Yes, by the skin of your teeth. And the only internship program you could get into was here in Wolfenbüttel. Frankfurt or Bonn would have been more prestigious."

"I don't need prestige. Wolfenbüttel is good enough for me. It's been good enough for you, and I didn't want to leave you all alone. Now, if you'd make an honest woman of Sophie . . . ."

"Oh, I see. You got lousy marks so you could keep an eye on your old father."

"That's not what I meant. Anyway, why don't we open the letter, see who it's from and what they want. Maybe they want to offer **you** a job. Maybe they heard of **your** stellar medical skills."

He tore open the envelope, looked at the signature. "It's from a Dr. Margot Brenner. Do you know a Margot Brenner?"

"I don't think so. Someone you went to University with?"

"Nope." He began to read out loud.

Dear Dr. Meinhoff,

You probably don't remember me, as I was only an infant the last time you saw me, but I'm sure you remember my father, Martin Brenner, and my mother, Claire. My father, as you must remember, never escaped from Germany, but my mother always spoke of how kind you and your wife were to us when none of their other friends . . ."

He turned to his father. "Who were they, Papa?"

"Martin was a friend, a colleague. You don't remember, Willy. You were a baby yourself, but they stayed with us for a few days before they left Germany. It was late, 1939. They should have left sooner, but Claire, Mrs. Brenner, hadn't wanted to leave her parents, who were sickly."

"What happened?"

"Their little boy got sick, and Martin insisted his wife leave with their baby daughter. He planned to follow when the boy—Peter, I think was his name. He was just about your age—was better."

"And?"

"And someone betrayed them. The Gestapo came and took them away. They arrested me for sheltering an enemy of the state. They wanted to take your Mama, too, but I talked them out of it, said she had to take care of you, a future Hitler Youth."

"And what happened to them? To the boy and his father?"

"I never heard. When I got out of prison I went into the army. Your mother and you moved to Kassel. And then after the war we came here. I never heard from Claire again either."

"Wouldn't you think she'd have written, tried to find out . . ."

"Your Mama wrote her after I was arrested. Then the war started. After that we couldn't have written even if we'd wanted to. I was being watched. We had to be very careful."

"I don't remember any of that."

"You were very young. He slept in your room while they stayed with us, the boy, Peter. He was a little, how should I say, a little slow. He was your age, but he didn't talk or walk."

"Who betrayed them? And why?"

"I don't know? I've always suspected Heinrich. He had wanted to buy Martin's office equipment, and he was mad that Martin gave it to me. Buy, hah! He wanted to steal it, practically. A lot of them did that in those days. The Jews had no choice, had to take whatever anyone offered. Martin said he'd rather give it to me, and he did. And Heinrich was angry. I always suspected he was a closet Nazi, anyhow. Not that he ever said anything—except what we all had to say in public, you know, *Heil Hitler* and all that swill. Anyway, I could never be sure."

"Why didn't you write her after the war?"

"What was there to write? I didn't know anything other than what your mama had already written her. And I was busy. I was trying to re-establish my practice. I had to go through that de-Nazification process."

"I'm sure she could have helped if you'd asked. After all, you went to jail because you did the right thing."

"Yes, and that's what got me cleared. But read me the rest of the letter."

Willy continued.

. . . when none of their other friends would even speak to them. My mother tried to find you, unsuccessfully, after the war. She died last January, and I decided to try to find you, to try to find out whether you knew what became of my father and my brother, Peter. The Medical Society gave me your name, so I am taking the liberty of writing.

I just graduated from medical school last week. My internship starts on July 1st, and I thought maybe I could come to see you before then. I would appreciate any information, any news, you could give me about my father.

You can call me at Wadsworth 8-8452.

Sincerely,
Margot Brenner, M.D.

"After all this time," the senior Willie said.

"How old is she, Papa?"

"Let's see, she was less than a year when they left in '39, so I guess about . . . twenty-four, twenty-five."

"Call her, Papa. She sent her phone number."

"I'll write her. Not that there's anything to tell."

"But you and Mama were her parents' friends. If it was me, I'd want to hear."

"She's a doctor, too, just like her father. They must have done well in America if she could go to medical school. The Jews always manage to land on their feet."

"Papa!!"

"I mean it as a compliment, Willy. They are hard-working people. And Martin was an excellent doctor. It was bad, especially after '38 when the Nazis wouldn't let him practice anymore."

"Then what did he do?"

"Oh, he still treated Jews, and some of them could still pay him. But Christians weren't allowed to use Jewish doctors. I helped him out. He worked for me—unofficially, you understand—and that helped. That was part of what got us into trouble, too. It's one of the things the Gestapo questioned me about. That could also be why Martin got picked up. If Heinrich told them he was working for me, treating Aryans."

"So call her, Papa. What time is it now in America?"

His father pulled his pocket watch. He refused to get a wristwatch, still kept his grandfather's old watch, smooth from years of rubbing against pockets, on a chain.

"It's the middle of the day in America. She's a doctor, she won't be at home now. I'll try her later."

"But I'm going out."

"Do I need you to make a call? I'm not senile yet."

"I know that. But I wanted to hear what she says, maybe talk to her."

"Why the interest? She's the one who wants information."

"I don't know, Papa. Anyway, you'll tell me what she says, right?"

"Of course. Where are you off to this time?"

"Brigitte wants to see the new Bergman film, *Winter Light*"

"You've been seeing a lot of her lately. Serious?"

"I could be. She doesn't want to be tied down, at least not to me."

"And what's wrong with you?"

"She's looking for more than a country doctor."

"Wolfenbüttel is hardly the country. And anyway, there's nothing wrong with a country doctor. Your mother was happy . . ."

"You weren't a country doctor then. And anyway, she wasn't very happy here in Wolfenbüttel."

"That had nothing to do with Wolfenbüttel. It was the war. She never really recovered from that. You don't remember, Willy, but your mother, before the war, she was . . . bouncy, full of spirit. She was plump, like a juicy currant." His eyes filled with tears, and he shook his head. "It's hard . . . to remember."

"Plump? She was always so thin when I knew her. I could put my fingers around the top of her arm, even when I was still a kid."

"Yes, the war changed her. Changed us all. And then, when there wasn't enough to eat . . . and then Oma and Opa died. People forget we suffered too."

"Yeah, well. We let Hitler happen."

"Not all of us."

"Enough of us. Anyway, I'm off to make Brigitte happy."

"Then be careful. Don't make her pregnant."

"Don't worry, Papa."

"I get paid to worry," he said, smiling. "It's what fathers do."

"Not most of the fathers I know. Not that I know that many fathers, come to think of it."

"Yes, men of my generation are scarce."

"Well, I'm glad you survived. Not only do I have a father, but the best father." He came over, and gave his father an unaccustomed hug. "Don't wait up for me. Maybe I'll get lucky tonight."

"You have protection?"

"Papa!"

After Willy left, his father finished the notes he had been working on, then put the papers into the patients' files in the wooden cabinets behind his desk. It was still light out, but the old chestnut tree that grew in the back yard had darkened his office, so he turned on the desk lamp, a modern fluorescent model Willy had bought him at Christmas to replace the antique he still kept on top of the file cabinets, out of sentiment.

He headed for the kitchen, where he made himself a sandwich, grabbed a bottle of beer out of the refrigerator and went into the den. He picked up the *Staatszeitung* and read the headlines.

The news, as always, was depressing: The Americans were sending technical advisers to Indo-China. More trouble between Russia and America. Hitler hadn't been wrong about that. Willi Brandt was being cautious. There was a terrible collision on the autobahn. A child was missing in Kassel.

His thoughts returned to the letter from Martin's daughter. She wanted to come. Well, what if she did? He'd welcome her. It was the least he could do for Martin. Ironic that her mother was dead, too, like his Eva. She'd not been the same after Martin's arrest. He'd told her he'd done what was necessary, but it ate away at her anyway, long before the cancer that finally took her. No matter how often he'd explained . . . oh, what was the use? You couldn't change the past, and Eva was gone.

He turned on the radio to his favorite classical station. That was better. The familiar notes of the *Trout Quintet* filled the room. He closed his eyes, the better to concentrate. The house, now that the sun had set, was chilly. He put on his old cardigan. Finished with his makeshift meal he lit one of the two cigarettes he still allowed himself daily.

The ringing of the phone startled him awake. The den was dark. He stumbled up and into the kitchen, turning on the light as he reached for the phone.

"Dr. Meinhoff?"

"*Ja?*"

"This is Margot Brenner. Do you speak English?"

"A little. Not so well."

"I can speak German."

"That's good," he said, in German. "I got your letter just today. I was going to call you later."

"That's all right," she said, having switched to German, too. "I suppose I'm a little eager. I was so glad to find you . . . after all these years."

"Yes, well, I wish I could tell you something you don't already know."

"But I don't know anything. How are you? How did you survive the war? How is your wife? Eva? And your son? My mother said . . ."

"Ach, so many questions. Those I can answer. My son is well. A good boy . . . a man, I suppose. He's a doctor, too. He followed his Papa, the way you followed yours. My wife, alas, died, it's more than ten years now. The war . . . she was never the same after I was arrested."

"You were arrested?"

"Yes. Not all of us were Nazis, you know."

"Oh, I know. My mother spoke of your courage in helping us. You were the only ones who . . ."

"Yes, well, we did what we could, what was right. You said in your letter that your mother is dead. I'm so sorry to hear that. She was still a young woman."

"Yes, but breast cancer didn't care."

"Ah. I'm sorry."

"Thank you. Dr. Meinhoff, I know this sounds crazy, but I'd really like to meet you and your son. I don't start my pediatric internship until July 1st . . ."

"You want to come here?"

"Yes. Yes." She stopped. "Now that I know where you are. I have so many questions about my father, about what happened."

"But I don't know what happened, other than that he was betrayed and I was arrested."

"But you knew him. What he was like, as a man, as a doctor."

"He was a good man, a good doctor."

"Yes, my mother said that, but . . . you really knew him, and Mom, well, how do you say it in German . . . she saw him through rose-colored glasses."

"Rose-colored glasses?"

"You know, idealistically. She idealized him. According to her they never even had a fight."

"Ah. Yes. But to come here? It would just . . . stir things up . . . for you, I mean."

"No it wouldn't. It would do the opposite, put things to rest." She paused. "I wouldn't make a nuisance of myself. I'd stay in a hotel. There are hotels in Wolfenbüttel?"

"We're not in the jungle."

"Oh, I didn't mean to . . . I just don't know anything about Wolfenbüttel. I looked in the Atlas, and I saw it's not that far from Braunschweig, or even from Hannover, but . . . you're a doctor. Is there a hospital there?"

"Yes. The Städtisches Klinikum, Georg-August. It's part of Göttingen University. That's where my son is training."

"Do you know whether there are any openings?"

"Openings?"

"Yes. I mean, I was just thinking. I'm just starting my internship here. There's no reason I couldn't do an internship in Germany instead . . . if I could get one."

"I don't know. Why would you want to? Just to ask me a few questions?"

"No. I don't know. It seems almost as if I need to . . . I don't know. Do you know whom I could call to find out?"

"Well, I know the head of the training program there. Klaus Prange. We were in medical school together. He knew your father, too."

"That would be helpful. Do you have his number?"

He gave it to her, "But I wouldn't get my hopes up. By this time all the programs are filled."

"Well, if not then not. But I could still come to visit before my internship starts."

After a few more minutes of polite chitchat she hung up, thanking him for everything.

Willie turned off the light and made his way back to the den. He switched on the floor lamp next to his chair. His cigarette had burned out in the ashtray. He lighted another since he hadn't, technically, smoked the last one . . . . There was still a little beer left in the bottle, and he drank that. The radio was now playing Wagner, *The Ride of the Valkyries*. He shook his head.

"It'll be all right," he assured himself. "There's no way Klaus will hire her. And if she comes to visit, what can I tell her? The Gestapo came. They took her father and the boy. Finished."

CHAPTER 4

New Haven, May 1963

John was on the platform when she got off the train. He took her overnight case from her, set it down, and pulled her into a hug.

"God, I've missed you," he said.

"It's only been ten days."

"With my parents it seems like ten years."

"They're not that bad."

"Try living with them."

He picked up her bag, and, taking her hand, pulled her to the parking lot where he dropped the bag next to a navy Porsche.

"Like the car?" he asked.

"Very classy."

"Graduation present from the 'rents."

"Very classy."

"Yes. But it has strings."

"Doesn't everything?"

"I suppose. And I guess these aren't so bad, as long as I behave."

"Why wouldn't you behave? Or, rather, how are you supposed to behave? You'll be so busy with the internship you won't have time to misbehave."

"You'd think. Actually they want me to . . . how did Father put it? 'Give myself a chance.'"

"To do what?"

"Uh . . . to get over my, uh, 'infatuation with that unsuitable woman.'"

"That would be me?"

"The same." He smiled wryly. "I'd like to unsuit you right here. Seriously. Why don't we just get married this weekend and put them out of their misery."

"You think it would?"

"Well, at least the uncertainty would be gone. And," he smiled wryly again, "once we're married we could start working on our divorce."

"Very funny. I don't think I feel very comfortable, though, staying at their house if that's how they feel about me."

"Oh, they like you, Margot, they really do."

"But I'm unsuitable."

"You don't understand. They like you. They think you're smart, and pretty, and nice. But that has nothing to do with anything. As Mother said, 'Just because someone's nice doesn't mean you should marry her.'"

"Certainly not. Look, I was going to tell you later, but I guess I might as well do it now. Something's come up."

"Come up?"

"Yes. Remember I told you I've been trying to find Dr. Meinhoff, that friend of my Dad's in Hannover?"

"Yeah . . . ?"

"Well, I finally found him. Mom had never gotten an answer when she wrote him after the war, but after she died I decided to try again. I wrote to the German medical association, and they gave me an address. He doesn't live in Hannover anymore, hasn't for years. I guess that's why Mom never found him. Anyway, I called him in Wolfenbüttel."

"What's a Wolfenbüttel?"

"It's a small city. I asked whether they have a hospital there, and they do. So I asked whether they might need an intern. He wasn't sure, but he gave me the name of the head of the program, and it turns out they have a vacancy. One of their surgical interns was just killed in an auto accident."

"I don't think I like where this is going."

"I airmailed them my credentials, John, and they said if everything checked out they'd give me a spot. A surgical internship."

"What about Sinai?"

"They won't have any trouble filling my spot. A peds internship there is a plum, and . . . ."

"Right. And you'd give up a plum for . . . what was the name of the place? Wolfen-something? That'll look great on a resume. And what about us?"

"We were going to be separated anyway."

"Yeah. But not by an ocean."

"John, you know as well as I do that once we start we'll both be so busy, and so exhausted . . . . How much would we see of each other? This way, when we have time off, you can fly over, and we can really be together."

"Sounds as though you've made up your mind."

"If they offer it to me I'll say yes."

He turned the key in the ignition and pulled out of the parking space. He said nothing as he maneuvered the car out of the lot and onto the street.

"Don't you see, John? It'd give me the specialty I really want, and I'd get a chance, finally, to meet Dr. Meinhoff, and to find out what happened to my father and brother."

"I thought you knew what happened to them."

"Only that they died, Dad at Auschwitz, and Peter before then; but after the war Mom couldn't find the Meinhoffs. So we never knew *exactly* what happened. Probably Dr. Meinhoff won't know either, but . . ."

"Wasn't your dad picked up before we got into the war?"

"Yes?"

"So this Dr. Meinhoff didn't write your mother and tell her then?"

"His wife did. But she only said the Gestapo had come and taken my father and Peter away, and that her husband had been arrested for 'sheltering an undesirable.' That's all she knew, and we never heard from them again."

"And he never wrote your mother after the war either?"

"Never. As I said, Mom wrote him at the only address she knew, but the letter came back stamped 'Addressee Unknown.' For all Mom knew he died in the war."

"Then what made you try to find him again now, after all this time?"

"I don't know. A feeling. After Mom died I just felt somehow that I owed it to her to give it one more try. And when I got my application for membership in the AMA it occurred to me that the Germans must have an AMA too, and that if anyone knew where he was—if he was still alive—it would be them. And I was right."

The streets were becoming less urban. The houses they passed were larger, on big lots with old trees and manicured lawns. The sun shone. Lilacs bloomed in profusion, deep purple, light purple, and white. After several blocks of what were now stately mansions, some barely visible behind fences, John turned into a driveway between two stone pillars. Curved and sloping uphill, the driveway led to a fieldstone house with a hipped slate roof. The front door was painted a shiny dark green, adorned with a brass knocker in the shape of a horse. The windows facing the front were leaded glass, behind which translucent white curtains hung.

"We're home," John announced, turning off the ignition. "It's large—but it's pretentious."

Margot got out and looked around. Behind the house she could just make out a garage. The grass on the lawn seemed to have been cut with a slide rule. There was not a dandelion or other weed to be seen. The borders of the driveway had been planted in an orderly array of colors, going from white to pink to red, and then back. To the other side of the house stood a huge white lilac bush, the leaves almost hidden by the profusion of blooms.

"It's lovely," Margot said.

"Yes, well Mother likes to garden. And the landscape service sees to the lawn. And the pool service sees to the pool, and the tennis court service . . . ."

The front door opened.

"Mr. John," a white-haired woman in a black dress covered by a white apron said with a warm smile, "your parents are waiting in the dining room."

"Hello, Annie. I was just showing Dr. Brenner Mother's flowers."

"I'm sure some of them will still be here after lunch," she admonished. "Why don't you leave Dr. Brenner's bag in the hall and I'll take it up to her room." She turned to Margot. "I'm Annie, and I've known this young man since before he was born. He's half the reason for these grey hairs." She looked fondly at John as she stepped aside to let Margot into a foyer graced by a chandelier and papered in silver and white stripes. To one side was a cherrywood table on which stood a silver tray with what appeared to be several calling cards in the bottom. *Did people really still do that?* Margot wondered.

"Would you like to wash up, Dr. Brenner?" Annie asked.

At her "Yes, please," Annie led her to a door just beyond the foyer.

"Your room has its own bath, but this is more convenient for now," she said.

Margot closed the door and turned on the light. The room had, in addition to the commode, a pedestal sink on which stood a china dish with an assortment of soaps in the shape of seashells in various pastel shades. On the towel bar hung three peach-colored linen hand towels with the monogram **vWs** embroidered in a slightly darker peach. Margot washed her hands, then dried them guiltily on one of the pristine towels.

John was waiting outside. He put his arm around her waist and steered her into the dining room where his parents waited at either end of a long white-linen covered table. John pointed her at the chair next to the sideboard, on which rested an assortment of sculptures, a Chinese vase, and an ornate set of silver candlesticks. Above the sideboard was a portrait of Mrs. Watt in a blue velvet chair, her hands resting loosely in her lap. Her hair was done in a long braid, which curled over her left shoulder. Her lips and cheeks were pink, her eyes a deep almond. A wry suggestion of a smile curved her lips. On her lap, next to her ringed hand, rested the head of a springer spaniel.

"I hope your trip wasn't too unpleasant," Dr. Watt said as John sat down opposite Margot.

"Not at all. It gave me a chance to read, something I didn't have much time for over the last year."

"What are you reading?" Mrs. Watt asked.

"William Shirer. *The Rise and Fall of the Third Reich.*"

"That's serious reading," Mrs. Watt laughed. "I'd think, after all your studies, you'd want something a little more . . . relaxing."

"You mean like *Peyton Place*, Mother?"

"I'm sure there's a happy medium. Shall I ask Annie to serve lunch, before everything is wilted?"

Lunch was delicious, and the conversation stayed light. Margot admired the portrait, and was promised a full tour of the house and grounds. After coffee and dessert, Dr. Watt rose and excused himself.

"I have a few things to take care of at the office. John, I could use your help. I'm sure Mother and Margot will manage without us for an hour or so."

John flashed Margot an apologetic smile, then rose. He bowed to his mother, leaned over and whispered "Behave" into Margot's ear before kissing her lightly on her cheek, and left the room on his father's heels.

Margot stood and began to gather up the coffee cups.

"Leave those for Annie," Mrs. Watt said. "She'd be hurt if you didn't."

Margot put them back and shrugged.

"Would you like to go up to your room and rest, dear? Or shall I give you that tour of the house?"

"I don't need to rest, but I'd like to hang up a few things."

"Annie will have taken care of that." She rose, gestured to the archway separating the dining room from the kitchen. "Shall we, then?"

The tour of the house required little of Margot besides an occasional "ooh" or "ah" when Mrs. Watt gave the pedigree of some artifact or piece of furniture. The floors in the living room gleamed, the rugs were oriental and thick. The furniture was upholstered in brocades and watered silk. The woods were polished to a high sheen.

Margot's bedroom was furnished in bird's-eye maple, with a double bed covered by a wedding ring quilt. The walls sported Currier and Ives prints, spaced between wall sconces with ecru shades.

"Your bathroom is through that door," Mrs. Watt said. "That other door is the closet." She opened it to show Margot's dress, jacket, and skirt hanging on satin-covered and sacheted hangers. On the closet floor stood her slippers, her pumps, and, on a luggage stand next to the dresser, her bag. Margot opened one of the drawers of the dresser, and saw her underwear neatly stacked. A whiff of lavender greeted her.

"John's room is down the hall," Mrs. Watt continued. "Would you like to see it?"

"Sure."

She was led, then, down the hall, papered in a muted floral print. "That's our quarters," Mrs. Watt said as they passed a closed door. She opened the next door they reached.

Like in the guest room the furniture here was bird's-eye maple. This bed was also covered by a quilt, but this one was simply a series of geometric shapes in reds, whites, and blues. On the walls were photographs of airplanes, from an early one of the Wright Brothers' to modern jets. The bookcase on one wall held a collection of sets, from *Winnie the Pooh* to Robert Louis Stevenson, Dickens, H.G. Wells, and Jules Verne. A couple of athletic trophies sat on the shelves as well, and a poster of the Beatles was taped over the bed. The closet door was slightly ajar, a loafer stuck in the crack. Mrs. Watt bent, pushed the shoe inside, and closed the door.

"We haven't really changed anything since John went to college. And since he'll only be here until his residency starts, I imagine he hasn't wanted to do any re-decorating either."

"You must be happy that he'll be back in New Haven."

"I'm sure he'll be very busy. And if he has free time I imagine he'll be spending it in New York."

Margot hesitated. She saw no reason to share her plans with John's parents just yet. She and John hadn't finished their discussion, although she knew she'd made up her mind. But she didn't have an offer yet, so why get Mrs. Watts all excited. Besides . . . to start that discussion with his mother before she'd finished it with John seemed more disloyal, somehow, than possibly committing to Wolfenbüttel and giving up her Mt. Sinai residency. She shrugged instead.

"Your flowers are beautiful," she said into the silence. "I especially love the lilac bush. My mother loved lilacs."

"They are lovely, aren't they? We have some others in the back yard, near the pool. Those are the deep purples, but I think I like the white ones best. Would you like to see the back?"

"Yes, please."

Back downstairs they stepped from the kitchen door onto a flagstone patio. To the right of the patio was a garden in which pansies, impatiens, nasturtium, and others she could not name flowed like a spectrum, from palest pink to deepest purple.

"It's lovely," Margot said. "It's . . ."

"Yes. It gives me a great deal of pleasure. Other women play bridge. I garden."

"What do you do in the winter?"

"I have a greenhouse. You can't see it from here. It's behind the pool. I've been trying my luck with orchids."

They walked down a path to the pool.

"The poolhouse serves the pool and the court," Mrs. Watt said. "Do you play?"

"Badly."

"John's an excellent player. It's the only game at which he can beat his father. Perhaps sometime we can play doubles."

"I don't think John would want me as his partner."

"Ah well. Did you bring a bathing suit?"

"I'm only here 'til tomorrow, and I didn't think to . . . ."

"Well next time you come. And bring your tennis clothes. Perhaps you and I can volley a bit."

"I'd like that." *Not*, she thought, *that I have tennis clothes*. The few times she'd played tennis, on the public courts near the George Washington Bridge, she'd played in gym shorts and a tee shirt. Somehow she didn't think that counted as 'tennis clothes' in New Haven.

"Shall we sit?" They were back at the patio, and Mrs. Watt waved a well-manicured hand at the wicker chairs surrounding a glass-topped wicker table. They sat, facing the garden, the lawn, and the pool and court beyond.

"It's so peaceful here," Margot said. "You'd think you were miles from civilization."

"If that's civilization. Yes. I enjoy the quiet. Of course it was even more so when I was a child. Ours was the only house here then."

"You've lived here all your life?"

"Yes, and my father before me. My grandfather built this house. It's his portrait over the fireplace in the living room. The Scott family has been here for almost a hundred years. When he came back from the Civil War he wanted quiet."

"It must be nice to be in a place where your family and their family, and your children and their children, all belonged."

"Yes, that's why John's father and I . . . ," she stopped. "Perhaps you'd like some iced tea?"

"No thanks. I'm fine."

Mrs. Watt rose, went to the kitchen door. "Annie," she called, "some iced tea, please." When she was reseated, she said, "John tells me you were born in Germany."

"That's right. That's why I envy the continuity."

"Yes. I can see that. Are your people still over there?"

"No. My father, brother, and grandparents were all killed. My mother and I came here in 1939."

"I'm sorry. And your mother lives in New York?"

"My mother died in January."

"Oh, John did mention that. That's why she wasn't at the graduation."

Margot bit back the retort, 'Right, she couldn't get away.' No point in being a smart aleck, even though she was finding this conversation wearing. What was it Mrs. Watt had been planning to say there, when she caught herself and offered iced tea? That that was why she and John's father wanted him to marry someone who also belonged? Someone suitable?

"Well, let's talk of something more pleasant, dear. Are you looking forward to your residency?"

"It'll be hard, but yes."

"I admire you, taking all those hard courses, all that unpleasantness. It must have been difficult for you, I mean as a woman."

"Well, it wasn't the courses so much. The hardest part was that there aren't many women in medical school, and some of the professors resent us. Some of them weren't very subtle about it. And of course some of the men, well . . . that's how I first got to know John. After someone stuck a . . . a body part"—(she decided not to specify the part for fear of sending poor Mrs. Watt into cardiac arrest) —"into my lab coat pocket, he was the only one in the lab who didn't think it was funny."

"I'm glad I raised a gentleman."

"He is that. Anyway, one of the professors told us we were just taking spaces away from some deserving man, that we'd all give up medicine and have babies anyway. And some of them thought that we were just emotionally unsuited, and tried to prove it."

"To prove it?"

"Well, in surgery once, the professor asked me for a Kelly clamp. When I handed it to him he slapped my face, said I didn't know a Kelly from a curved clamp, and that I was a menace in an OR."

"He slapped you?"

"Yes."

"He must be . . . not one of our . . . I mean, clearly, no breeding."

"I don't know about that. He once reminded us that his ancestors didn't come on the *Mayflower* because they wanted the servants there first to chill the martini glasses."

Fortunately for continued amicability, Annie came out then with a tray holding a pitcher of iced tea, two glasses, and a plate with an assortment of cookies. In each glass was a piece of lemon and a sprig of mint. Annie poured tea into each glass, handed one, and a linen napkin, first to Margot and then to Mrs. Watt, who took a sip and sighed contentedly.

"No one makes iced tea the way you do, Annie," she said. Annie just nodded, left the pitcher, and retreated to the kitchen. Margot took a sip of the tea as well, and winced inwardly. No sugar.

Not too long afterward, John and his father returned.

CHAPTER 5

Wolfenbüttel, May 1963

They had breakfast together before Willy left for his hospital rounds. It had been their custom since he came back from the war. Before Eva had died she had made the coffee and oatmeal, boiled the eggs (once they could get coffee and eggs again, or even oatmeal). In the early days after the war they were lucky to have a slice of what passed for bread, and he and Eva had often gone without so that Willy could eat his fill. Being a doctor had helped, because grateful patients, who had no money either, would sometimes bring them an egg or three, or even a chicken, a bottle of milk, or a piece of meat when they butchered. It helped, and they were never in danger of starving, but Eva was skin and bones when the war ended. Her clothes hung on her like a scarecrow, and she never gained back her weight. She pooh-poohed it when he worried, said she wanted to stay slim so he wouldn't look at other women (as if he would). By the time the pains started and she could no longer hide them, it was too late.

He rose and cleared the breakfast dishes. They were part of Eva's dowry—Rosenthal, white with a delicate floral pattern—and he handled them like the treasures they were to him. As he was putting them back into the cabinet, the phone rang. He hung the last cup gently before picking up the receiver.

"*Ja?*" he asked.

"Willie? It's Klaus. I just had a phone call. From Martin Brenner's daughter, can you imagine?"

"As a matter of fact, yes, since I gave her your number."

"She wants to come here, to the hospital."

"I know. She told me. But you're all filled, I imagine."

"Well, we were. But I just found out yesterday that one of my new surgical interns missed a curve on the Autobahn. Pity. He was a bright young man, the most promising of the lot."

"Is . . . but she's going into pediatrics, not surgery."

"We talked about that. She told me that wasn't her first choice. She really wants to do surgery, but apparently in America, in spite of all the fine words . . . anyway, she said she'd love to do her surgical training here."

"So you're hiring her?"

"I'm not a total idiot, Willie. She's air-mailing me her credentials. I don't buy a pig in a poke. Even if she is Martin's daughter."

"And if her credentials are good?"

"Then why not? If it meets our needs?"

"You wouldn't rather have a German, someone who really speaks the language?"

"For surgery you don't have to be a Cicero. And besides, all the decent German doctors already have their placements. The ones who are left, well, would you want them to operate on your cat?"

"I don't have a cat. But I see your point. Well, I'll be interested to hear what you think of her credentials."

"I'll do better than that. When they come I'll let you help me evaluate them."

"I'm not a surgeon. What do I know about surgery?"

"She's not a surgeon either. Yet. But you're a good judge of character. When you were on the board here and used to sit in on interviews, you had a way of seeing through the crap. Remember that guy, Horst something? Impressive credentials, very smooth? We were all set to offer him a staff position, and you voted no. Later I heard from a friend at the Frankfurt hospital that they took him, and he was a disaster. They dismissed him in the middle of the year. Something about missing drugs. And trouble with female patients."

"I don't remember him, but . . . I guess something about him didn't feel right. That doesn't make me . . ."

"Look, you don't have to. I just thought you'd be interested. You were Martin's best friend. His only friend, by that time, I'm ashamed to say."

"We all did things we're ashamed of, Klaus. They were bad times."

"Yes, but you had the guts . . . and you paid for it."

There was an awkward pause, and then they chatted for a few more minutes before Willie agreed that he'd look at Margot's papers when Klaus got them.

A feeling of dread followed him into his office. *After all this time,* he thought. He shook his head. We all did things we're ashamed of,' he had said to Klaus, and Klaus had praised him for his guts. If he only knew . . . . He shook his head to clear it. There was nothing to worry about, he told himself. So Martin's daughter would come. They'd have her over for dinner. He'd invite Sophie—a woman's presence was always good. He'd tell the girl—the woman, he had to remind himself—he'd tell her what he could about Martin, what a fine man he'd been, a fine doctor. He'd tell her about the knock on the door, the Gestapo. He would not tell her about the last real conversation he'd had with Martin.

He was busy all day with his patients. They were mainly elderly. The young people wanted young doctors, those trained in the new ways, those with shiny offices. One of these days, they'd have to get a shiny office, too, so that Willy wouldn't become obsolete before he ever was in vogue. The young people wanted machines, tests, penicillin if they so much as sneezed. They didn't have time. They didn't want to sit and answer questions for half an hour before their doctor examined them, but that was the way you could tell what the problem was. Willie's patients had time. They were just glad someone would listen to them. Their children were busy working, trying to build from the ruins. Willie was willing to listen, so his waiting room was always full, and his days passed too quickly.

His growling stomach reminded him he'd never had lunch. He made a note on Frau Kohl's chart—was she really 83? Aside from her insomnia she was in better shape than some of Willie's contemporaries, who were dropping in their tracks with coronaries and strokes with depressing regularity. He put away the patient charts, turned off the light, and made his way to the kitchen.

He took a beer out of the refrigerator and sat down to look at the paper. He skipped all the national and international news, and turned instead to the local goings-on. Those he could, maybe, deal with.

Time to think about supper, he told himself. Willy was on call and was staying over at the hospital. He could go down to the Rathskeller. He hadn't had a decent meal in days. But he didn't like eating alone. Was it too late to call Sophie? Probably, but he went to the phone anyway.

"Oh, Willie. If you'd called a half hour earlier . . . . I just finished my leftovers."

"That's all right. Just a thought."

"You could come here. I still have some pot roast and red cabbage. And I could put up some noodles."

"No, don't bother. I should have called earlier. Sorry."

"I'll keep you company at the Rathskeller, if you'd like. I could have a beer."

"That would be nice. I'll come and pick you up."

"Not necessary. By the time you walk here I can meet you there. Say half an hour?"

She was standing outside the restaurant by the time he arrived. A slim woman, almost as tall as his five-nine, she wore a pair of grey slacks with a man-tailored white silk blouse, which did not hide her full breasts. A soft gray sweater was draped over her shoulders. Her blond hair had a streak of gray at the front and was pulled back in a French knot. The pearl studs in her ears matched the strand around her long neck. She smiled when she spotted him, and turned up her face to give him a kiss on the cheek. She smelled subtly of lavender.

"Thanks for coming," he said, giving her a quick hug. "I didn't feel like eating alone—again."

"Poor Willie."

They went inside, down the two stone steps into a cavernous room with dark wooden beams. The windows were stained glass; the walls were adorned by pewter beer steins, wooden staffs, deer's heads with huge racks. The tables, made of the same dark oak as the beams, were filled with noisy groups.

"*Guten abend, Herr Doktor, Frau Doktor,*" said a portly man with a walrus mustache and red face. His white apron covered his stomach like a canvas on a stretcher, ready for the artist to paint his landscape. *And a large landscape it would be.* Willie thought, with a smile.

"Good evening, Kurt. Do you have a table somewhere away from all the *Sturm und Drang*?"

"If you don't mind the corner near the kitchen."

"Sounds fine to me. All right with you, Sophie?"

Kurt led them to their table, presented menus longer than some books, and went off to take care of other customers.

"So," she asked, "how was your day?"

"Uneventful. The usual aches and pains. And yours?"

"The usual. Lots of earaches, two cases of chicken pox, a sore throat or two, and the usual quota of hysterical mothers who forgot to make an appointment but think if they don't bring their child in for their checkup today the world will end."

"That's what I like about my practice. My patients make appointments. It's the high point of their month."

He looked at her face. A good ten years younger than he, Sophie was approaching fifty. She could easily pass for forty. While there were smile crinkles at her eyes, her skin was smooth. She wore no makeup, as far as he could tell, but her cheeks and her full lips were red. Wisps of her hair had escaped the French knot and curled around her ears. She wore her nails cut short, covered with clear polish. Her fingers were long and strong. Aside from the pearl earrings and necklace, she wore only a sports watch and a wedding band on her right hand for accessories. Her husband, whom she had married while they were both in medical school, had not come back from the Russian front.

Sophie was the head of pediatrics at the Georg-August. Willie had met her when they moved from Kassel, after the war. Eva had still been alive then. He had gone to work at the clinic, and while his specialty was not pediatrics, he and Sophie had become friendly. Before Eva became too weak, Sophie had occasionally been to their house for coffee and cake and, when times improved, for dinner. Eva felt bad for Sophie. "Such a young woman to be widowed," she'd said to Willie. "Don't you know someone for her?"

After Eva's death Willie had been smothered in attention. Widowhood was the prevailing state for the women of his generation (*für das konnen wir unsern Führer danken*—'for which we can than the Fuhrer'), and even before Eva was cold, even before she was dead, truth to tell, the food came: roasts, cakes, *Kartofelshalet*, herrings, hearty soups. It was months before Willie had to worry about a meal for himself and young Willy. And they were solicitous, these bearers of meals. Could they clean his house? take care of Willy for an afternoon? warm his bed? This last was never stated, of course, but who would knock on a door at ten in the morning, hands in potholders carrying a steaming iron pot, and perfumed and made up as for … the opera? an audition? The stream of visitors slowed to a trickle after several months, when it became apparent that the proffers were, while gratefully accepted, not producing the expected reciprocity.

Sophie had not come bearing casseroles. She had sent a note, saying if he needed anything . . . . It wasn't 'til several months later, when they had bumped into each other at a lecture at the hospital, that he'd asked her, impulsively, to come for dinner. After that . . . .

"You're very quiet, Willie."

"Sorry. I had an interesting call last evening, the daughter of an old colleague."

"A phone call?"

"Yes. From Martin Brenner's daughter. You know, the friend who stayed with us 'til they were picked up by the Gestapo.

"And she's the baby girl?"

"That's right."

"Why is she calling now, after all this time?"

He took a bite of his fish, chewed.

"Her mother died recently. She's just graduated from medical school."

"You don't sound happy about it."

He smiled. "Ah, you know me too well. It's not that I'm unhappy. Just, why stir things up?"

"What would she be stirring up?"

"Memories, bad memories. You know I was jailed. It was no picnic."

"But you were a hero . . . ."

"Hardly. Anyway, it wasn't a happy time. I'd just as soon not think about it."

They sat in silence for a few minutes while he ate.

"It wasn't a happy time for us, either," Sophie finally said. "Alex knew he'd be drafted, and he really didn't want to go. He wasn't political, but he thought Hitler was insane. We should have left, the way he wanted to, but I was afraid. We were just getting established in our practice. Even if we could have gone, we would have had to start all over. I was a coward. And I lost Alex."

She twisted her ring, something she did when she was upset.

"How could you know? We all thought it would pass."

"We should have known. We should have read *Mein Kampf*, taken him seriously before it was too late."

"Yes, well, if we had crystal balls . . . . Anyway, the girl, Margot, wants to come here."

"What was her father like?"

"Martin? A good man. A good doctor. We were in medical school together, and it wasn't easy for him, as a Jew. But he never complained. He did what he had to, never put on airs. After a while everyone accepted him. Of course that was in the twenties. He was very much in love with his wife, very idealistic. Didn't even want a dowry. The irony is that, even though he was Jewish, he didn't believe in all that 'hocus pocus,' as he called it. Didn't even have the boy circumcised. His boy was a little slow, didn't talk or walk although he was almost two, but Martin adored him."

"It should be interesting, meeting his daughter."

"I suppose. Well, she's not here yet. But let's talk of happier things." And they did. Willie passed up dessert, although he was tempted by the strudel with *Shlagzahne*. He paid the bill, and then, hand in hand, they walked back to Sophie's house.

It had rained earlier in the day, but now the stars were out, and the smell of the trees with their new leaves was pleasant. When they got to her door Sophie asked, "Would you like to come in for a nightcap?"

"Willy's staying at the hospital. He's on call tonight," he answered, following her inside.

CHAPTER 6

Wolfenbüttel, May 1963

Willy unfolded himself from the front seat of his Volkswagen Beetle and stepped out. He bounded up the four steps leading to Brigitte's front door and rang the bell. Although it was past eight, it was still light, and the bushes on either side of the house were flowering. Insects buzzed and somewhere a bird was chirping. Willy looked at his watch. The movie started in half an hour. He hoped Brigitte was ready. On the other hand, if she wasn't, and if they missed the movie, it was no big deal. They could always go for a leisurely supper and then go back to her place afterwards, and . . . . He felt stirrings as he thought about that and adjusted his slacks so as not to offend. He pulled himself up to his full six feet, straightened his tie, and tapped his foot.

"You look stunning, as always," he said. She did. She was small, no more than five-one or -two, with a figure that turned heads. Her straw blonde hair was cut close to her skull, emphasizing the good bones, and her cornflower eyes sparkled, sometimes with amusement, sometimes with anger, but always with intelligence. She practiced criminal law, did courtroom work, and she hadn't lost a case yet. Opposing counsel, looking at the package, always underestimated her . . . the first time.

"You don't look bad yourself, Herr Doktor," she smiled.

"Like my jacket? It's a Harris tweed."

"Very British. Very proper. All that for a movie?"

"Well, not for the movie, but for the company. After all, when one escorts an attorney . . ."

"I'm underdressed," she said. She wore a beige skirt which came just above her knees, showing off her good legs in impossibly high heels. A cotton sweater, in a blue that matched her eyes, covered a white silk tee shirt. Gold hoop earrings were her only jewelry.

"Not at all. But if you want to go inside we could dispense with the clothing issue . . . ."

She grinned. "Movie," she said. "I've heard good things about it. Afterwards we'll see."

The Bergman movie turned out to be a bore, and halfway through he whispered, "I'm having problems staying awake."

"Shh," she said, "don't disturb the fans. Do you want to leave?"

"Do you?"

"I thought you'd never ask."

Outside she took his hand. "I'll never take Helli's recommendation again," she said.

"It wasn't that bad," he mock sang.

"Yes it was," she said back, in a solemn Bergmanesque tone. They laughed.

"Want to get something to eat?" he asked.

"Sure."

Hand in hand they walked down the street, past the stores that, by day, set up tables outside to entice passersby. Now, with the exception of a bookstore, all were closed.

They came to a restaurant, where groups of young people stood outside, talking.

"We won't get a table," he said.

"We could sit at the bar. I don't want to eat much anyway."

"We could try somewhere else."

"It'll be the same everywhere. Now that people have a little money again . . . ."

They went inside, past knots of people talking animatedly.

"Brigitte," a voice called out. She looked around, saw a man standing and waving.

"It's Dieter," she told Willy, "from my office."

Dieter, a round young man with thinning hair, pushed through the crowd. His shirt sleeves were rolled to the elbow, exposing a thick thatch of blond hair. The collar of his blue-striped shirt was open, his navy tie pulled to half mast.

"Join us?" Dieter asked. "Hilde and I have a large table, and by the look of things you're not likely to get seated until past your bedtime."

Brigitte looked at Willy. "Up to you," she said.

"Sure, thanks." They made their way past the throngs. Dieter said, "My wife, Hilde. This is Brigitte. I've told you about her. And this is . . . ?"

"Sorry," Brigitte said. "Willy Meinhoff, Dieter Strunk."

The men shook hands. Willy half-bowed to Hilde, then pulled out a chair for Brigitte before sitting down himself.

A waiter materialized, and stood expectantly, pad in hand.

The waiter shoved a menu at Willy, mumbled, "I'll be back," and went off into the crowd.

"Are you a lawyer too?" Willy asked.

"Oh, no. I'm a *hausfrau*. The law is no profession for a woman." She put her hand to her mouth when she realized her gaffe. Dieter studiously avoided looking at her. Brigitte smiled.

"The times are changing," she said.

"Oh, I didn't mean . . . and of course if one is single . . . But those long hours, and the weekends. Poor Dieter never knows when he'll be home, and when he has a trial . . . . Sometimes the children ask, 'Who is that man?' when he comes into the house."

Their food arrived before Brigitte had to answer, and they tucked in. They talked about the movie they'd walked out of.

"Oh, I loved it," Hilde said.

"I missed it," Dieter said. "One of those long nights. Hilde went with her sister. Sounds like one I'm not sorry I missed."

"Really, I loved it," Hilde said again. "So, what do you do, Willy? Are you an attorney too?"

"No, I'm a doctor."

"Oh, that's exciting."

"Sometimes. But the hours are long, too."

After another long pause Brigitte asked, "So, how many children do you have, Hilde?"

At that she was off and running, and there was no further need for anyone else to do more than nod or grunt or smile when she paused for breath.

When they were outside again Willy said, "God, that was painful."

"We should have stood at the bar," she said.

"What kind of a guy is Dieter. He didn't get a chance to say much."

"A good lawyer. Sharp. Works hard. No wonder he stays at the office late."

"Let's not go out with them any time soon."

They walked hand in hand back to her house. At the door she took her keys out of her purse before turning to him.

"You have any plans for the rest of the evening?"

He pulled her to him, kissed her enthusiastically.

"Want to hear what they are?" he asked.

She unlocked the door, and pulled him in after her.

CHAPTER 7

New York, May 1963

"Here's my address at the hospital," Margot said, handing Chris a sheet of paper. "Is there anything I forgot to tell you?"

Christopher O'Rourke put the paper into the drawer under the phone. "I think I got it all. The rent gets paid on the first of each month. The phone bill and electric get paid when they come in. The super, Eddie, knows I'm subletting, and the neighbors hear no evil and see no evil. Oh, and no wild parties."

"That's about it."

"This is really great, Margot. It's so close to the hospital I may actually be able to sleep in my own bed occasionally."

"Interns don't sleep, Dr. O"Rourke."

"Especially when there's no housing for them. I don't know what I'd have done if . . ."

"Well, it worked out for us both."

As they talked Margot tightened the strap on one of the bags standing near the front door.

"I still don't get it, why you're giving up a spot at Sinai to go to some two-bit hospital in nowheresville, Germany."

Chris shook his head. He looked about fifteen, with a round face, blue eyes, and a cupid's bow mouth. His red hair was cut close. The freckles on his nose and cheeks stood out in sharp relief against his white skin. A fuzz of red hair covered his cheeks. At 5'9" he was not much taller than she, but he was broad in the shoulder and his arms were thick with muscles. He, John, and Margot had been good friends since their first year of medical school, had studied together, pulled all-nighters, supported each other through all the ups and downs of those grueling four years. Chris was the son of a building superintendent, the first in his family to have gone to college. Graduating from CCNY with a straight-A average, he had won a Salk scholarship and been admitted to every medical school he'd applied to.

"You sound like John."

"Maybe because he's right. If it were my girl . . . ."

"Girl? More like *girls*, isn't it." In spite of his stellar academics, Chris was a legendary Lothario, and the halls of the hospital were littered with the corpses of his conquests. "And anyway," she went on, "he's in New Haven."

"At least it's not across an ocean."

"Second, it's a surgical residency, Chris. You know I really wanted surgery."

"Yeah, and it sucked that I got one at Presby and you didn't get one at all. But still, Sinai isn't Podunk, and peds is . . ."

"Yes, I know. A great residency for a woman. But it's not surgery. And anyway, this is something I need to do."

"Why now? Why all of a sudden? I mean I know you've always wondered about your dad and your brother, but still, the timing . . ."

"Is perfect, Chris. It all came together. And if not now, then when? After I finish my residency I'll need to get a real job, and then I'll be busy. There'll always be a reason why the time isn't right. And people don't get younger."

"You're twenty-four, for pete's sake."

"I don't mean me. I mean Dr. Meinhoff, my father's friend. If I put it off, and then when the time was 'right,' whenever that was, he was dead, I'd never forgive myself. No, this is the time. And your subletting my apartment is just serendipity."

"Glad to be of service. Is John majorly pissed?"

"He's not happy. But we're all going to be so busy anyway . . . and besides his parents are probably rubbing their hands in glee."

"Huh?"

"They don't think I'm suitable."

"Your non-Mayflower ancestors? Yeah, whenever I'm up at his place I feel as though they want me to use the servants' entrance. But hey, you're not marrying them."

"At the moment I'm not marrying anyone. And they're hoping out of sight, etc."

"You're not worried about John, are you?"

"No. If we're meant to be . . . but right now neither of us is ready for marriage. I've got to do this, Chris."

He leaned over and hugged her, kissed her cheek.

"All right, kiddo. I'm on your side. And I'll keep John on the straight and narrow."

She smiled. "You? Now maybe I *am* worried."

He put his hand on his heart. "Yes, well . . . ."

"I'd better get downstairs. John will be here any time now."

He picked up the heavier of her suitcases, while she took the smaller one and her medical bag, shiny and new and ready for use. She sighed. Her mother had looked forward to buying it for her as a graduation present. She hadn't lived long enough to do it.

"What's wrong?" Chris asked.

"Nothing. Just thinking about my mom."

"Yeah. That sucked, that she couldn't see you graduate. She was a neat lady."

"Yes, she was, wasn't she."

"She was so proud of you, Margot. Whenever we were at your house, you could see it. And she baked a great cake, too."

"She didn't pass that on to her daughter."

"Who knows. Maybe in Germany . . . ."

"As if I'll have time to bake."

"I miss her, too. I always felt I could talk to her. I mean my mom is okay, but I wouldn't go to her for advice. She'd just tell me to ask the priest."

Margot looked around one last time. "You've got the keys?" she asked. He showed them to her and she closed the door behind her.

John was just pulling up when they came to the front door. He got out of the car and took her bags, putting them into the trunk. She hugged Chris one more time, then got into the front seat. He stood on the sidewalk, and as the car pulled out she watched him turn and go back into the house.

"Sure you want to do this?" John asked.

"I have to," she said.

"I'll miss you."

"I know. I'll miss you, too. But it's not so long 'til Christmas, and we'll go somewhere nice. Somewhere warm, and we can lie on the beach and relax. By then we'll both be cross-eyed."

"With frustration?"

She laughed. "I meant with overwork. I don't know, maybe in Germany they don't work their interns thirty hours a day, but I doubt it. And they'll run you so ragged in New Haven you won't even have time to miss me."

"Don't bet on it. I miss you already."

She put her hand on his arm, squeezed it. "I know. I *will* miss you. And I'll write. And we'll call. And it's not so long . . ."

". . . 'til Christmas," he finished.

By the time they got to Idlewild International Airport, she felt weepy. John parked the car, and they carried her bags to the check-in counter where Margot presented her ticket and passport. Then they walked toward the gate.

"It's early," he said. "We could get a drink before you have to board."

They found a bar in the main terminal. It was dark, and the bartender, a man whose shirt looked as though he'd been wearing it for several days, was drying glasses and stacking them on the shelf behind him. The shelf also displayed bottles with liquids of assorted colors, as well as rows of conventional liquors. Several men sat on stools at the bar, separated from each other by the empty stools on either side. They were staring into glasses, or space. One was reading a paperback book.

John and Margot settled themselves at a small table in the corner, on high-backed stools.

"What would you like?" he asked.

"Actually, a cup of coffee. But if they don't have that, then maybe just some tomato juice."

"Then we should look for a restaurant. I'm not having a drink. I have to drive home."

So they got up, and walked around the terminal, past people scurrying in all directions, past stewardesses in groups of two and three, looking either perky and well scrubbed, or showing the wear of transcontinental flight.

Finally seated in a coffee shop, they looked at the menus a harassed waitress shoved at them.

"Have a sandwich," John suggested. "This may be the last decent meal you get for years."

"Oh, I imagine they cook in Germany, too. And they're serving dinner on the plane. Breakfast, too."

"Yes, but not American food."

"That's true. Lufthansa probably doesn't serve American food. I'll just have some coffee."

After they gave the waitress their order, John opting for a slice of apple pie with a scoop of vanilla ice cream, they held hands.

"You're not going to date anyone else, are you?" he asked.

"I told you I wouldn't."

"I know. I won't, either. But there'll be all those guys in their *lederhosen*."

"Right. And there'll be all those cute nurses. C'mon, John, don't do this."

"I just don't want you to go."

"I know that. I love you."

"My father says if I was a real man I'd have insisted you stay."

"Tell your father you are a real man."

"It's hard to tell my father anything."

"Well, I think you're a real man."

"How do you know. We never . . . ." He blushed. She smiled.

"No, we never quite did, but not because you're not a real man. I appreciate that you never forced the issue. And," she looked down at their clasped hands, "right now I'm feeling pretty stupid that I never . . . you know . . . ."

"When does your flight leave?" he grinned.

"We'll be together at Christmas," she said.

Afterward they walked to the gate and sat together, holding hands, not saying much, until it was time for her to board. They clung to each other then and kissed so passionately that the attendant at the gate finally said, "Buddy, if you feel that way maybe you want to buy a ticket."

She walked with her head turned, watching him 'til it was time to climb the steps onto the plane. She waved one last time, then went through the door and found her seat. She took a paperback out of her carry-on bag,. A rather obese man slid over an elderly woman sitting in the aisle seat, and plopped into the seat next to her. He was formally dressed, jacket and white shirt, with a striped gray-and-navy tie. He fastened his seat belt before reaching into the pocket of the seat in front of him to take out the safety card.

"Mike Adler," he said, sticking out his hand.

"Margot Brenner."

"So, you going on vacation?"

She wasn't really interested in sharing her life story, so "Sort of," she said.

"You should read the safety instructions. Just in case. Not that anything will go wrong," he added hastily, "but it's always good to be prepared."

"I suppose." Dutifully she extracted the card, glanced at it, and then opened her book.

Awhile later there was an announcement that the doors were being closed, and the passengers were instructed to pay attention to the stewardess who went over the safety instructions, announced that the expected flight time to Hannover was fourteen hours. Margot went back to her book.

"They'll serve a snack in a while," her seat companion told her. "The food is excellent on Lufthansa. You won't go hungry."

She smiled at him, and went back to her book.

"What are you reading?"

She held the book up, showing the cover.

"*Pride and Prejudice*? Never heard of it. Is it a best seller?"

"It probably was when she wrote it . . . a hundred years ago."

"Ah, you must be some kind of egghead. Me, if it's not on the best seller list, forget about it." He grinned. "But that's okay," he continued grandly, "live and let live is my motto."

She said nothing, hoping that he wouldn't feel the need to talk constantly. It was bad enough that his body slopped over into her seat, forcing her to edge toward the window, but if he expected conversation for the entire flight . . . . She went back to her reading. Maybe he'd take the hint and make friends with his other seat-mate.

The engines rumbled to life, and Margot put down her book to watch the plane taxi out of its parking slot. She watched it roll down the runway, then felt it pick up speed. She understood the principles of aerodynamics, physics having been one of the required pre-med courses, but she wasn't sure she quite believed this huge bird would really lift off. It did, though, and she was awed as it went up and up, and the city below got smaller and smaller, until the water of the bay was lost under the clouds.

When the captain announced that he'd turned off the seat belt and no smoking signs, Mike Adler rose, took off his jacket, and rolled up his shirt sleeves. He climbed over the woman in the aisle seat, took a pack of Luckies and a silver lighter out of his jacket pocket, folded the jacket into the overhead bin, then settled back into his (and Margot's) seat before lighting up with a sigh of contentment.

"Cigarette?" he offered.

"Thanks, I don't smoke."

"There's nothing like a cigarette if you're nervous. Or after a meal, or after other pleasant experiences." He smiled suggestively. She went back to her book.

Shortly afterwards the stewardess appeared at their seats. "Sir," she said, "the flight isn't completely filled. Perhaps you'd like a seat to yourself."

"I'm comfortable here," he said.

"But maybe the young lady . . . and the *g'naëdige frau*, Ma'am? "

"Yes," Margot said eagerly. "That way we can stretch out, get comfortable, if we want to sleep later."

Mike looked offended. "Well," he said, "I guess I can take a hint." He picked himself up, retrieved his jacket from the overhead compartment, and followed the stewardess. The woman in the aisle seat gave her a warm smile.

"Better, I think," she said.

"Much," Margot agreed before retreating happily into Jane Austen. Her companion, too, went back to her reading.

Fourteen hours on a plane is a long time, Margot found, longer than fourteen hours on call. On call, at least, one is busy, and while one may sleep standing up, the time passes quickly. Here the motors droned. The stewardesses came with snacks, first coffee and sticky pastries wrapped in cellophane. A while later they offered cocktails, for a price, or more coffee or juice or water, and salted peanuts in little foil packets. When they finished clearing the cups and napkins from that round they came around with dinner. While they ate she and her seat-mate struck up a conversation. The woman, who introduced herself as Phyllis Hatcher, taught German at Hunter College. She was going to the university at Halle for the summer.

"I used to go every year before the war. I stopped in '38. I didn't like what was happening there. Terrible. Don't let anyone tell you people didn't know what Hitler was doing. My friends knew. Those who could get out did. The ones who couldn't . . . but they knew. I started going again three years ago. I still have a few friends there. We don't talk much about the war.

"The ones who were my friends are ashamed. The ones who supported Hitler . . . well, now they say 'Hitler who?' but I have no use for them. Some of my friends in the states ask why I go back. But I have to keep up my German, you know. And the Germans are trying."

"Trying?"

"To overcome their history."

"I suppose. They are paying reparations."

"Yes, that too. And they're Israel's strongest ally. I suppose they've learned their lesson."

When Margot said she was going to Wolfenbüttel, Phyllis said she had friends there, and that when she went to visit she'd look her up.

By the time dinner was over and the detritus collected it was dark outside. Margot switched on her overhead light and went back to her reading. The next thing she knew the sun was coming up on her right. She looked at her watch. It said twelve o'clock. She wondered why it was already getting light, then realized she hadn't set her clock ahead to European time. She needed to pee, but didn't want to disturb Phyllis who was still sleeping. She watched a beautiful sunrise.

CHAPTER 8

Wolfenbüttel, May 1963

Dr. Meinhoff did not have a secretary, office manager, or recep-tionist. When the phone rang while he was with a patient, he let it ring. Emergencies belonged in the hospital anyway, and his regu-lars knew not to telephone during office hours. Also during office hours he left the front door unlocked, and his patients knew to ring and then enter—and wait. Willy often scolded about this.

"Anyone could walk in," he said.

"That's the point."

"I mean anyone. Not just patients. Wolfenbüttel isn't as safe as it was when I was a boy."

"There's nothing here anyone would want."

"Don't be naive. You have drugs . . . ."

"And a secretary would keep me safe?"

"No. But you could keep the door locked."

"Right. And when someone rings? She'd buzz them in. If it's a robber he'd come in when she buzzes."

"All right, Papa. Wouldn't it make your life easier, though?"

"No. Because then I'd have to find work for her. I'm fine, Willy, but it's nice you worry about me."

And that had, for the time being, been that. Truth be told, he liked the life of a country doctor. He earned enough to be comfort-able. He had enough patients to keep him busy, and not so many that it was a strain. Yes, he had been ambitious once, but that had been before the war, when he and Eva were young. Afterwards . . . well, afterwards he was glad to be able to make a living, to take care of his family. It was more, maybe, than he deserved.

He was washing his hands, having just finished examining Hermann Klebe. As Hermann dressed they chatted.

"Nothing wrong with you except you're not twenty anymore," he told the octogenarian. "But you have the heart of a twenty-year-old."

"*Ja,* and the head of an old man. I go in the bedroom and I don't remember why."

"Hella doesn't remind you?"

Hermann smiled.

"I don't mean that. That I still remember."

"Then you're a lucky man. Many of your contemporaries . . . well, they may remember but the equipment doesn't cooperate anymore."

"*Ja.* What I meant, though, I go into a room and when I'm there I don't remember what it was I wanted to get."

"Happens to us all."

"Not as often as with me, though. But I guess I shouldn't complain. I'm still here, and Hella is all right, and the children call occasionally."

He finished buttoning his shirt. "What about you, Doctor? You ever think of remarrying?"

"Sometimes. But I've gotten used to my life."

"You could get used to another life. You're still a young man."

"I'm sixty-three, not so young"

"A boy. Wait 'til you're my age," he chuckled. "Then you'll realize how young that is."

Willie sat at his desk. Hermann sat in the chair opposite. His hands were knotted with arthritis, his face wrinkled. But he had a full head of gray hair, and his eyes were clear and sharp. His pants were old but the crease was razor sharp, and even though he had been retired from the postal service for many years, he still wore a tie with his dress shirt.

"So . . . I'll see you in November. We just want to keep a check on that little bump on your neck. Not that I think it's anything to worry about, but . . . and no more than two cigars a day."

"Ach, you want to take away all my pleasures?"

"Well, not all of them. You said Hella remembers."

They shook hands and Hermann left. Willie walked with him to the front door, then ushered Irmgard Metz into the examining room.

And so it went, and the day passed, and by the time he walked the last of his patients to the door, and locked it, and went back into his office to finish up his notes and put away the files, it was evening again.

He was preparing supper when Willy bounded in.

"Guess who came to the hospital today, Papa?" He took off his jacket and pulled off his tie, throwing them over the back of one of the kitchen chairs. He rolled up the sleeves of his blue shirt, then went to the refrigerator and took out a beer.

"Brigitte Bardot? I don't know, Willy. Who?"

"Margot Brenner. The daughter of your friend. And I hear she's a knockout."

"Ah. She's here already?"

Willie finished peeling the last potato, and put it into the pot with the others.

"She came today. I didn't meet her yet, but Otto told me about the new American intern, and the whole place is buzzing. Has she called you yet?"

"Not so far. I'm sure she will."

"You'll invite her to dinner when she calls, won't you?"

Willie sighed. "Yes, Willy. I'll invite her."

"You don't sound very excited."

"What's to be excited?"

"She's your friend's daughter."

"Yes. And it was a long time ago, and it brings up memories I'd rather leave buried."

Willy went to the sink and washed his hands. "It's not good to bury things. They come back and bite you in the ass some other way."

"Thank you, Dr. Freud. Some things are better left buried."

"Yes, and that's why they never mentioned the years from 1933 to 1945 in school. Somehow in history we went from the election of Hindenburg to the election of *der Alte* without anything in between."

"That's not so. I remember when you had to do a report on Buchenwald."

"Yes, but that wasn't until Gymnasium, and then only after there were those graves in the Jewish cemetery that were desecrated. Suddenly the government decided maybe they couldn't just skip those years after all."

"Some things are better forgotten, Willy. What's the point of . . . ."

"What's the point!" His voice rose. "You, of all people, ask that?"

"Yes. They were bad times. People didn't always do the right thing, and . . ."

"You did."

"Not always."

"When it counted. You took in the Brenners."

"Yes. I did do that. Come, let's eat. And you can tell me all about Dr. Brenner."

"There's nothing to tell. I haven't met her. But I want to."

They ate their supper and talked of other things.

The next morning he was in his examining room. Fräulein Maas, a bony woman with sparse hair dyed an improbable shade of red, lay on the table. Willie had known her since they had moved to Wolfenbüttel. Her parents had been his patients. Fräulein Maas had been a nurse during the war and had come back from the front with her lips permanently set, so it seemed, in an austere line. She held the sheet to her thin breasts while he palpated her abdomen. There was a lump where no lump belonged. She winced as he palpated.

"That hurts?"

"A little."

"Sorry. I think maybe we should get a picture. I'll give you a referral, you'll go to Georg-August."

"Do you think it's serious."

"Let's get a picture."

"It's not the liver, I don't think. The liver . . ."

"Let's not pre-diagnose. Let's get that picture." He stood up, draped the sheet back over her lower body. "You can get dressed now, then come into my office and I'll have that referral for you."

He washed his hands, then stepped through the adjoining door to his office, leaving her to get dressed. When she came back into his office her navy skirt and white blouse were hanging on her thin frame. Her sensible shoes were shined, the seams on her stockings ruler straight. She clutched a large navy handbag to her chest.

"Cancer?" she asked when she was seated opposite him. The doorbell rang, and he ignored it.

"Not necessarily. Let's not jump to conclusions."

"It's what killed Mama."

"Still. We don't necessarily repeat our parents' history. Here." He handed her the referral. "Get it done as soon as you can. No sense worrying longer than you have to. They'll call me when they have the results, and I'll call you as soon as I hear."

"If it's cancer . . . ."

"Let's not anticipate."

"No. But if it is, I'm not waiting around. I've seen too much to want to go that way."

"Fräulein Maas," he said gently, taking her hand, "even if it is cancer, they've got all sorts of new treatments. And there are all sorts of cancers, some not much worse than appendicitis. Let's not anticipate."

She removed her hand. "Thank you, Doctor. I'll make that appointment." She drew herself up from the chair, rested her hand on the back for a moment, straightened, and head held high, walked out.

Willie followed. In his waiting room Ernst Becker sat nervously, twisting his cap around and around in his hand. Across the room sat Frieda Strumm, knitting a pair of booties for another of the grandchildren that her children seemed to produce with metronomic regularity. Next to her, reading a paperback book, was a young woman in her early twenties. Willie shook his head. She looked exactly like her mother.

"Dr. Meinhoff?"

"You're Dr. Brenner." He offered his hand, and she took it in a firm grasp.

"I'm sorry to have barged in like this. Maybe I should have called, but after I finished filling out papers at the hospital this morning, I asked someone where Wilhelm-Buschstrasse was, and they said it wasn't far. So I walked over."

She smiled, showing even white teeth. Clearly she had been adequately nourished and cared for during the war, he thought, unlike some of the German children. He shook his head to clear it, smiled back at her.

"It's not a problem . . . if you can wait. I have to see my patients."

"Of course. I can wait. Or I could come back."

Willie took his watch out of his pocket. It was just after eleven.

"I usually have lunch at about twelve thirty. Why don't you come back then? I only have a piece of bread and cheese, but I'm sure I can find something . . . or we could go to a café."

"I don't want to impose, or mess up your schedule."

"I *do* eat. Where are you staying?"

"Near the hospital, on the Alterweg. I was lucky. The hospital put me in touch with an elderly nurse who has an extra room."

"Well, if you want to wait, you're welcome. Otherwise, we could meet at the cafeteria on the corner of Alterweg and Wilhelm-Buschstrasse. That way you can do what you need to, and I'll be able to get back in time to see my afternoon patients. Unless you're willing to take a chance on some bread and cheese here."

"Whichever is easier for you."

"We'll eat here, then." He turned to his patients, both of whom had been studiously *not* listening to the conversation. "Who was here first?" he asked.

"She was," Ernst Becker said, pointing to the still knitting Frieda Strumm.

"That's all right," she smiled, "this is much more peaceful than my house."

Ernst Becker stood, stopped twisting his cap, and followed Willie into his examining room. Neither Ernst Becker nor Frieda Strumm required much of his medical expertise, but they were happy for a half hour of his undivided attention. With all the commotion in her house, Willie guessed no one ever heard Frau Strumm. Becker was another situation. A childless widower, whose wife had been killed in one of the raids, he had spent time in a POW camp and had come to Wolfenbüttel upon his release. Quarrelsome, opinionated, totally out of step with today's world, he had few acquaintances and fewer friends. Willie thought this might have been the first time he'd used his voice since his last office visit.

After these two he'd seen a two-year-old with an ear infection and a farmer, smelling of the manure pile, who'd stepped on a rusty nail. A prescription for penicillin and a tetanus shot and his office was clear. When he escorted the farmer out, Margot Brenner was still sitting in his office reading her book. She looked up when the door closed behind this last patient.

"You have a varied practice," she said. "You don't specialize?"

"Actually most of my patients are elderly. The young ones usually go to the younger doctors. This was an exception. But I've always been a generalist. It's just circumstances that have turned me into a geriatrician."

She rose, put her book into her briefcase, a dark leather one that looked as though it was of pre-war vintage. She saw him looking at it.

"It was my father's. I've used it all through college and medical school. Maybe it brought me luck."

"He was a fine man, your father." He opened the door to his living quarters, ushered her through. "I usually eat in the kitchen when I'm by myself."

"That's fine. I usually eat in the kitchen, too."

"Please, sit." He pointed her at one of the chairs at the kitchen table, a round clawfoot made of oak. It was shiny, but scarred with use. In the center stood a wooden salt-and-pepper shaker, and a small glass vase filled with cornflowers.

"May I help?" she asked.

"That's all right. Sit. I know where everything is, and as I said this won't be fancy. Another time we'll invite you for a more formal meal."

From a glass-fronted cabinet he took plates, cups, saucers. He opened the refrigerator, which stood next to a fairly new stove.

"Let"s see what we have."

He came to the table with a butter dish, a jar of preserves, and two kinds of cheese wrapped in wax paper. Limburger," he smiled. "I hope you don't mind."

"My mother loved it."

"And you?"

"I eat it."

"Hardly a resounding endorsement. Well, there's gouda, too. That's less pungent. And wait: One of my patients brought me some *Kochkäse*. Well, then. Some bread, and I think we're set."

He sat across from her. She studied him, and he fingered his old dueling scar. He hadn't thought about it for years.

"From the war?" she asked.

"From being young and stupid," he said. When she looked puzzled he continued. "It used to be a rite of passage in medical school. To duel. If you didn't have a scar it meant you flinched, and it branded you a coward."

"Did my father . . . ?"

"No. Jewish men weren't in those clubs. By the time we were in medical school the practice was really dying, but it was a family tradition, and my father would have been mortified if I hadn't acquired the badge. *Noblesse oblige.*" He smiled self-deprecatingly. He proffered the plate with the cheeses. "Help yourself."

"I think I'll try some of the *Kochkäse*. My mother used to make it, and I love it." She spread some of the cheese, buttery and full of caraway seeds, onto a slice of the dark bread, took a bite.

"Wonderful," she said.

"Good. The coffee should be warm by now." He rose and filled their cups. She added milk to hers, took a sip. It had been standing around too long, but it was hot.

"So," she said when he was seated again, "tell me about my *father*."

"There's not much to tell. Someone betrayed him. The Gestapo took him and your brother away. They arrested me."

"I know that part. I meant, tell me about my father—what he was like as a man, as a doctor, as a husband, a friend, a father."

"Ah." He took a long sip of his coffee. "What can I tell you? We went to the Medizinische Hochschule in Hannover together. This was in the early twenties. Your Papa was one of a very few Jews there. Most of the others were . . . clannish, kept together. I can't blame them," he added hastily. "My fellow students didn't make it easy for them."

"Like my fellow medical students didn't make it easy for us few women."

"I'm sure. The other Jewish students, they kept to themselves, swallowed the insults, the ruined experiments, the body parts left in their lockers. Your Papa? When he found a . . . ," he stopped, blushed, "a man's . . . uh, member . . . in his lab coat pocket? He held it up and said, 'Is one of you fellows missing something?'"

"I see some things are universal," she laughed. "Good for my dad."

"A few instances like that, and my comrades decided your Papa was all right. Not really a Jew. It helped that he wasn't religious. The others, they wouldn't take calls on their Sabbath, and that caused resentment too. Your father never shirked and by the time we graduated he was one of the more popular students. Graduated at the top of the class, too."

"And you stayed friends?"

"Yes. We were both on staff at the hospital in Hannover, and we had our practices not too far away from each other. When your father married, and I married my Eva, we all became friends. And when my Willy and your brother were born, the mamas were always together. We went to the theater, to concerts, to each other's houses. We had some wonderful times."

"And after 1933?"

"Yes, after '33 things changed. Of course you children weren't born then. Willy was born in September '37. Your brother was born a month earlier. He was a beautiful boy. When they were together with one of the maids, people always thought they were twins . . . both blond, both blue-eyed."

"But you were still all friends?"

"Of course. At first it didn't matter. Then, in '35 things began getting bad. The Jews lost their citizenship. Jews and Christians weren't allowed to marry or have relations. Some of our friends began to draw back. They stopped inviting your parents to parties. They stopped referring patients to your Papa."

"Yes. My mother says my dad wanted to leave then, but she didn't want to leave my grandparents, and she thought it would pass."

"Yes. We had many discussions. We all thought it would pass, that Hitler was a clown, and that the German people would soon come to their senses. Unfortunately we were wrong."

"So tell me more about my dad. What was he like, I mean, as a person."

"He was totally ethical. If we went to a restaurant and they undercharged us your father would point it out and insist on paying the full price. And he had a wonderful sense of humor. You know how it is in medicine. Sometimes things are bad. Your Papa always found a way to make a joke, to lighten the mood."

He took a bite of his limburger cheese sandwich. "Ahh," he said. "He liked good food, good wine. He said your mother made the best *Hefekuchen* in Hannover. And he loved to read, not just medical journals, although he kept up with the latest in medicine, but he loved Goethe, and Heine, and Busch, and Tolstoy. And Freud. He told me if he had to do it over again, he would have become a psychoanalyst."

"I didn't know that."

"Well, I don't know that he talked about it a lot. He didn't want your mama to feel bad, that she was holding him back because he was a husband and father. That's the kind of man he was. And he loved you and your brother. People called him a *Kindernarr*. Do you know what that means?"

"I think so. Isn't it someone who's overly fond of children."

"Sort of. A fool for children. Not a pederast, though. Anyway, any chance he got he'd wheel Peter in the park. And you, after you were born. In those days men didn't do that. It wasn't considered manly. But your Papa didn't care. Of course, by the time you were born he couldn't wheel any baby in the park anymore . . . ."

"Why not?"

"Parks were off limits to Jews."

"Oh, right."

"But he still wheeled you both whenever he could. And played with you, and put you to bed."

"And then things got so bad that my parents decided to leave?"

"Right. After '38 he lost his medical license, but because of his profession he was still able to get a visa, even though it was hard. And he had an offer of a practice in New York, once he got his license there."

"Yes, my mother said a friend of theirs who had left in the early thirties put up the affidavits and wanted him to go into practice with him. But he never got out."

"No. Your brother got sick. And then someone betrayed him."

"Betrayed him how? That's one of the things I never understood. I mean, I know he was Jewish, but that was no secret. And
he was leaving, and had the papers and everything. What was there
to betray?"

"Ah, who knows? They were bad times. People turned on their
fellows. It didn't have to be true. Your father was working with me,
treating Aryans. That wasn't allowed. I think one of our colleagues,
a man who was always jealous of your Papa, made a call to the
Gestapo."

"And said he'd been treating Aryans?"

"That's what they questioned me about when they arrested
me. If it was the man I think it was, he was also angry because he
wanted to buy your father's equipment, and your father wouldn't
sell it to him. He gave it to me, instead, and I suspect that angered
Heinrich." He took a sip of his coffee. "I could be wrong, of course.
It could have been someone else. A patient maybe, who wasn't
satisfied, or who thought he shouldn't have to pay the bill after
being treated by a Jew. People thought all sorts of strange things."
He took another sip of coffee. "Some more coffee?"

"No, I'm fine." She drank some of the now-tepid coffee. "And
after the Gestapo came? You never saw him or Peter again?"

"Never. They took me to Buchenwald after a while, and then
the war started in earnest and they gave me a chance to join the
Wehrmacht."

They chewed in silence for a few minutes.

"So, this Heinrich. Is he still alive?"

"I don't know. I haven't kept up with any of the people from
that old life."

"What was his full name?"

"Heinrich Speer. It's funny. The rumor was that he wasn't so
Aryan himself. Not that it was ever proved, but maybe that's why
he was so . . . . Anyway, I have no proof."

"Maybe I'll try to find him. When I go to Hannover."

"If he's even alive."

"Nothing ventured, nothing gained."

"I'm afraid I haven't been very helpful. But I told you that when you called."

"No. It is helpful. And I'd like to hear more, about my father, the man. I don't mean today, because I know you're busy. But I'll be here awhile."

"I imagine you'll be busy, too. Internship doesn't leave you much time, if I remember correctly."

"I'm sure not. But I'll have some time off. May I call you again?"

"Of course. You'll have to come and have dinner with us, and meet my Willy. When do you start your internship?"

"In two weeks. Until then I'm just sort of hanging around at the hospital, getting my bearings. Exploring the town, things like that."

"Well then we should have that dinner before you go into the internship hole. Let me check with Willy and see what his schedule looks like. Do you have a telephone where we can call you?"

"I think Frau Lindemann has a phone, but I don't know the number. But Willy could leave a message for me at the hospital. Or I could call you in a day or so."

They agreed that that's what she should do. He offered some fruit, which she declined. She offered to help wash up, which he declined. She thanked him for the lunch, and for seeing her, and shook his hand and left.

That went all right, Willie told himself after the door closed behind her. *I don't know what I was worrying about. And even if she finds Heinrich, what can he tell her?"*

CHAPTER 9

Wolfenbüttel, June 1963

Margot walked down the street, lined with linden trees. Their leaves, a bright new green, shaded the sidewalk, but it was warm enough so that she put down her briefcase and took off her jacket. She folded it over her arm and resumed her walk. The street was busy with pedestrian and bicycle traffic, interspersed by the occasional car. There was not nearly the vehicular traffic, though, that she was used to in her Washington Heights neighborhood. She remembered that during the war there had been practically no cars on the streets. Between the poverty of the neighborhood residents and gas rationing, a car was a rarity. Her older cousins told her they'd been able to roller skate up and down the streets without worrying about getting run over. They'd been able to play stickball in the street, using the manhole covers as bases, and they'd always been annoyed when, toward evening, the lone car returned and, with a whole street to choose from, parked on one of their bases. Nowadays kids couldn't use the streets like that in Washington Heights, or, she guessed, anyplace in New York. Whenever John came to visit he had trouble finding a place to park his car. Here, though, there were plenty of parking spaces.

Walking along she thought about her lunch with Dr. Meinhoff. She hadn't learned much new, although it was interesting that her father had wanted to switch to psychoanalysis. And she'd heard from an independent source what her mother had always told her, that her Dad was a special person. What a waste.

When it became clear, after the war, that neither her father nor Peter would be coming back, and when her mother's letters had been returned, her mother, and then she, had tried to find out more. Through inquiries to the German government and the various refugee agencies, they had learned that her father had, eventually, been transported to Auschwitz. Peter had died shortly after they were arrested 'of natural causes,' the government had said. This date of death had been a source of grief for Claire. "Poor Martin," she had said when she'd learned it, "he would have blamed himself that he couldn't keep him safe." Martin, according to the government, had lived until 1944. How had he survived until then? Had his position as a doctor helped? If so, what happened then?

She wondered whether there was a way, now that she was here, to find more specifics. Maybe before she started her internship she could go to the city hall in Hannover. Maybe they had records there.

"Look out," someone called, just as a soccer ball came flying in her direction, followed closely by a freckled boy in scruffy short pants and a once-white tee shirt. She stepped out of the way, and the boy, maybe ten or eleven, deftly kicked the ball before it hit the sidewalk, and with a mumbled *"Entshuldigung,"* followed its arc back into the street where his comrades continued their game.

She stood and watched them for a minute, enjoying their energy and skill. In America they'd be playing stickball, or stoop ball if they didn't have a broomstick. Here they kicked the ball, raced after it with balletic leaps, reversed direction, and did it again. The boys were of assorted sizes, some almost as tall as she, others still clearly pre-pubescent. They were all skinny, all dressed in clothes that had been through many washings. Their shoes were scuffed, worn at the heels and toes. Most of them were blond, although there was one boy whose dark skin suggested his mother had met an American G.I.

She continued her walk, and her thoughts. What would she say to him if Dr. Speer was still alive? "Did you betray my father?" wasn't likely to win friends and influence people. No, she'd do what she'd done with Dr. Meinhoff, just say she knew he'd known her father, and she wanted to find out as much about him as she could. Maybe he'd talk to her. Maybe, too, the next time she spoke to Dr. Meinhoff, she could get the name of some of the patients her father had treated.

Did that come under patient confidentiality? She was sure they had that here, too. She'd have to ask. She'd have to know that anyway when she started work. If Dr. Meinhoff did give her some of the patients' names, maybe she could talk to them, too, if they were still alive. If they were still in Hannover. She knew the war and its aftermath had caused great upheaval. People moving, people dead. Hannover, she knew, had been bombed to smithereens. She wasn't sorry about the bombings, but it meant that it was less likely she'd find anyone.

Her musings had made the blocks evaporate, and she found herself back at the two-story row house that would be her home for the next two years. Frau Lindemann lived on the ground floor and let rooms on the second to supplement her meager pension. The tenants were all hospital personnel, although Margot was the only doctor. The others, Frau Lindemann had told her, were two nurses, an orderly, and a lab technician. Margot had not yet met any of them.

She looked around at the well-kept yard. There was a currant bush to one side, its fruit still green but beginning to show signs of pink. The red and yellow flowers at the borders of the path were free of weeds and stood like sentries guarding the walk. The grass on the small lawn looked as though it had been cut with manicure scissors. She shuddered when she remembered her Uncle Oscar telling them that when he'd been at Dachau after Kristallnacht one of his labors had, indeed, been to cut the grass with manicure shears. She shook her head. Maybe coming here hadn't been such a good idea.

She took out the key Frau Lindemann had given her and opened the door. The smell of ammonia and floor wax greeted her. The floors shone. Her landlady might be retired, but she hadn't lost her reverence for antisepsis.

Margot climbed the stairs and turned right, to her room. It was small, no more than 12' by 15', and contained a mattress on an iron bedstand, a dark wood dresser, and a night table with a lamp, whose shade was still covered by the cellophane that had encased it back in the pre-war days of its purchase. The cellophane was brown at the edges, although Margot didn't think the heat from the 40-watt bulb was the cause. The base of the lamp was in the shape of a shepherdess in flowing skirt and low-cut bodice, with a beribboned bonnet adorning her blonde curls. Under the lamp was a lace doily, the twin of which covered the top of the dresser. The floor was a dark wood, also shining within an inch of its life, and covered by what might, in its younger days, have been an oriental rug. Now it was so threadbare that it was hard to tell.

The mattress, she had discovered last night when she'd moved from the Ramada hotel on Bahnhoffstrasse, was firm and the linens were clean. The pillow was down, as was the comforter.

She didn't have cooking privileges. Frau L. had been clear about that. She didn't want any food in her upstairs rooms. "It attracts vermin, and I won't have that." But for an extra thirty marks a week she could eat breakfast and dinner with her landlady and whichever of the other tenants chose that. She didn't know what her schedule would be once she started her internship, but until then she had opted for the meal plan. For lunch she'd be on her own. Since she planned to spend most of her days at the hospital anyway, she didn't think that would be a problem.

She took off her 'working clothes' and put on a pair of jeans and a polo shirt. She wasn't sure whether that was appropriate attire for a Fräulein Doktor, but it was comfortable. Her mother's Aunt Ella hadn't approved of her jeans in New York, either, but it was what she liked to wear when she didn't have to dress up. She'd always thought girdles and stockings were just another way to keep women in their place, like binding feet in China.

She picked up her towel and cake of soap, and made her way to the communal bathroom. This, too, sparkled and smelled of disinfectant. After using the toilet and washing her hands and face, she took the rag from under the sink and wiped off any water spots. She wasn't going to violate Frau Lindemann's hygienic standards, no sir!

Dinner was served promptly at six. Frau L. had been clear on that. If you weren't there you didn't eat, and she'd appreciate it if you let her know if you were planning not to be there. Margot had said, "I don't know how that will work once I'm at the hospital. Emergencies come up."

"I know about emergencies. I worked there for forty-three years." The landlady had pulled herself up to her full five feet, and Margot had half expected her to salute. Her bobbed hair, dark brown streaked with white, lay obediently against her skull. Her eyebrows, a straight unbroken line, were also dark brown, and her green eyes sparked behind thick glasses. Her thin lips were set under a stubby nose, and her back was the kind of straight Margot's mother had tried, unsuccessfully, to instill in her by making her walk with a yardstick between her shoulder blades.

When Margot entered the dining room now Frau Lindemann sat at the head of the table set for six and covered by a blue-and-white-checked oil cloth. The dishes were the same blue willow Dr. Meinhoff had served on. Margot wondered whether that was the Wolfenbüttel pattern. Besides Frau Lindemann three other people were already seated, two women and a man. Margot took one of the empty seats to Frau L.'s left, nodding to everyone as she did.

"This is Dr. Brenner," their landlady said. "She's from America, but she speaks passable German." Margot smiled. "This," the landlady went on, indicating the young woman to her immediate right, "is Renate Kühn. This is Ilse Shäffer, and this," she pointed to the lone male, a short, pudgy redhead with skin the color of putty, "is our only rooster (*der einzige Hahn im Korb*), Alex Weerbel."

Frau Lindemann rang a bell, and a girl of fifteen or sixteen stuck her head through the door.

"You can serve, Irmgard."

The girl curtsied and left, returning shortly afterwards with a tureen of soup, which when ladled into the bowls, proved to be pea soup. Before Irmgard had finished serving, the last of the roomers entered, a tall dark-haired woman of about Margot's own age. Her cheeks were flushed and she was breathing heavily.

"Sorry I'm late, G'nädige Frau," she mumbled. "An emergency just when I was getting ready to leave."

"Well you just made it," Frau Lindemann said. "This is Hedwig Krantz. She's a nurse in the emergency room. We have to make allowances for her. This," she indicated Margot, "is Dr. Margot Brenner. You may cross paths in the hospital. Dr. Brenner is training for surgery."

Hedwig smiled hello, and sat down at the empty place next to Margot.

"Nice to meet you. Thank you, Irmgard," she said when that young woman had ladled some soup into her bowl.

No one talked while they concentrated on their soup. There were a few pieces of sausage in the soup. Margot, who had a knee jerk aversion to pork (her mother had said "pork, pfeh!" once too often) pushed the pieces aside. She tried not to dwell on the fact that the sausage, having been cooked in the soup, had seeped its porkness into the liquid. She had a hunch she'd be doing a lot of mental gymnastics over the next three years.

"So you're going to be a surgeon?" her neighbor asked. "But what made you come to Germany?"

"I had a chance of a surgical internship here. In America I'd have had to settle on pediatrics."

"The head of pediatrics at Georg-August is a woman. Dr. Sauer. She's very nice, very approachable. Unlike most of the male doctors she doesn't treat us nurses as though we're all idiots."

"Or servants," said the plump woman across the table from Margot, who had been introduced as Renate someone.

"Yes. Some of the male doctors and professors treated us women doctors the same way."

"You must be strong," the rooster, Alex was it? said. "I mean, to be able to stand all that blood and flesh. Me, when I mop the floors, if there are bodily fluids I try . . ."

Ah, the orderly, Margot figured.

"Not at the table, Herr Weerbel." This from Frau Lindemann.

"Sorry," he mumbled, blushing and looking down at his empty plate. Fortunately for everyone, Irmgard came with a bowl of cabbage mixed with potatoes, which she ladled into everyone's soup bowls. That done she retreated and came back with a platter of sliced meat swimming in gravy. As she served each thin slice, she asked, "Gravy?" and where the answer was yes she ladled some onto the meat and over the vegetables. Margot, unsure of the provenance of the meat, declined.

"Ah, sauerbraten," Alex said, digging in.

"So where in America are you from?" asked the woman who had not, until now, said a word. That would be Ilse Shäffer, the lab technician, by a process of elimination. She had wiry black hair, red cheeks, and slightly protruding eyes behind horn-rimmed glasses.

"New York."

"I have an uncle who lives in Milwaukee," she said. "Is that near New York?"

"Not very. It's about a third of the way across the country, I guess sort of like from here to Rome. Have you ever been to the States?"

"No. I've never been out of Wolfenbüttel. But maybe some day . . . ."

"I was in Italy during the war," Frau Lindemann said. "Filthy place. Filthy people. I was glad to get back home."

Margot said nothing. Everyone ate quietly for a few minutes.

"So . . . ," Hedwig finally said, "but why Wolfenbüttel? In fact how did you ever even hear of Wolfenbüttel? I don't suppose we're in the tourist books."

"An old friend of my father's lives here. I spoke to him. He gave me Dr. Prange's number. I called, and they'd just had an unanticipated vacancy . . . ."

"Yes, we heard about that. Horst Shüler thought he could turn his new Porsche into an airplane. There's a lot of babies who'll grow up without a father now."

"Fräulein Krantz!" Frau Lindemann admonished.

"Well it's true. I knew Horst in Gymnasium, and . . . ."

"*De mortuis nihil nisi bonum*," intoned the landlady. Hedwig, officially chastened, went back to her sauerbraten.

"Your father came from Germany?" Renate asked. "But you must have been born in America. How is it you speak such good German?"

"I studied it at school. And spoke it with my mother."

"Not with your father?" Alex asked.

"My father died when I was a baby."

That quieted everyone again, and the conversation for the rest of the meal, which ended with stewed pears, required no further admonitions. As Irmgard cleared the plates, the roomers retreated up the stairs.

"My room is at the end of the hall," Hedwig told Margot. "If you need anything . . . ."

"Thank you, at the moment I'm all right."

CHAPTER 10

Hannover, September 1939

Another sunny morning. Willie had gone to the office. Eva had made oatmeal for the children and was spooning it into little Willy's open mouth. Peter sat on several medical books. A bib was tucked under his chin. He happily dipped the spoon into the bowl, then brought it to his mouth. Half the cereal went in, the rest dribbled onto his chin and onto the bib. He laughed with delight, dipped the spoon back into the bowl, and repeated the process. Eva spooned another mouthful into Willy. Martin sat next to Peter, watching Eva and the two little boys.

"Still no passage," he said after a while.

"I know. Willie has tried everything, everyone."

"Did Willie talk to you about his proposal? About the boys?"

"Yes." She sighed and bit her lip.

"And what do you think?"

"It's an impossible choice. Not just for you. For us too."

He nodded.

"I could take Peter and go somewhere else. I hear there are people who'll help Jews get to the border."

"And then what?"

"And then we could cross. To Switzerland, or to France."

"Switzerland isn't letting anyone in. And France is at war with us, with the Germans."

"But from there maybe we could get to America."

"Are you willing to risk Peter's life on that maybe? It's one thing for you alone, a strong man. But with a little boy . . . ."

"But if we stay here . . . ."

"Yes. That's why Willie made the suggestion. It's a terrible choice, but at least we can keep Peter safe."

"You'd give up Willy?"

Tears sprang to her eyes.

"It's a terrible choice."

Martin took a swallow of the coffee that was, by this time, lukewarm.

"I'll take good care of little Willy, but . . . ."

"I know. But he's not safe here either. Even if you and Peter were deported. Willie heard from one of his friends about a top secret place. They talk in whispers. It's called *Sonnenstein*. Did you ever hear of it?"

"*Sonnenstein*? No. What is it?"

"Willie says it's a place where they kill mental defectives, an extermination center. And he heard that Nazi doctors are going into all the hospitals and nursing homes, and sending patients there."

"There are all sorts of rumors, Eva. Willy looks fine."

She sighed, wiped her cheek with the fringe of her apron.

"Yes, he looks fine, but with the war we'll all be called to service. If I have to put Willy in a nursery, how long before they find out? And then . . . . Oh, Martin, what a world, what a country."

He said nothing.

"Papa, more oatmeal," Peter chirped. Martin scraped the oatmeal off Peter's bib, and spooned it back into the bowl, then went to the stove and added another dollop to the bowl.

"More sugar," Peter said. Martin added more sugar, and a splash of milk. Willy, like a little bird, opened his mouth for Eva to feed him.

"He can't feed himself. He still wears diapers. He can't even walk, Martin."

Martin shook his head.

"I don't know, Eva. If I have to leave, and if I take him, then . . ." He couldn't bring himself to finish.

"Then he's doomed. Don't you think I know that? Do you think it's not driving me crazy? I can't sleep. I can't eat. He's my baby, Martin. But if he's doomed anyway . . . ."

"We don't know that."

"We don't want to know that. Did you ever read *Mein Kampf*?"

"As a matter of fact, yes."

"The Master Race doesn't have room for defectives of any kind. That includes you and Peter, it includes Frau Krebs on the third floor, and it includes Willy."

"Who's Frau Krebs?"

"A neighbor. She has tuberculosis. She was in a sanitarium in Karlsruhe. Her daughter got a letter last week saying she'd died."

"People die of tuberculosis."

"True, but Willie says she was getting better, and he heard of three other tuberculosis patients who suddenly died last week."

Martin scraped another blob of oatmeal off Peter's bib. Eva shoveled another spoonful into Willy's open mouth.

"We should have left years ago, after '33," she said.

"You had no reason to."

"We had every reason, once Hitler came to power. Sure, we're not Jewish. Germany was going to be a glorious place for us. But what they started doing in our name, even before we realized about Willy, we should have left."

"We certainly should have left. I wanted to, but Claire, she didn't want to leave her parents."

"She did anyway, in the end."

"Yes, that's the irony. When they were deported after *Kristallnacht* she realized we had to go."

"Do you know what's happened to them?"

"The last letter we had from them they were back in Warsaw. That's where they were from originally, although they hadn't lived there since before Claire was even born. That letter came a few weeks ago. Now, with the war . . . ."

"Take Willy, Martin.'

"It may not come to that. Now that the war has started, Hitler has other things to do than chase Jews."

"I hope so, but I don't believe it. Anyway, if nothing happens nothing happens. But if they come for you . . . ."

Martin took another swallow of coffee. He put the cup down, sighed deeply.

"All right. But then I think we need to prepare. Peter," he said, turning to his son, "we're all going to play a game of pretend. Can you do that?"

"Pretend," the little boy said.

"Right, pretend. We'll *pretend* that Tante Eva here is your mama. Can you say that?"

"Mama," Peter said.

"Right, from now on, you'll call Tante Eva 'Mama.' All right?"

"Mama?" Peter said tentatively.

"Right. And from now on you'll call me 'Onkel Martin.' Can you say that?"

"Onkel Martin," Peter giggled.

"And when Onkel Willie comes home this evening you'll say, 'Hello, Papa.' Can you remember that?"

"Hello Papa."

"I'd better feed Willy," Martin said. He turned away for a moment, swallowed hard. Eva put down the spoon, rose and went to sit next to Peter. Martin sat in her chair, and spooned oatmeal into Willy's waiting mouth.

CHAPTER 11

Wolfenbüttel, July 1963

The first days of her surgical internship passed in a whirl. From the time she arrived at the hospital, usually before six in the morning, until she fell into bed—sometimes her own, sometimes the cot in the on-call room—she was on her feet. Some of the surgeons were patient and explained procedures as they went. Others just barked. Barking in German, she thought, was even worse than in English. On the other hand, no one had . . . so far . . . slapped her. And she was learning. A few of the surgeons actually let her near the patients, let her do a retraction, or tie off vessels. Dr. Olendorff had let her remove a hot appendix and had told her she'd done a good job. Dr. Speisser, on the other hand, had called her a '*Sheiss Dumbkopf*' because she hadn't wiped the sweat off his brow quickly enough.

This morning she'd been called on to assist Dr. Sauer at a tonsillectomy. She'd met Dr. Sauer when she had dinner at the Meinhoffs, and she'd liked her a lot.

"Call me Sophie," she'd said, and Margot tried, but found it difficult, both because Dr. Sauer was old enough to be her mother and because she was a staff physician at the hospital. At the hospital, of course, she used the title, as, indeed, Dr. Sauer reciprocated. Margot was still getting used to being called Dr. Brenner. In the social setting of the Meinhoff house Margot compromised by trying not to call Dr. Sauer anything. That worked all right when they were face to face at the dinner table.

The tonsillectomy was routine, Dr. Sauer said, and the whole operation lasted less than half an hour. Margot had marveled at the smoothness and efficiency with which Dr. Sauer proceeded. There were no histrionics, no shouting. The O.R. nurse handed her instruments almost before Dr. Sauer called for them. She used them coolly, then dropped them into the waiting receptacle. When it was time to tie off the bleeders, she stepped back and let Margot finish up. When they stripped out of their bloody scrubs and washed up afterward, Dr. Sauer said, "Well done. We'll make a surgeon of you."

"I didn't do much," Margot said.

"You didn't pass out, either. I've had more than one surgical intern, not to mention medical student, on the floor at my feet."

"Really. You'd think by the time they got this far . . . ."

"You would, wouldn't you? But you'd be surprised. Sometimes the bigger they are . . ."

"The first couple of times were hard for me. But now I tell myself it's just meat."

"And that works for you?"

"Most of the time. The worst thing I ever saw was once when I was in medical school doing my general medicine rotation. There was an alcoholic they brought in. You could smell him from outside the examining room. He had all sorts of sores on his feet and legs, and when we examined him the sores were alive, crawling with maggots. That was the one time I almost fainted."

"I can imagine. That's one of the good things about pediatrics. Not too many alcoholics."

"If I hadn't gotten this offer from Georg-August, I'd be doing a pediatric internship. But I've always wanted to be a surgeon."

"Really? It's never interested me. I mean, I don't mind the occasional tonsillectomy, but that's not really surgery, it's so routine. But surgery? With all those opinionated men . . . ?"

"Well, there is that, but it's so . . . neat. To take out a part that's not working, and fix it."

"Sort of like auto mechanics," Dr. Sauer laughed.

"I suppose. But to make people well again."

"I'm teasing you," she said. "Whatever you like. My late husband couldn't understand how I could look at sore throats and give shots all day. He was an anesthesiologist."

"That way he didn't have to talk to patients at all."

"I used to tease him about that. Said it was almost as good as pathology."

She grew quiet for a moment, looking at her reflection as she applied a light dab of lipstick.

"Well, back to the sore throats," she said.

Margot was due to assist at a gall bladder removal in an hour, not enough time to catch a quick nap. She ran a comb through her hair, put on a clean pair of scrubs, and made her way down to the cafeteria.

Some things were universal, she thought. Cafeterias smelled the same, and looked the same, in New York and in Wolfenbüttel. She wondered whether that would be true in China, too. She got herself a cheese danish and a cup of coffee. After adding milk and picking up a napkin, she looked around for an empty seat. Since it was still early, not even 8:00 a.m., there were empty tables, and she headed for one near a window. Around her were a few civilians who looked as though they'd slept in their clothes. There was a scattering of nurses, and a few people in scrubs.

The nurses were all women; the people in scrubs were all men. There were also a few people in the uniforms of the maintenance staff, clearly fueling up before starting their day. With the doctors and nurses, of course, you couldn't tell whether they were coming, going, or in between as she was. She amused herself trying to guess, by looking at the men, what their specialties were. That big one, who looked like a football player (oops, *soccer* here) was an orthopedic surgeon. That skinny one there, with the glasses thick enough to stop bullets, was a psychiatrist. *But then why is he wearing scrubs?* she wondered. *Maybe a dermatologist, then. And that one there . . . ?*

"Mind if I join you?"

Margot looked up to see Willy Meinhoff, a tray in his hand, standing next to her table.

"Not at all, but I can't stay long."

He dropped into the seat next to her, flashing an Ipana smile. His blond hair was tousled, as were his scrubs. His stethoscope and the cap of a pen protruded from his shirt pocket.

"I'm on lunch break myself," he said. He pointed at his plate, filled with a generous helping of scrambled egg, home fried potatoes, and knockwurst.

"You were on call last night?"

"Yeah. Thank goodness not as often as in my first year, but . . . it puts a crimp in my social life."

"Interns and residents aren't supposed to have social lives."

"I've noticed. So, how are you finding Wolfenbüttel?"

"I don't really see much of it, but it seems like a nice little city. Mostly I see the hospital and my room."

"Poor Margot. You should let me take you to some of the high spots."

"In my spare time, you mean."

"Yes, well, you're not always on call. And I'd like to get to know you, about your life in America. All that. After all, if it hadn't been for the war, we'd be old friends, right?"

"I'd like that." She finished the last of her danish, and washed it down with the coffee. Neither was particularly good, but the danish was sweet, and almost made up for the fact that the coffee tasted as though it had spent at least the night boiling in a tin pot.

"I'm off on Friday. How about you?"

She took her calendar out of her purse, and shook her head.

"Nope. My next night off is Sunday."

"I think I can arrange that. Let me call you."

"Just leave a note for me in my hospital mailbox. I'm more likely to get that."

"Trouble with your landlady?"

"No. But she doesn't like us to get messages, so she tends not to pass them on. Not that that's been a problem for me, but some of the others have complained."

She rose, picked up her tray.

"Good seeing you, Willy," she said. He stood and gave a half bow, before sitting down again and tucking into his meal.

Is that a date I just agreed to? she asked herself as she took the stairs to the surgery floor. Did she want it to be? She and John had both assumed they'd be too busy and too tired. For all she knew John was, at this very moment, seeing someone 'suitable.'

She stopped herself. That wasn't fair. It was his parents, not he, who wanted him to find someone else. On the other hand, being shown a bit of her new surroundings was hardly a date.

And Willy had said that had things been different they'd have been old friends. She looked at her watch. 8:15. John would probably be asleep in any case, and undoubtedly alone. Unless he was on call.

She missed him. While she'd become somewhat friendly with her two fellow boarders, Hedwig and Renate, there was no one here she could talk to, really talk to, the way she could to John and to Chris. And she missed him physically. Suddenly it seemed a long time until Christmas. John was looking into places, in southern France and in Spain, where they could lie on the beach and just be together, someplace not too expensive or too filled with tourists.

"Will I be booking two rooms or one?" he'd asked when they'd discussed it shortly before her departure.

"One," she'd said, realizing that she was crossing a line.

"Then why wait?" he'd asked, not unreasonably, and had asked again on their last night together. She couldn't really give him a reasonable answer. Somehow, she thought, it would be different in Europe.

"You mean," he'd teased, "it's like being drunk? 'When I'm in Europe I'm not responsible.'"

"When you put it like that it does sound pretty silly. But humor me."

"Haven't I?" he'd asked.

Now it seemed even sillier to her, and she wished he were here.

Once in the OR, she had no time to think of John, or of Willy, or of anything but the woman on the table. She was obese, and the layers of fat in her belly made the operation more complicated. The surgeon was Dr. Rausch, a silly, pompous rooster who was not above pinching bottoms. He was short, had to stand on a stepstool to perform, and, it was rumored, took pride in having a nurse unzip his fly and hold his penis while he urinated during surgery.

He had nodded curtly at her when she'd taken her place next to him. The patient, already anesthetized, lay like a whale, her belly exposed, her privates draped in a sterile sheet. The anesthesiologist, an Ichabod Crane-like figure under his mask and gown, fiddled with his dials.

Margot was holding the retractors when arterial blood spurted out of the woman's belly, a geyser spraying them all.

"Clamp that artery," Dr. Rausch screeched. The next few minutes ... hours, it seemed ... flew by in a kaleidoscope of instruments, blood, hands, shouts. Margot finally found the artery, which Dr. Rausch had, apparently, nicked, and was able to clamp it. The geyser subsided. The anesthesiologist said, "Pressure is low, but steadying," and Dr. Rausch was finally able to excise a severely diseased gall bladder. He let Margot sew the patient up, and after the nurse wheeled her to the recovery room, and Dr. Rausch, the anesthesiologist, and Margot were discarding their bloody scrubs and washing up, the little doctor put his arm around Margot's shoulder.

"So," he said, "is this your first misadventure in the operating room?"

Before she could answer 'MY misadventure??' he continued, "Don't worry about it. You'll learn, and since I was able to salvage it there's no harm done. It'll be our little secret, hmm?"

Margot was speechless. She looked at Ichabod Crane, who was busily washing his hands, looking at the foam on his hands, at the ceiling, anywhere but at her. He dried his hands quickly and hightailed it out of the scrub room.

"Our little secret, hmm?" Dr. Rausch repeated.

She nodded. He patted her on the rump, a friendly pat, and she cringed. She finished washing up, and went to the women's locker to find another pair of scrubs for her next scheduled surgery.

The rest of the day was routine, if you could call assisting while a surgeon found that surgery was useless because the patient's cancer was so widespread, routine. She was allowed to sew that one up, too, and was glad that she wasn't the one who would have to tell Herr Meyer's family the bad news. The last surgery of her day was a hernia repair, and that went off without a hitch.

By the time she was back in her street clothes, she was so tired she could hardly drag herself the few blocks to her rooming house. She thought of skipping dinner and falling straight into bed, but she'd told Frau Lindemann that she'd be there for dinner, and she knew that she'd better show up. She hoped she didn't fall asleep into the soup.

The soup was mushroom and barley, and she managed not only to keep her head out of it, but actually to eat it. She managed the kale and potatoes, and the boiled beef as well, and even enjoyed the applesauce and *lebkuchen* that Frau Lindemann served for dessert. She let the dinner conversation go on around her without contributing to it. It was all she could do to chew and swallow; speech was beyond her.

After finishing her meal she placed her napkin back in the napkin ring, excused herself, pushed back her chair, and staggered to bed.

In the morning she was almost human again, and because she wasn't due in for the earliest surgery, she got to eat breakfast. Unlike the hospital coffee, Frau L.'s was hot and strong and fresh. She ate a boiled egg and a piece of dark bread with butter and homemade gooseberry jam, "From my own bushes," Frau L. said proudly. Hedwig, the emergency room nurse, was having breakfast as well, and after they'd finished they agreed to walk to the hospital together.

"So," Hedwig asked as they walked, "how's it going?"

"All right. Some of the doctors are really good about letting me do things. Others aren't."

"Who've you been working with?"

"Yesterday with Dr. Sauer, and with Dr. Rausch."

Hedwig grimaced. "That little pig?"

Margot looked at her. Her brown eyes sparkled, as though sun was glinting off stone.

"You've worked with him?"

"I used to work in the OR. Rausch is one of the reasons I shifted to the ER."

"Why?"

They were nearing the hospital grounds. The flowers in the beds surrounding the entrance swayed in a slight breeze, their reds and whites making a pattern of pink. Hedwig looked around cautiously.

"Lots of reasons. I got tired of trying to avoid his hands, for one thing. He was always touching me, accidentally ... ha! ... brushing my breasts. For another, he always made mistakes and blamed someone else. If he could blame a nurse, he did. If there was no nurse within range, he blamed the intern or the anesthesiologist. Once he even blamed the patient, who was already knocked out and totally immobile. He said she moved."

"Didn't anyone ever report him?"

"Whom would they believe? An experienced doctor, or some nurse? Or a new intern? Why do you think it's only the new interns who get to assist him? As soon as a doctor has a little experience he finds a way not to work with Rausch."

"And the hospital administration? Dr. Prange? They don't notice?"

"What do I know? I'm just a nurse. But I hear that Rausch is married to the sister of the chairman of the hospital board. Who, by the way, is supposed to be a real battle-ax."

"Ah," Margot said.

"I saw her picture once. They were having a big party for the hospital, you know, diamonds and fancy dresses, and the men in evening clothes. There was Dr. Rausch, standing next to a woman about twice his height and weight. She looked like one of those female wrestlers. Her fat arms were encased in long black gloves, and her white flesh spilled over them. She was wearing a sleeveless dress, can you imagine, and enough jewels to decorate a Christmas tree. Quite a picture. And she had a look on her face like the witch in *Hansel and Gretel*. You know, as if she was waiting to eat some children for a snack. I almost felt sorry for Dr. Rausch, I mean, no wonder he tries to feel up good-looking women." She giggled. "Am I terrible?"

"No. But tell me, how do the interns get out of working with him?"

"Any way they can. They suck up to other doctors so they'll ask for them, or they look at the OR schedule and try to work their schedules so they're not on when Rausch is doing surgery. Fortunately he doesn't do too many anymore. I think some of the patients have heard about his high 'accident' rate." She gave Margot a searching look. "Did you have a problem with him, too?"

Margot hesitated. Finally she said, "It's our little secret."

"Oh, he pulled that on you, too? What'd he do, nick a vein?"

"No, an artery."

"Did the patient die?"

"No, I was able to clamp it off, but it was touch and go for a while."

"And then he blamed you? I told you he was a pig."

By this time they had reached the elevators, and they parted company. Margot felt a little better. Not only was she not alone in her assessment of Dr. Rausch, but, more important, Hedwig had given her a way to avoid him . . . maybe. While she couldn't switch to the ER, she could certainly try to work around him. Let some other new intern have the experience. Once was enough for her. More than.

As she scrubbed up for the morning's first—for her—case, she thought of the letter she would write to John as soon as she had a spare moment, and could stay awake long enough to hold a pen.

CHAPTER 12

Wolfenbüttel, July 1963

"I won't be home for supper tonight, Papa," Willy said as they sat in the kitchen, eating a leisurely breakfast.

"The lovely Brigitte"

"No. I'm going to show Margot Brenner the non-medical side of Wolfenbüttel."

"Oh?"

Willy sighed, took a swallow of his coffee, before saying ,"You don't approve?"

"I thought you and Brigitte . . . ."

"I told you, she's just waiting for Mr. Right. I'm a diversion." He smiled. "Not that I mind."

His father shook his head. "Young people today. In my day . . . ."

"Yes, Papa. In your day women saved themselves for marriage, but now we have the pill. It makes it a lot easier to get laid."

His father shook his head again. He would never have spoken to his father that way. On the other hand, it was good that Willy felt easy enough with him. True, when Willy'd reached puberty, his father had taken him to an apartment where a woman initiated him into the mysteries of sex, after which the topic was never mentioned between them. Times have changed.

"Anyway, Papa, what have you got against Margot Brenner?"

"Who said I have something against her?"

"The way you said 'oh.' The way you asked about Brigitte."

"I just don't want you to get hurt."

"And why would I get hurt. First of all, I'm just being friendly, showing her Wolfenbüttel."

"That's how it starts."

"How what starts?"

"A relationship. She's a pretty woman. You're a young man . . ."

"And? For all I know she's married, Papa."

"Then she wouldn't be here. I'm just saying, I don't want you to get hurt. You know she'll go back to America eventually."

"Papa. You're making a mountain out of a molehill. Even if it leads to bed, which I'm not saying it will, that doesn't mean anything. Don't worry, I won't get hurt. But what about you? When are you going to make an honest woman out of Dr. Sauer?"

"I don't know that she wants to be an honest woman." He smiled. "I mean, she likes her life, her independence."

"I wouldn't mind, you know. I mean, I know you loved Mama, but I think even Mama would want you to have someone, not be alone. Have you thought about it?"

"About marrying again?"

"No, about taking up football. Of course about marrying again."

"I don't know, Willy. It'd be a change for you."

"For heaven's sake, Papa, I'm twenty-five. One of these days I'll even get my own place. I won't be on a hospital salary forever."

"There's plenty of room for you here."

"I know, Papa, but eventually I might even find the right woman and get married. And I'd feel better if you weren't alone."

"All right."

"All right you'll ask Sophie?"

"All right, I heard you. So where are you taking young Dr. Brenner?"

"I don't know. I thought, if she likes jazz, maybe to that new club downtown."

"Does she like jazz?"

"I don't know, but I'll find out. So far all I know is that she's not on call tonight."

They talked of other things, and after breakfast Willie went into his office to catch up on some paperwork. Young Willy went in to watch the tennis matches at Wimbledon on the television.

Why hadn't he asked Sophie to marry him? he wondered. Did he love her? Certainly not the way he'd loved Eva, but they weren't teenagers. He enjoyed her company, was comfortable with her. Even in bed it was good. Okay, not fireworks, but it was good, companiable, and when, from time to time, the plumbing was slow, she was understanding, patient. But she seemed satisfied with things as they were. He was afraid to rock that boat. What if he asked and she said no? Then could they go on as they were? Or, what if she said yes, and they married? That would change things too. No, better leave things as they were. It wasn't as though Sophie was pressuring him to marry her. On the other hand, since Willy wouldn't be home for dinner . . . . He went to the phone.

When Willy arrived at Frau L.'s, Margot was waiting in the front parlor. They had had their Sunday dinner after Frau L's return from church: vegetable soup, sauerbraten with spätzel and red cabbage, and stewed apples and ginger cookies for dessert. The evening meal would be light, just bread and butter and some cheese, and Margot had told her landlady that she'd not be there.

"A young man?" Frau Lindemann had asked.

"Yes, a doctor from the hospital."

"Ah." The landlady had smiled. "I wondered what was taking them so long."

"Oh, it's not like that," Margot had protested. "He's an old family friend. He just wants to show me something of Wolfenbüttel."

"Is he young?"

"Yes."

"Single?"

"Yes."

"Then it's like that. You mark my words. I've been around young doctors long enough. You be careful."

Margot smiled. It felt good to have someone worrying about her. She hadn't had that since her mother had died.

"You look nice," Willy said, taking in her navy skirt and light blue scoop-necked blouse, her bare legs in flat sandals. Willy was dressed in neatly pressed chinos, an open-necked shirt, with a navy sweater knotted by the sleeves around his neck.

"You look nice, too."

He smiled, and held the door for her. They walked out into the warm summer evening.

"So, what would you like to see?"

"I don't know. What is there to see?"

"Ah, this is a swinging city. We have a museum, we have churches. We have a library. We have cafes and restaurants, and a movie theater, five book stores, a concert hall, and a couple of clubs that have some good jazz. The museum and library are closed. I don't suppose you want to go to church, so that leaves the rest. Although, I'm not sure there's a concert tonight."

She laughed. "What would you like to do?"

"Well, I'm torn. On the one hand I'd like to take you to hear some jazz. But if we do that we won't get a chance to talk much, so maybe we could save that for another time and we could just have dinner someplace. Is that all right?"

"Sounds fine to me, but I don't know that I'll want to eat very much. Frau Lindemann served a hearty lunch."

"*Ja*, Sunday lunch. So you'll be a cheap date." He smiled again. He had a wonderful smile, she thought. It crinkled his eyes, and produced deep dimples. His blond hair fell onto his forehead, and he brushed it back. "I know a quiet place. They have good food, but you can order small portions."

"Sounds fine."

They walked down the street heavy with pedestrians out for a stroll in the warm evening. There were young couples in jeans and tee shirts, arms entwined, elderly women in sensible shoes and hats, walking sedately. There seemed to be few elderly men.

"So," Willy said, "tell me about life in America."

"I don't imagine it's much different from life in Germany. People work, go to school. Children play, except the boys play baseball instead of your football—which we call soccer. I live in New York City."

"What's that like? I mean I know about the Empire State Building, the Statue of Liberty, and the United Nations. But what is it like living there?"

"Well, the buildings are taller than they are here. In my neighborhood most of the buildings are six stories, and have elevators, although in some of the other boroughs . . . ."

"Boroughs?"

"Well, New York City is made up of five boroughs . . . sections, I guess you could say. Originally they were separate cities, and then in 1898 they joined into one city. There's Manhattan, that's where I live, and where the Empire State Building and the UN are, and there's the Bronx, and Brooklyn, and Staten Island, and Queens. In Staten Island and Queens there are lots of private houses, like here."

They had come to a restaurant, *Der Weisse Hase*. "Here we are," Willy said. He pushed open the door and waved her into a room with six tables, each covered with a white cloth and sparkling glasses and flatware. White napkins were standing in the wine glasses. A short round woman with bright red cheeks and sparkling brown eyes bounded up to greet them.

"Ah, Dr. Willy. Good to see you."

"Good evening, Frau Lempke. This is Dr. Brenner. She's from America, working at Georg-August, and I thought I'd show her what a good Wolfenbüttel restaurant is like."

"Pleased to meet you, Dr. Brenner. Where would you like to sit, Dr. Willy?"

He pointed to a table in the corner, near the window, whose curtains kept the street out. Frau Lempke waved them over, past several tables where the diners were tucking into ample meals.

Willy pulled out her chair and waited until she was sitting before seating himself across from her. Frau Lempke returned with large menus covered in leatherette.

"How is your father?" she asked Willy.

"He's good. He said to say hello."

"A good man," Frau Lempke said to Margot. "He saved my Gunther's life."

"How is Günther?" Willy asked.

"Good. He's working in Stuttgart, at the Mercedes factory."

"Good for him," Willy said. "So, what's good tonight?"

"Everything."

"So, tell me about your life," Willy said when Frau Lempke left.

"All of it?"

He grinned. "Sure." He thought for a moment, then continued. "Do you remember anything about your life here?"

"No. My mother told me lots of stories, but no, no memories. I was just a baby when we left. Do you remember us?"

"No. And I was older. I was almost two."

"What's your first memory?"

"I think when Papa came back from prison."

"How long was he in prison?"

"It seemed like a long time to me, but he says it was just a few weeks. Then he went into the army, and we didn't see him again until the war ended."

"What do you remember about the war?"

"The air raids. Mama and I spent a lot of time in the cellar. There were quite a few kids, and we thought it was fun. We played games, 'til one day there was a direct hit on our house. We were lucky. The ceiling fell on the other part of the basement, so we were able to get out. But after that it wasn't so much fun. Then we moved to Kassel to stay with Oma and Opa, and we stayed there 'til Papa came back. Kassel wasn't a picnic either, but Oma and Opa lived on the outskirts, so it was safer."

"We had air raid drills in New York, too, my mother said, but I don't really remember them. By the time I was aware of my surroundings, the war was winding down."

"What's *your* first memory?"

"I think . . . when I was about three. I had the measles, and my mother sat at my bedside practically the whole time. I remember she brought me an ice cream on a stick. If I close my eyes I can still taste it."

"What did your mother do in America? How did she earn a living? Or were you able to take money out with you?"

"None. By the time we left we were lucky to get out at all. My mother said they had to leave everything—the silver, the good dishes, her jewelry. She even had to smuggle out her wedding band. For some reason, they let her take her sewing machine, and that's how she supported us. She worked as a dressmaker. I was the best dressed kid in my class, and I hated it."

"Why?"

"Because everyone else wore these wonderful clothes from Grant's or Woolworth's, and I wanted to look just like them."

"Ah . . . so did you learn English right away?"

"I wasn't even talking when we left Hannover. My mother spoke some English, so she made a real effort to speak English to me. It was hard for her, but I guess it helped her, too, because it made it possible for her to get work. Some of my aunts and uncles had a harder time. Actually German is my second language."

"You speak it well."

"Yes, well, Mom spoke German to her friends and relatives, so I picked it up. But when I was growing up, when we walked down the street and she spoke German, I made believe I didn't know her. I very much wanted to be a *real* American. But enough about me, tell me about yourself."

"Ah, I lead a boring life. I live at home with Papa, as you know. I was an indifferent student, as Papa will be happy to tell you. I'm overworked and underpaid at Georg-August. But I always wanted to be a doctor. How about you?"

"Yes. Ever since I can remember. I don't know whether it's because of my father, or because I was sick a lot as a kid and decided it's better to be the injector than the injectee."

"Do you have a boyfriend?"

"Yes. John. He's doing an internship in orthopedics at Yale. You've heard of Yale?"

"Yes," Willy said. "Impressive. He didn't mind your coming here?"

"He accepted it. We both knew we'd be so busy that it's not that big a deal."

"If you were my girlfriend I'd mind."

Their wine came, brought out by Mrs. Lempke, who opened the bottle deftly, poured a little into Willy's glass, and waited for his nod of approval before pouring for Margot, and then filling Willy's glass.

"Your dinners will be out in about ten minutes. Is that all right?"

"We're not in a hurry," Willy said. When their hostess had left he went on. "Is . . . John? Is he an immigrant, too?"

"Not hardly. His ancestors came over on the *Mayflower*."

"The *Mayflower*? Those little white bell-shaped . . . ?"

"Oh, lilies of the valley?" She laughed. "No, the *Mayflower* was a ship. It brought the first pilgrims from England to the new world. John's family has lived in America since then."

"Ah. And in democratic America the parents don't mind that their son is involved with—what? a newcomer?"

"Well . . . let's say they hope my being here will make John see the error of his ways."

"So then maybe America isn't so different from Germany. Here family still means a lot. You'd think after what happened it wouldn't, but you'd be surprised."

"I don't think I'd be so surprised."

"Not my Papa, of course. He really doesn't care who I date, as long as she's nice and makes me happy."

"And is there someone nice who makes you happy?"

"For the moment. But it's not serious. She's waiting for Prince Charming."

"And why aren't you Prince Charming? You're good looking, you're a doctor? You're . . . ."

"Thank you. Brigitte and I . . . we're good friends . . . well, a little more than friends, but we both know we're not the one." He shrugged. "And I'm not ready to get serious. I want to finish my internship. Then I'd like to travel a little, see the world. Maybe visit you in New York. That is, if Papa weren't alone."

"I'm sure he could cope."

"Oh, I know, but I'd feel guilty. Since Mama died he's always put aside his own pleasure for me, and I'd feel like a louse just taking off. I wish he'd marry again."

"Dr. Sauer?"

"Yes. That's right, you met her at our house."

"And I've scrubbed with her. She's a pleasure to work with."

"And I think she makes Papa happy. But he says he doesn't want to upset my life. I told him he should go ahead. Well, maybe he will, one of these days. Did your mother ever remarry?"

"No. For a long time she didn't accept that my father was really dead, and even after that, well, I don't think she ever found anyone who measured up. And she wasn't going to settle for second best."

"Did you hope she'd remarry?"

"The truth? No. I mean I *said* I did, but I knew if she did I wouldn't get all her attention. I felt like a hypocrite whenever I told her she should go out and meet someone. Oh, there were a few men, but some of them didn't want the responsibility of me. And some of them were creeps."

"Creeps?"

"Not nice. One of them always wanted to kiss me on the mouth. Mom got rid of him in a hurry."

"It must have been hard for her."

"Yes. But she never made me feel deprived, or poor. I mean, I knew what our circumstances were, and I started working—baby sitting and stuff—when I was quite young, but I never felt bad about it. It was just what it was. My cousins, who had two parents, had things I didn't have, but I had my mother, and I wouldn't have traded with them for the world."

Their food arrived, and they began to eat.

"This herring is wonderful," Margot said. "It tastes much fresher than what I'm used to."

"The liver is first class. Would you like a taste?"

"That's all right. I'll stick to the herring. I really meant it about not being very hungry, but the truth is I don't eat bacon or pork."

"Are you religious?"

"No. It's a psychological thing. My Mom said 'pork, yech,' once too often. Are you religious?"

"Not at all. We never were, even when Mama was alive. My father says your father was a free thinker, too."

"That's what my mother said. But to the Nazis it didn't make a difference. He might as well have been wearing sideburns and *tzitsis*."

"*Tzitsis?*"

"The fringes that orthodox Jews wear. To remind them to keep the commandments."

"Anyway, I don't see how anyone can believe in a God after what happened."

"I agree, but that wasn't God, that was people," she said.

"Yeah, but if there's a God, he let it happen."

"The religious people say he gave us free will."

"And what do you say?"

"I say the same thing you do. If there's a God and he let that happen, then I don't want to worship him."

"So what do you believe?"

"That we have to do what we can to make sure Hitler never happens again, anywhere."

"How do we do that? Look at Russia. Stalin was no better than Hitler."

"We can't control everything. But we have to do what we can where we are."

"But even in America. Look how you treat the black people."

"Yes, and some of us are trying very hard to change that."

"How are you doing that?"

"Last summer I went down to Mississippi to register voters. And I give money, when I have any, to organizations that are working for change."

"Mississippi is where that little boy was murdered? For whistling at a woman?"

"You heard about that even here? Yes, it was scary being there. And my mother really didn't want me to go, but I said, we, of all people . . . ."

"That was very brave of you."

"Maybe if more people had been brave like your father, early on, we never would have had to leave."

"You're right. But most people aren't brave. They just want to be left alone."

"They don't understand that if it can happen to someone else it can happen to them too."

"They don't want to hear that. Even in little things. Haven't you noticed, people don't want to . . . . Like one time, in my Latin class, the professor told us not to study the ablative, that we'd get to it later. Then on an exam there was a whole twenty-point question on the ablative. I didn't say anything during the exam, because I wanted to check my notes to make sure I was right, and when we left the room, and I mentioned it to my classmates they all agreed. They said, 'Tell him, Willy, next session.' So at the next session I raised my hand, and reminded the professor. He looked at the rest of the class for confirmation, and not a single person backed me up. For me it was the difference between an 1 and a 2 on the exam, but for some of them it was the difference between a passing and failing grade, and still they didn't say a word. The professor shrugged. That was that."

"That makes it even more important that we speak up. My mother was always telling me not to rock the boat, we're not native-born citizens but if I learned anything from history it's that we have to speak up."

"I think we've learned that here. Well," he smiled, realizing he was contradicting himself, "some of us. But enough serious talk for one night. Do you like jazz?"

"I don't really know it much. I like classical music, except the modern stuff."

"Another night I'll take you to hear some really good jazz. There's a group at a club here, the clarinetist played with Ellington, and they're excellent. Maybe we can convert you."

They had finished eating. Margot declined dessert. When the check came and she tried to pay for her own meal, he said, "Next time. This time I can be a big shot. You hardly had a thing."

They walked back to Margot's rooming house, and Willy took her hand and kissed it.

"Thank you for a nice evening, G'nädige Frau."

"I enjoyed it too, Willy. Thank you."

CHAPTER 13

Hannover, April 1940

Martin was awakened from a fitful sleep by the pounding on the front door. His sleep had been uneasy since the night he had put Claire and Margot on the ship. Little Willy, now officially Peter, slept soundly in the crib on the other side of the room. He was a sweet little boy, good natured, always smiling. He was content to sit for hours clutching his Steiff teddy bear and watching the activities around him. He was especially delighted when Peter, now officially Willy, played near him. At two and a half, he was still not talking, although he now walked and was starting to feed himself.

Peter had had a hard time with this game of "pretend," especially when the sleeping arrangements were changed so that his place was usurped in Martin's bedroom. All the pep talks about having his very own room had not convinced him. He also had a hard time calling Martin "Onkel" and Willie and Eva "Mama" and "Papa." Martin's stomach still knotted when he remembered how harsh they'd had to be with him until he'd capitulated. *Poor little guy,* Martin thought, *how can he understand?* He wondered, for the umpteenth time, whether they were doing the right thing.

The pounding continued, and he heard shouts. His door was flung open, and a red-faced storm-trooper yelled at him, "Get up, Jew."

Martin jumped up. "Don't wake the boy," he said quietly.

"Get dressed, *Dreksjude,*" the trooper bellowed. Several others appeared at the door, one not much more than a boy. That one pushed Willie into the room. Willie, his hair tousled, clad only in a nightshirt, his feet bare, looked . . . bereft.

Martin quickly put on underwear, pants, and a shirt. He took a pair of socks out of the drawer, and when he bent to put on his shoes the storm trooper kicked him in the kidneys. Martin grunted with pain. 'Peter' slept on. When his shoes were laced he straight-ened painfully, and reached for his suit jacket.

"Get the boy dressed," bellowed the storm trooper.

"What do you want with him? He's hardly more than a baby."

"You're both under arrest, *Dreksjude*."

"Arrest? For what?" Willie asked.

"Shut your trap," the young storm-trooper said. "You're in deep shit yourself. Don't you know that harboring Jews is a crime?"

Martin stood, unmoving. The leader reached into the crib and yanked 'Peter' roughly. He snuffled, and turned away from the light. The Nazi pulled him roughly by the arm, flipped him up, and shoved him at Martin.

"He stinks. Either get him dressed now, *Sheisskopf*, or we'll take him like this. It's all the same to me. We've wasted enough of our time on you vermin."

'Peter' began to bawl. Martin quickly found some warm clothes, and a diaper (he wasn't toilet trained) and cleaned and changed him before dressing him in woolen pants, a shirt, and sweater.

"All right. Let's go," the leader snapped.

'Peter' continued to bawl. Martin held him and patted him gently.

"Can I at least get him a bottle, so he goes back to sleep?"

"Make it snappy."

Martin, holding the boy, went to the kitchen, accompanied by one of the Nazis, who watched his every move while he poured milk into the bottle, put on the nipple and nipple ring, and put the milk into a water-filled saucepan to warm. 'Peter's' bawls were subsiding to whimpers, hiccups, and gulps.

By the time the bottle was warm Willie reappeared, Eva behind him dressed in her wool bathrobe. She clutched at his arm. Willie was now also dressed, his hair plastered down with water.

The storm-trooper shoved Martin, still holding the now-sleeping boy, roughly toward the door. Another shoved Willie.

"Where are you taking them?" Eva asked.

"Where they belong," the Nazi barked. "Just thank the Fuhrer that we're not taking you, too."

"What have we done?" Eva wailed.

"Shut your mouth, woman. If you didn't have your boy you'd be coming too. Now say goodbye to your husband. And remember, we're watching you."

Eva clung to Willie. "Be brave," he whispered to her, "for the child. I'll be all right."

Eva nodded. She tried to shake Martin's hand, but the storm-trooper pushed her aside. She was able to stroke 'Peter's' hair briefly as the group marched out of the apartment. She sank to the floor of the hallway, weeping uncontrollably. When there were no tears left she rose and staggered into the room where Peter (now irrevocably Willy) slept undisturbed.

"Oh, God," she whispered, "what have we done?"

In the morning the sun shone. Outside the buds were opening on the trees. The birds sang. Willy, now Peter, came into the kitchen where Eva was going through the motions of making coffee. She had not slept, and her face was still swollen and red.

"Where's Papa? Where are Onkel Martin and Peter?" he asked.

"They had to go away?"

"Why?"

"Some men wanted to ask them some questions. They'll be back soon, I'm sure."

Willy was quiet for a minute. In his pajamas, his blond hair tousled, his face still creased with sleep, he looked like an advertisement for the Aryan race. Eva bent to hug the boy, and to plant a kiss on his blond hair.

"Why would they ask Peter questions?" Willy asked. "He can't even talk."

Eva sighed. "I don't know, sweetie. I suppose they have their reasons."

"I had a bad dream last night," the boy said. "I thought I heard monsters yelling and banging. I hid under my quilt."

"That's a good thing to do when there are monsters," Eva said. "The quilt will protect you. Come, let's get you dressed, and then we can get you some breakfast."

Willy followed her into his room where she took out underwear, shorts and shirt, and a pair of socks. She led him into the bathroom, and waited while he peed, then helped him wash up. When she was satisfied with his cleanliness, she wrung out the wash cloth and dried him briskly with the thick towel before handing him his underwear.

"Now brush your teeth."

"I brushed them last night."

"Of course, but you have to brush them in the morning, too. You know that. While you sleep there are all those germs, and you need to get them out so when you grow up you'll have good strong teeth."

"Like you and Papa? And Onkel Martin?"

"That's right, darling. There now, brush up and down. In the back, too."

"It tickles my mouth when I do that."

"That's all right."

In the kitchen she asked, "Would you like some jelly on your oatmeal, as a special treat?"

His face broke open in a huge smile, and when the bowl was set in front of him, he ate happily.

Eva had trouble swallowing even the coffee, but she knew she had to eat.

Since Suze had left, Eva had done her own housework. She was glad of it now. It kept her busy. While Willy played with his blocks, she mopped the floors, dusted the furniture, cleaned the bathroom. She tried to keep her mind on the tasks, scrubbing the toilet vigorously, washing the sink and bathtub.

Finished in the bathroom she went into the bedroom she shared with Willie. She shook out the down quilts and opened the windows, laying the quilts on the sill to air. She fluffed the pillows. She took off and replaced the sheets. She dusted the dresser and armoire. She dusted the wedding photo of herself and Willie and set it back on the dresser. Then she went to the drawer where she kept her underwear. Sachets encased in silk released the scent of lavender. From the silk case where she kept her handkerchiefs she withdrew a photo of Willy. It had been taken just before the war. He was dressed in a white suit with leggings and matching hat she had knitted for him. He was clutching his teddy bear and smiling happily. She kissed the picture, then gasped as though someone had hit her in the stomach. Tears ran down her cheeks. She held the picture to her breast another minute, then secreted it again between her handkerchiefs and finished her dusting.

When she had put Willy's quilt on his window sill to air, and had dusted in his room, she said, "Let's go to the store and see what we can get for supper."

Willy was busy with his blocks. He had built a tower, which tottered precariously, before he knocked it down with enthusiasm. Then he began to build it again.

"Can we get some chocolate?"

"We'll see," she said.

She handed him his jacket, which he proudly put on all by himself. She took a sweater out of the hall armoire for herself, and put on her hat, securing it with a hat pin. She reached for her gloves, handbag, and shopping bag, and they were ready.

She locked the door behind them. As they descended the stairs Frau Schmidt was coming up, panting, a shopping bag from which a cabbage and some beet tops stuck out held in one hand. With the other hand she held on to the banister.

"Good morning, Frau Schmidt," Eva said. "I see they have vegetables at the market."

Frau Schmidt looked pointedly at the stairs, clamped her lips tightly together, and kept on walking. Eva repeated her greeting. Frau Schmidt hissed "Jew lover," and continued up the stairs.

"Why is that lady talking mean?" little Willy asked.

"Maybe she had a bad dream, too," Eva said.

They walked down Humboldtstrasse, and turned onto Wieland. Eva nodded to neighbors as they passed. Willy skipped ahead of her, stopping dutifully when he reached the street to wait and take her hand. On Wieland they passed two Gestapo officers. The older of the pair smiled at her. The younger said, "Gnädige Frau," and patted Willy on the head. "He'll make a fine Hitler youth," he told Eva. She nodded, took Willy's hand, and walked on.

At the market the bins were more wood than vegetable. Sad and wilted cabbages, a few shriveled carrots and some potatoes were all that remained.

"Ah, Frau Doktor," the greengrocer greeted her. An apron that had once been white draped his ample belly. He wore a woolen brimmed cap from which a few strands of grey hair peeked. His nose and cheeks had the red broken veins that spoke to many years of shnapps.

"Good morning, Hans," she said, forcing a smile.

"You're late this morning," he said.

"Yes, I was cleaning."

"I saved you some vegetables," he whispered. He thrust a bag into her hands. She opened her purse to get out money, but he waved his head.

"No. Make a nice soup for the doctor and the little one." He patted Willy's blond curls.

"Thank you," she said.

"It's nothing. But next time come earlier, before everything is gone."

"Thank you," she said again.

"And take care of yourself . . . and the boy."

She nodded, took Willy's hand.

"Can I have some chocolate, Mama?" he asked.

"We'll see. We'll walk to Baum's and see whether they have any. But with the war . . ."

They walked down near the park, and crossed the street to Baum's. The sign in the window still read *Juden Unerwünscht* although, Eva thought, since there were no longer any Jews around, it was redundant.

They walked into the store. Before the war Baum's had had glass cases displaying all sorts of wonderful pastries, rich with chocolate and whipped cream. Other cases had displayed chocolates, pralines, cream filled truffles, some wrapped in foil, others sitting in their little pleated cups. The glass cases remained, but now the shelves were almost empty. There was one bin in which half a dozen nonpareils rested in the bottom, another housed a lone chocolate bon-bon, and on one of the shelves rested two sad bars of milk chocolate, covered in foil.

Frau Baum, looking as tired as Eva felt, sat on a high stool near the cash register. She forced her mouth into a smile as Eva and Willy walked in.

"Good morning, Frau Baum," Eva said.

"Is it?"

"Well, the sun is shining."

"So it is. Since Oskar was called up I don't notice the weather. Or what day it is."

"It's hard, I'm sure," Eva said.

"And I can't get any stock. I don't know why I bother to open the store."

"Things will get better," Eva answered, although she didn't believe it for a minute.

"For you, maybe," she said bitterly. "They're not calling up doctors."

Eva bit her lip. She bent down to Willy.

"What would you like, sweetie?" she asked. "The bon-bon? The non-pareils?"

He shook his head, pointing to one of the chocolate bars.

"Might as well take them both," Frau Baum advised. "Lord knows when I'll see any more."

Eva extracted money from her purse and handed it to Frau Baum, who proffered the two bars. Then she reached into the case, took out the lone bon-bon, and handed it to Willy.

"Here," she said. "Somebody might as well be happy."

Willy took the chocolate eagerly and popped it into his mouth.

"Say thank you," Eva said.

"Thank you," he said, a little stream of chocolate dribbling out of his mouth.

As they exited the store Eva saw Frau Baum come from behind the counter to lock the door, and shaking her head.

Three weeks later, Willie came home, briefly. His head was shaved, he was thinner, and his eyes, ringed by dark shadows, looked haunted. He hugged her to him, and she felt his ribs through his shirt.

"I leave for the army in the morning," he told her. "You should go to your parents."

CHAPTER 14

Hannover, September 1963

Margot debarked from the train at the Hauptbahnhof in Hannover, and made her way to the street. While the tracks and platforms had been restored, the facade of the station still showed the scars of the bombs that had leveled much of the city. *Good*, she thought. *I'm glad they suffered, too*. Outside the station both pedestrian and vehicular traffic moved briskly. Volkswagen Beetles were in the majority, but there were also Opels and Mercedes, and a few Renaults and Citroens.

She flagged a VW taxi and gave the driver the address. She had wangled two whole days off call by trading with other surgical interns, and sucking it up to work a procedure with Dr. Rausch. Luckily this time he hadn't nicked any major organs or vessels, and she'd managed to stay out of arm's reach. Minor victories! Now she was on her way to see Dr. Speer, the person Dr. Meinhoff suspected had betrayed her father. What would she learn, she wondered?

"You're not from here?" the taxi driver intruded.

"No, from Wolfenbüttel. I'm just visiting a . . . friend of my family's."

"But you're not originally from Wolfenbüttel, either," he persisted. "American?"

"Yes," she sighed.

"You speak good German," he said.

"I studied it at school."

"Most Americans don't bother. They think if they speak English louder we'll understand."

"Yes, well . . . ," she said.

"Don't get me wrong. I love the Americans. They saved us from the Russians. And from Hitler, too, of course."

"Of course," she said. "Were you here during the war?"

"No. I was in the army. The infantry. I didn't volunteer, I assure you, but as soon as I turned sixteen I was called up. It was hard."

"I'm sure," she said.

"I was on the Russian front. Never shot at an American. I love America."

Margot said nothing. Of all the Germans she'd met since she'd come over, not one who'd been in the army had served on the western front or shot at an American. They'd never heard of Hitler, either. Amazing.

"I came back here when I was discharged. It was all rubble. Terrible. We Germans suffered too, you know."

"I'm sure," she said again, thinking *but not enough*.

"But that's over, and I hope when we fight the Russkies you Americans will know this time who your friends are. Anyway, right now things are good. Look how we've rebuilt." He pointed at the row of apartment houses rising on his right, at the shops with shiny plate glass displaying all manner of wares.

"Tell you what," he said. "I'll take the scenic route. Pay me what's on the meter now, and I won't charge you for the rest."

"That's okay," she said. "Another time."

"There may not be another time, G'nädige Fräulein, and I could show you the *Leibnizhaus*, the Hannover Rathaus, the *Bibliothekspavillon*, the new *Stadthalle*. It's amazing what German industry has accomplished in such a short time."

"I'd love to," she lied, "but I promised I'd be there by"—she looked surreptitiously at her watch: 11:18—"by 11:30. And I don't want to be late."

"Well, let me give you my number. If you have more time later, or next time you come, call me and I'll give you a tour—and a special rate."

"That would be lovely," she said, thinking *when hell freezes over*.

A brief five minutes later he pulled up in front of an apartment building, clearly post-war. She handed him the fare, with a precise 15% tip. While she counted out the marks he wrote on a slip of paper, and handed it to her in exchange.

"My number," he said. "It's a lovely city, Hannover."

"Yes, thank you." She watched him pull away from the curb, wondering whether the Germans had, in fact, learned anything. She knew she shouldn't generalize. Most of the people she was working with, at least those of her generation, were horrified by their past. The older ones were mainly . . . what? circumspect? reformed? ashamed? For that matter, her relatives, in spite of what they'd gone through, weren't so wonderful either. While they mostly voted Democratic (a reflex response to their gratitude to Roosevelt), their social attitudes had caused many an argument on the rarer and rarer occasions that Margot saw them. They certainly wouldn't want their daughter marrying a Negro—even if he was Jewish, and they were sure that Negroes were happier living in their own neighborhoods. Why would they want to live where they weren't wanted? When Margot pointed out that they, of all people should know better, that others had said, and still said (look at John's parents) the same things about Jews, they replied that that wasn't the same thing at all: "Look what we Jews have accomplished since we've come here. Negroes, on the other hand, are all on welfare, don't want to do an honest day's work," and so on and on. Margot would grow apoplectic; her mother would try to change the subject and would lecture her on the way home about not stirring things up.

"I don't start it," she'd retorted, "but I can't not say anything when they say such outrageous things."

"You're not going to change their opinions."

"But I don't have to agree."

Now that her mother was gone she saw her relatives less and less. She shook her head, brought herself back to the present, and looked up at the gray stone building. There was a wooden front door, a rich dark brown, with a beveled glass window in the upper half. A brass plate with a row of brass buttons next to a series of name plates was attached to the left. Margot looked for the name and, finding it next to 3C, rang the bell. After a brief pause a buzzer released the front door, and she pushed it open. Inside there was another door, this one of heavy glass, and another set of bells. She rang again, and was again buzzed into a hallway. A mahogany table, covered with a lace runner, stood to her right. On top of the runner sat a bowl filled with dried hydrangeas. Beyond the table was the elevator. She pressed the button, and the door opened. She got in, pressed 3, and when she got off, she looked for 3C and rang the bell.

The door opened. Heinrich Speer, she assumed, dressed in a gray suit with vest, a white shirt, and a navy-and-white-striped tie, said, "Dr. Brenner?"

"Dr. Speer?"

He bowed and ushered her into a foyer that was twice the size of Margot's room at Frau Lindemann's. The floor was parquet, covered by a dark red oriental rug. To one side was a polished cherrywood table covered by a lace cloth, and a silver bowl in which rested assorted keys, business cards, an odd pencil, and various envelopes. Across from the table was a closet, and on the other side a built-in bookcase, on which books and magazines were scattered. A light fixture on a brass chain illuminated the foyer.

"Welcome," Dr. Speer said. "May I take your bag? Your jacket?"

It had been cool when she'd left Wolfenbüttel, and she'd dressed in a blazer, beige skirt, and pale pink silk blouse. By now the day had warmed, and she gratefully shrugged out of the blazer. She held on to her briefcase, and after Dr. Speer placed the blazer on a hanger and put it in the closet, she followed him into a large living room.

"Sit," he said, indicating a sofa that was placed between two wall to ceiling windows. The sofa was covered in a dark green brocade. A round glass-topped coffee table stood in front of it, and on either side of the coffee table stood two wingback chairs, one covered in the same brocade as the sofa, the other in a dusty rose-striped silk. At the front of the room, just past the entrance, stood a grand piano, a book of music open on the front. Atop the piano was a shawl of a dark maroon wool and several pictures in gold, silver, and wood frames. Both sides of the room were filled with floor-to-ceiling glass-enclosed bookcases.

"So," Dr. Speer said, sitting in the brocaded chair and looking her up and down. "You're Martin's daughter. You look like him, I think."

"Do I? I don't remember him."

"You have the same eyes, the same hair color. And the same briefcase," he smiled.

"Everyone says I look like my mother."

"Ah. How is your mother? I remember she was a lovely woman. Beautiful."

"She died last January."

"My sympathy . . . . But I'm a boor," he said, standing suddenly. "I should offer you something. Coffee? Tea? It's a bit early in the day, but something stronger? A shnapps?"

"No, that's all right. Maybe a glass of water."

"Of course." He walked to the living room entrance, stuck his head out, called, "Flora?"

A small, birdlike woman appeared. She wore an apron over a brown silk shirtdress. Her gray hair was pulled back in a bun.

"This is Dr. Brenner. The daughter of one of my colleagues from before the war. Dr. Brenner, my wife, Flora."

Margot stood, extended her hand. "Nice to meet you, Frau Doktor." Mrs. Speer nodded, took the proffered hand, and smiled shyly.

"Did you know my father, too?" Margot asked. Mrs. Speer shook her head.

"We didn't marry until later, after the war. My first wife was killed in one of the air raids," Dr. Speer explained.

"I'm sorry," Margot said. They were all standing awkwardly.

"Flora, a glass of water for Dr. Brenner?"

Mrs. Speer nodded again, turned, and left the room. She had still not said a word, and Margot wondered whether she was, perhaps, mute. Dr. Speer folded his lanky frame back into the chair, and Margot sat as well. She was wearing pumps with heels, and was glad to get off her feet.

"So," she said, "I'd like to hear about my father."

"I don't know anything. I told you that on the telephone. Only what I heard, and that was all rumor. There were so many rumors."

"Well, I'd be interested in what you heard, but really, I'd just like to hear about my father, from what you knew of him. As I said, I never knew him, and all I have are my mother's stories."

"Of course. Well, let me see . . . Martin was . . . he was an idealist. He took his oath seriously."

Margot nodded.

"We worked together at the hospital. He was the one, if there was a problem, we called him. He was a good doctor, and he deeply cared about his patients. It wasn't just about the money with him, not like some of . . ."—Was he going to say *Jews*? Margot wondered—". . . like some of those louts who just went into medicine because it would get them a better dowry. And pretty girls."

He smiled, ran his long fingers through his still thick gray hair.

"When he couldn't work at the hospital anymore we all missed him. And then, when he couldn't practice anymore, it was a shame."

Mrs. Speer came back with a glass and a pitcher of water on a tray. There was also a white napkin, FSM embroidered in white silk. "Did you want ice?" she asked, placing the tray on the coffee table.

"No, this is fine, thanks," Margot said.

"I'll leave you, then," she said. "When you're ready for lunch . . . ."

"Oh, I don't want to impose."

"We insist," Dr. Speer said, "don't we, Flörschen?"

"Absolutely," she said.

She left the room, and Margot poured herself a glass of water.

"Where was I? Oh, yes. When he couldn't practice anymore, Willie Meinhoff took him into his practice. Unofficially, of course. But you know that."

"Yes. I've seen Dr. Meinhoff. That's how I ended up in Wolfenbüttel."

"How is Willie? We lost touch after the war."

"He's good. His wife is dead, too. His son is also a resident at Georg-August, although not in surgery."

"Little Willy? A doctor? Who would have thought?"

"Why do you say that? It's not unusual for a son to . . . ."

"Of course not. It's just, well, Willy was a little—how should I put it—? Well, your brother was the same age, and he was way ahead of Willy. How is your brother? Is he a doctor, too?"

"My brother never got out. He was killed shortly after my father was arrested."

Dr. Speer seemed to wince, then coughed.

"I'm so sorry. I guess I did hear that, but there were so many stories . . . ." He shook his head. "Anyway, your father. We were never close friends, and after the Nazis came to power, well, I was a coward. I admit it. I admired Willie, but I couldn't take chances. I had a great-grandmother, you see."

"A great-grandmother?"

"A Jewish great-grandmother. It was only that one little bit of blood, but if someone had denounced me it would have been enough. So I joined the Nazi party and kept my mouth shut, and *sieg heil*ed along with everyone else. Well, almost everyone else. Willie didn't. But we can't all be heroes."

"Someone betrayed my father," Margot said carefully.

"I don't doubt it," he said. Then he added, a bit too defensively, "But it wasn't me. I may not have been brave, but I admired your father. He was a good man. Funny, dedicated, a masterful diagnostician. One time we had a case, no one could figure out what the problem was. The patient, a young woman, kept getting sicker and sicker. No one could find anything. Everyone thought she was pretending, a hypochondriac. Your father wouldn't give up. He did tests; he asked questions; he read textbooks. Eventually he found the cause, a rare pancreatic tumor. Of course he couldn't do anything for her either, and she died, but at least she got someone to believe her."

"Dr. Meinhoff says he really wanted to go into psychiatry."

"I don't know about that, but he would have been good. He was a good listener. Funny, I haven't thought about him for years. I'm sorry. I try not to think about those times. They were terrible, and I'm ashamed that I wasn't braver."

"You weren't the only one."

"Thank you. But that doesn't make me feel less ashamed. I knew better. For those who really believed in Hitler I suppose you could make an argument. At least they acted on conviction. I acted on cowardice."

"None of us knows what we'd do unless we're there," she said. In spite of herself, she found herself liking him, defending him against himself.

"But some people did the right thing. Willie did." He paused. "Why didn't your father leave when you and your mother did?"

"My brother got sick. My father thought they'd follow as soon as Peter was better. He had a promise of a job in New York. And then the war started."

"And then the war started. And then that madman had free rein." He shook his head again. "Does Willie have any idea who betrayed your father?"

"Not really." She paused now, then said quickly, "He thought it might have been you."

"It wasn't. I swear. But I suppose I can see why he might think that. I wanted to buy your father's practice and equipment, and he gave it to Willie. I understood that. After all, Willie took him in, but I can see that Willie might think I'd be angry. Lots of people turned in their former friends for less."

Did she believe him? she wondered. He sounded plausible, but he'd had many years to work on the story. She sat quietly, looking at him. He was still a good-looking man, in spite of the sadness that the bifocals covering his deep brown eyes couldn't hide.

They sat uncomfortably for a few minutes, then, "So little Willy is a doctor. Who would have thought . . . ? What does he look like?"

"Willy? Tall, blond, blue-eyed. Good looking."

"And he's all right. Normal?"

"He seems to be."

"Well, just goes to show, doesn't it. There were so many whispers at the hospital."

"Whispers?"

"About little Willy. Especially at that time. You know about the euthanasia programs?"

"I've read about them. The Nazis killed old people, the infirm, mental defectives. Is that what you mean?"

"Yes. Well, at the hospital, there were whispers that Willie had better be careful, keep the boy under wraps. But I guess it was just development. They say children all develop differently. It was just . . . . I guess the contrast with your brother . . . . They were the same age . . . . I even remember, now that I think of it, one of the doctors saying . . . ." He stopped.

"Saying what?" she asked.

"Nothing," he said. "It was just a stupid remark. People said all sorts of stupid things about the Jews in those days."

"What did he say?"

"That it was a pity the Jew—he meant your father—didn't have the imbecile."

"Was Willy an imbecile?"

"Apparently not, if he's a doctor now."

I know some doctors who are imbeciles, she thought irreverently. Dr. Rausch came to mind. Well, he wasn't exactly an imbecile. Just incompetent.

"I don't know what else I can tell you."

Margot realized she'd been wool-gathering.

"Do you know anyone else here, in Hannover, who knew my father?"

"There are very few of us left. Let's see. Klaus? No, he came after your father was already . . . . Hermann? No. He was a dyed-in-the-wool Nazi. He made it a point not to have anything to do with . . . ."

"Could he have been the one who betrayed my father?"

"It's possible. But he didn't know that he was staying with Willie. Believe me, we only ever talked about the weather when Hermann was around."

"But there must have been others who . . ."

". . . were Nazis? Of course. But they're not here anymore. After the war, the ones with something to hide, those of us who were even still alive, made it a point to relocate. You know. In another town, where there was no one to contradict you, where it was easier to say, 'I only went along.' We all had to get de-Nazification certificates, and if someone came along and told the Brits that so-and-so was a collaborator, or worse, well . . ."

"So is this Hermann still practicing?"

"Yes. It took him awhile to get clearance. And today of course he says he was never for Hitler, but there are still a few of us who know better."

"Do you think he'd talk to me?"

"I'm sure he would. But I wouldn't believe a word he said."

"Still . . ."

"I'll give you his number. In fact, I'll make the call. How long are you planning to stay in Hannover?"

"I'm planning to take the train back this evening. But I could stay over if I had to."

He rose. "Well, let me try calling."

While he was gone Margot took another sip of water. The sun streaming through the windows warmed her back. She got up, went to one of the bookcases, and looked at the titles. There was a section of medical books, bound journals, but there was also a complete set of Goethe, of Schiller, Lessing, Heine, and even *Die gesammelte Shakespeare*. There were also novels, some clearly old, but others that seemed to be modern. She recognized Günter Grass among the authors.

"You like my collection?" Dr. Speer asked. She hadn't heard him come back into the room.

"It's quite extensive."

"Actually Flora is the reader in the family. I read when I get the chance, but Flora is the literary one. She writes poetry. I think she's very good, but she won't show it to anyone. Anyway, Hermann says he'd love to meet Martin's daughter. He always admired him." His voice dripped with sarcasm. "He said he could see you this after-noon, after he's finished seeing his patients. Is that all right?"

"That would be fine. Thank you." She rose.

"You'll stay for lunch, I hope?"

"I don't want to put you out."

"It's no trouble. Flora would consider it *eine Beleidigung*, a huge insult, if you didn't stay. Besides, Hermann can't see you before four, so there's plenty of time. His office is just two blocks away."

"Well, in that case, thank you."

"That's settled then. Let me just tell Flora . . .". He left the room again, and when he returned he said, "Hannover was a wonderful city before the war. We had concerts, theater. Of course we have them again now that times are getting better, but we lost so much talent."

Here we go again, Margot thought. *Here's where we get to the 'We suffered, too 'speech.* "Yes," she said.

"I don't mean that the way it came out," he said. "I know there are a lot of Germans who play that tune . . . 'We had it hard. Look at the bombings. At Dresden.' I have no patience for that. Whatever we suffered, we deserved. We voted for Hitler. We cheered him on. It wasn't until we started to lose that suddenly people said, 'We were never Nazis.' No, I meant we lost the talents of the people who left, who couldn't play, or write, or sing, or practice. Or the ones, like Mann and Dietrich, who wouldn't."

"Were you friends with my parents before . . ."

"There was a group of us: Willie, your father, me, Hermann, Julius Stahl, Max Brandt, Oskar Bendler. We all went to medical school together." He absently fingered his dueling scar. "We all were on the staff of the hospital. As we got married some of us remained friends. Hermann, as I said, was a Nazi from the beginning, so after '33 he had nothing to do with your parents. But Willie, Oskar, Julius, and Max and I . . . then Julius married. His wife belonged to the BDF."

"The BDF?"

"*Bundt Deutsche Frauen*. The German Women's Association. So she and Julius dropped out of our circle. Max never married. The rumor was that he was, how to say it, *einen warmer Bruder* . . . a homosexual. Of course no one said it out loud. In those days. And Oskar. I haven't thought of him in years. He died at Stalingrad, which was ironic because before '33 he was, if not a Communist, then certainly close . . . Anyway, yes. Sophie, my first wife, and I stayed friends with your parents for a while. Until it got too dangerous."

"So what else can you tell me about my father?"

"He was a good man. When your brother was born he was so proud. He brought him to the hospital sometimes. He was a beautiful child, bright, cheerful. He was the only man I knew who didn't think it was unmanly to push him in the carriage."

"Yes, my mother told me that. His mother, my grandmother, thought that made him a *washlappen*, a wimp. But Mom says he didn't care."

"We never had children. Sophie, couldn't . . . and by the time Flora and I married, well . . . . But I don't think I could have been that kind of a father. By the time you were born, of course your father was no longer on the hospital staff, and we no longer had any contact, but I'm sure he was as proud of you as he was of your brother." He paused for a moment, then said, "Let me see. What else can I tell you? He had a wonderful sense of humor. Even in medical school, at the beginning, it was hard for him, being Jewish. But he used humor, and after a while the others left him alone."

"Yes, Dr. Meinhoff told me about the penis in the pocket."

Dr. Speer turned a deep red. *Oops*, Margot thought. "That seems to be a common medical school prank," she said. "In our class it was directed against the women."

"I suppose some things don't change," he said. "But the point was that your father had a good sense of humor. He could tell a good joke. And he could take one. Oh, he was a serious fellow, but he could see the funny side of things, too."

He looked at his watch, rose. "Come," he said, "let's see what Flora has prepared for us."

She rose, too, picked up her briefcase, and followed Dr. Speer into a formal dining room, where a table that could comfortably have seated a dozen was covered by an ecru damask cloth and laid for the three of them.

"I know Flora will want to sit there by the kitchen," he said, seating himself at the head of the table. On cue Flora appeared with a china tureen and a silver ladle.

"I know it's warm out," she said, "but we like a bowl of soup at lunch, right Heinrich?"

She spooned soup into each of their bowls then sat to her husband's right. Over the course of the lunch, Flora asked Margot about America, about how she liked Wolfenbüttel, and what it was like to be a woman doctor.

"I never had any ambitions like that," she said. "I did study at the university before the war, but I only ever wanted to write."

"Your husband said you write poetry."

"Oh, I dabble. What else do I have to do all day? It's not as though I'm trained for anything. And besides Heinrich likes me to be at home."

When lunch was finished, and Margot knew she wouldn't eat another bite for several days, Dr. Speer said, "I imagine you'll want to go see Hermann now. I've written down his address."

He handed her a slip of paper.

"May I help you clear?" Margot asked.

"Thank you, no. It's nothing," her hostess said quickly. "It's been a pleasure meeting you."

She thanked them both, promised to keep in touch. Dr. Speer helped her on with her blazer, then waited at the door until the elevator came. Outside she looked at the slip of paper. It gave an address on Listerstrasse. Dr. Speer had told her to turn left after leaving their house, then to walk two blocks and turn right. She followed his instructions, noting that most of the houses were new, clearly post-war.

When she got to number 5332, a tan brick six-story building, there was a shiny brass plate next to a side entrance. The plate said Dr. Wolfgang Hermann. She rang the bell, and was buzzed into an office that looked like every doctor's office on both sides of the Atlantic. There was a desk at the front, at which a stout woman with her gray hair pulled back into a severe bun, looked at her over thick glasses held by a silver chain.

"Yes?" she asked.

"I'm Dr. Brenner. I have . . . ."

"Oh, right. The young lady from America. Please, sit," she smiled. "Doctor has his last patient, but he should be finished soon."

Margot sat in one of the straight-back chairs, opened her briefcase, and took out a copy of *JAMA* with an article on fibroids that she had started to read on the train. A study had shown that surgery was not always indicated, since they tended to shrink after menopause. She was looking at the statistics when a door at the far side of the room opened and a middle-aged woman came out, holding a handkerchief to her red eyes. Behind her was a short, stout man in a white coat. His hand was patting the woman's shoulder, murmuring, "It'll be all right, it'll be all right."

The woman nodded her head. She stopped at the front desk, and opened her handbag.

The doctor turned to Margot. "You must be Dr. Brenner, *ja?* I'm Wolfgang Hermann. Come in, come in." She got a whiff of his breath, peppermint with an underlay of something unpleasant. He motioned her through the door, turned and said. "You can go home after you're finished, Trude."

Margot followed Dr. Hermann down a long hallway, on which hung several framed prints, one of dogs playing cards, another of a mother holding a fat naked baby, another of several horses in a snowy field. There was an oriental runner on the floor. She entered Dr. Hermann's office, which smelled of cigar, and he indicated a leather-covered wingback chair facing his desk. The floor was carpeted in a dark green, and that was covered with an oriental rug. She settled into the leather, and he scurried around the desk and seated himself in a matching chair. The desk was covered by a leather-framed green blotter, a leather-covered cup holding several pens and pencils, an empty wire basket, and a prescription pad. A heavy glass ashtray held ashes and a dead cigar. Behind the chair, on the wall, were the framed diplomas indicating Dr. Hermann's pedigree. Since they pre-dated the Third Reich, they were free of swastikas. She wondered what graduates of that unfortunate period did with their diplomas. Had the state re-issued them, sanitized, after the war? Margot looked at the other walls, which were painted a pale green, and which held several paintings, landscapes of no particular artistic merit.

"So," Dr. Hermann said, "you're Martin's daughter."

She nodded.

"I remember him well. A good man, a good doctor. He emigrated, yes?"

"No, as a matter of fact, he . . . ."

"I heard he emigrated. Lots of people did. Who could blame them. Those weren't good times."

"Certainly not for my father. Were you good friends?"

She watched his eyes. Behind thick glasses they were a pale gray. Did she detect a spark of something? His eyebrows were bushy, with practically no space between them. That was the only hair he showed. His skull was shiny, and his hands and the little of his arms that showed below his white cuffs and brown suit jacket were also hairless

"I wouldn't say good friends," he said slowly. "More colleagues. We moved in different circles."

"Yes."

"I wasn't married then."

"Ah."

"And then, of course, when things got bad one couldn't— I mean, not without causing real problems. My parents were elderly, I was their only son. One had to be careful. But in my heart I was never a Nazi."

"I'm sure not," she lied.

"So, your father didn't emigrate? I was sure someone had told me he'd gone to New York."

"He was supposed to. But my brother got sick, so they stayed behind. My mother and I left."

"Ah. Did he . . . ? Was he . . . ? Were they?"

"Both killed. We're not sure just how it happened. Someone betrayed them."

"That's terrible," he said, looking suitably solemn and horrified. She had a hard time keeping a straight face, not saying anything, but if she wanted information she had to play along.

"Do you have any idea who might have done that?" she asked him.

"Who knows? Those were bad times. Anyone could have . . . . When did you say this happened? Was it before the war?"

"Sometime in 1940, we think."

"Mmm. They rounded up the Jews when the war started, sent them to camps to keep them safe. There were some people who were angry at the Jews, and the Führer wanted to protect them, especially after *Krystallnacht*. So much property damage then. He didn't want that to happen again. At least that's what they told us then. Of course, after the war, when we found out about the camps, we were shocked. Horrible. Who could have imagined?"

"Were you in the army?" she asked, not wanting to hear any more self-serving crap. 'Who could have imagined?' Oh sure!

"Not at first. I was in the SS, I'm ashamed to say. Had to join, of course, to stay on the hospital staff, but still . . . so I wasn't called up for several years. They needed doctors here, too."

"I didn't realize joining the SS was mandatory," she couldn't help saying. "I mean, I know people had to join the Nazi party to keep their jobs, but . . . ."

"Yes. Well, it's not well known, but there was extraordinary pressure brought to get me to join. I resisted, of course, but as I said, I had elderly parents, needed my job. And besides, I thought maybe I could do some good from the inside. You know, internal resistance."

"Mm."

"And I was able to. Sometimes I could mitigate the . . . severity. But you don't want to hear about that, and after the war, I was eventually pardoned. They took my good works into account."

"So you don't know who might have betrayed my father? He was living with the Meinhoffs at the time."

"Willie? That's right. They were good friends, I remember that. I wonder what happened to Willie."

"He's practicing in Wolfenbüttel. So is his son."

"The imbecile?"

"He's not an imbecile. He . . ." .

"Another son then?"

"As far as I know there's only the one son."

"Well, what do I know? As I say, we moved in different circles. And there were so many rumors going around in those days."

"And you have no idea who might have turned my father and Dr. Meinhoff in?"

"Willie, too? That's a shame. I mean . . . but he wasn't Jewish . . . still, no one was really safe in those terrible days."

She stood up. She wasn't going to get anything here, and he was making her feel more and more nauseated the longer she stayed.

"Thank you for your time," she said.

"Not at all." He extended his hand. She ignored it, stooping to pick up the briefcase she'd placed at her feet. "I'm sorry I couldn't be of more help, but I'm glad to see that you did all right. A doctor, eh?"

"Yes."

He got up from his chair, came around the desk, and walked with her down the corridor. His bad breath increased her feeling of nausea.

"Say hello to Willie for me if you see him. I don't know whether he'll remember me."

Outside she stood for a moment, leaning against the brick of the building. She felt dirty, as if something were crawling up her back, down her arms. What, she wondered, had she hoped to learn? If he was the one who'd betrayed her father, had she expected him to confess it? Internal resistance, my foot! If Hitler came back today he'd be *sieg heil*ing in a hot minute.

She looked at her watch. It was not yet four-thirty. The train she was planning to take back to Wolfenbüttel didn't leave until 6:45. She could find a cafe, have some coffee and a piece of pastry. Or she could go to the town hall and look at records, see what she could find there. She was still full from the ample lunch Frau Doktor Speer had served, and after her session with the Nazi she wasn't sure she ever wanted to eat again. So the town hall, then.

CHAPTER 15

Hannover and Kassel, September 1942

Eva gave a last look around the apartment. She hated leaving the furniture, but there was no way she could take it to her parents' house. They hardly had room for her and Willy. No, better to leave it with Lore Merz, who was glad of a place to live since her house had been destroyed last week. Lore and her daughter, Helga, had moved in with Eva and Willy then, and she would take care of the apartment until things settled down, Willie came home, *so Gott will*, and they could all go back to a normal life. If that ever happened.

In every letter she got from Willie he told her she should go to Kassel, she'd be safer there. He never wrote about himself, but as long as his letters came he was at least all right. Lore's husband, Klaus, had been killed on the eastern front, and from what Eva heard from the few friends who didn't believe the official news stories, the war wasn't going all that well. While the official news was that Russia was about to surrender, people who listened to the outlawed short-wave radios said that the German army had been turned back at Stalingrad, a big defeat. Since America had entered the war, the British had also gotten a second wind. There were whispers that Rommel had been defeated in North Africa, and the bombing raids had gotten worse in Hannover.

She had been resisting going home to her parents, but after the bomb that destroyed the other half of their building, she realized that it was selfish to stay here. Besides, in Willy's school there was more and more pressure on him to join the Pimpf, a sort of apprenticeship to the Hitler Youth. In Kassel things might be less . . . political. She certainly hoped so. So she had offered Lore the use of the apartment, and now she stood with her suitcases, and went to Willy's room.

At five he had grown into a big boy, with long thin limbs and big feet. His face had lost its baby look, and his blond hair was cut short, soldier fashion. He sat in a chair next to the window, reading one of the Karl Mai books he devoured.

"It's time to go, Willy," she said.

"I just want to finish this chapter, Mama."

"You can read it on the train. We have to get to the station."

He got up reluctantly, put the book into his leather backpack, and put his arms through the straps. He picked up the suitcase standing next to the door, and looked around.

"Don't you want to take Franz?" Eva asked, indicating the rather threadbare Steiff teddy bear that still sat on his bed.

"I'm too old for bears."

They said goodbye to Lore, who held her three-year-old in her arms.

"Helga can play with my toys," Willy said.

"Thank you. I'll take good care of things here, Eva."

"I know you will. Take care of yourself, too."

"Maybe you'll be back soon. Maybe things will get better soon."

"I'm afraid they'll get a lot worse before they get better. Take care."

They embraced briefly, and then she and Willy walked down the stairs, their suitcases bumping at each step. Mrs. Schmidt stood outside her door. Eva pointedly said, "*Auf Wiedersehen*, Frau Schmidt," and received a snorted, "Hmpff," in return.

"Why doesn't Frau Schmidt like us?" Willy asked.

"She's a Nazi," Eva blurted.

"We don't like Nazis, do we Mama?" he asked.

"Shh, Willy. Let's not talk about that right now. When we're with Oma and Opa . . . . Do you remember them?"

"No. But I've seen their picture, so I'll know them. Will they know me?"

"They'll say how much you've grown. The last time they saw you, you were just a baby. That was before Papa went into the army."

"Will Papa know me when he comes home?"

"Of course. He's your Papa. And besides I sent him a picture at your last birthday. In your long pants, remember?"

"They don't fit me anymore."

"Yes, you're growing so fast. I can let them out at the waist and make them into knickers for next year."

Her father met them at the Kassel station. After they embraced, he held Willy at arm's length.

"I can't believe this is the same boy," he said.

Eva winced. "Yes, he's grown big, hasn't he, Papa?"

"And handsome," her father said. Eva looked at her father. In the three years since she'd last seen him he'd turned into an old man. His suit—he always wore a suit, as befitted a civil servant—hung on his frame, and the collar of his white shirt looked several sizes too big for his skinny neck. The shirt, that her mother had always prided herself on keeping a sparkling white, was now dingy, yellowed at the loose collar, and frayed.

"You've lost weight, Evaschen," he said.

"Well, it's not always so easy to get food in the city," she said.

"We'll have to see what we can do about that. Mama managed to find a chicken . . . . Do you like chicken, Willy?"

Willy grinned. "We haven't had any chicken in a long time, have we, Mama?"

"Then it's good you've come to the country."

"Kassel is hardly the country," Eva said.

Her father picked up her suitcase, and Eva took Willy's. They left the station, and crossed the street to a horse-drawn cart.

"Have you ever ridden in a horse and wagon, Willy?" his grandfather asked.

"No, sir."

"Neither had we 'til we couldn't get gasoline any more. Luckily my neighbor—Eva, you remember Paul Hack?"

"Hello, Mr. Hack," Eva said. He clambered down from the front seat, and tipped his hat.

"Paul and his horse offered to pick you up. It's a long walk," he explained to Willy.

They stowed the suitcases at the bottom of the cart, then Eva and Willy climbed in. Her father got onto the front seat with his neighbor. Willy, wide-eyed, watched as the horse trotted along the cobbled streets.

Her mother stood in the doorway when they approached. Her hair, pulled back into its customary bun, had gone completely gray, and she, like her husband, seemed to have shrunk several sizes. Her dress was covered by her usual apron. She ran down the steps, and threw her arms around first Eva and then Willy as they alighted.

"I can't believe this is Willy," she said.

"Believe it," Eva said. "Three years in a child's life is a long time. Over half his life."

Her father dismounted, retrieved the suitcases, and shook the driver's hand.

"Thanks, Paul, I owe you . . . ."

"Glad I could help. After all you've done for us."

"Let me show you where you can wash up," his Oma told Willy. "Then we'll have some lunch, yes?"

She led him down a hallway to a small room, no more than a closet, really, that held a sink and a toilet. The toilet had a wooden seat, and, near the ceiling, a wooden tank from which a chain descended. Several pipes ran down the wall from the tank to behind the toilet.

"Don't flush after you make pee-pee," his Oma said. "We have to conserve water, so we flush only when you make number two. Can you remember that?"

"Of course."

"And be sparing with the paper." She pointed to a pile of torn-up newspaper.

"What's that?"

"Toilet paper. But we only get the newspaper on Sundays, so it has to last."

"Where's the other toilet paper?"

"Gone with the war. Maybe your Papa, wherever he is, has real toilet paper. But here we can't get it anymore. Anyway, do you have to make pee-pee?"

Willy shook his head, embarrassed. He hadn't been asked about his toileting in years.

"Sure?"

"Yes, Oma. I'm five, you know. I'm going into second grade."

"So your Mama says. That's wonderful. She says you can read."

"Of course I can read."

"Well that's good. Wash your hands, and we'll see what there is for a big five-year-old to eat."

That evening, after Willy was asleep in the room he would share with his mother, Eva and her parents sat in the kitchen. The curtains were drawn, the black cloth pulled tightly over the windows so that the light wouldn't leak out.

"We haven't had any air raids here, so far, but we have to be careful," her mother said. "I'm glad you finally decided to be sensible."

"If it had only been me . . ."

"You'd have stayed in Hannover?"

"It's our home."

"It *was* your home. For the time being this is your home."

"Oh, Papa. Mama! What's going to happen to us?"

"We'll survive. We'll keep our mouths shut and our necks in, and we'll survive."

"You really believe that?"

"We survived the first war."

"That was different. This time . . . I don't know. In the first war, from what I read, neighbors were still neighbors. We were all Germans together, and when we suffered we were still all Germans. Now, this morning, we have a neighbor, Mrs. Schmidt. She's a dyed-in-the-wool Nazi. Ever since Willie was arrested she's been rude. Nothing worse, so far, than not saying hello, and muttering 'Jew lover,' but another of our neighbors told me . . . ."

"Yes, there are people like that all over. That's why we're careful."

"That's not the worst, though. In school they fill Willy with all sorts of garbage, want him to join the Pimpf, and he likes the uniforms, and the songs, the camaraderie."

"By the time he's ten, *so Gott will*, all this will be over."

"I hope here in school there'll be less, uh, enthusiasm. I tell him to be careful with what he says and does. But he's just a child, not much more than a baby. One day he came home from school telling me the Führer wants children to be vigilant against spies. I asked him whether the teacher had told them what spies look like. He said, 'Oh, Mama, he said spies could look like anyone, even your mother or father.' So I asked him what the teacher thought they should do if their parent was a spy, and he said the teacher told them to report them, that that was what good Germans did."

"You explained it to him, didn't you?"

"Of course. But that's what they're filling their minds with. What happens to the children whose parents believe that garbage?"

"They'll join the Hitler *Jugend*. They're the ones who got us into this mess in the first place," her father said. "What I don't understand is how an educated *Volk*, a country that produced Bach and Beethoven, Goethe and Schiller, bought that crap in the first place. And your brother . . . who certainly should know better, and certainly never learned it at home . . ."

"What about Ullie?"

"He's out there saluting with the rest of them. Couldn't wait to join the *Luftwaffe*."

"He'd have been drafted anyway, Karl," her mother said quietly. "At least this way . . ."

"At least this way he gets to bomb innocent children in London. Don't make excuses for him. He bought the whole package. Remember Heinz Cohen, Eva?"

"Ullie's friend?"

"Right. They were in and out of each other's houses, inseparable. Well, Ullie separated himself all right. On *Krystallnacht* he was out throwing stones at the Jews gathered around the synagogue, even throwing stones at Heinrich! I'm ashamed he's my son."

"Don't say that, Karl," her mother said. "He wasn't much more than a boy . . . ."

"Those 'boys' killed eight people that night. And then he married that cow, Metz's Inge. All she does is produce a baby a year, for the Führer. I'd keep Willy away from them, Eva."

"So Ullie's turned into a Nazi?"

"I'm afraid so. Goes to show it's not just upbringing. He never learned that here."

"I know, Papa. Where is Ullie now?"

"I don't know where he's stationed. It's a big secret, but he comes home every now and then, just long enough to put another one in the oven. If it weren't for the children I wouldn't have anything to do with her, but . . . ."

"She's not a bad person, Karl."

"No. As long as you don't get her started spouting that garbage. And she's filling the children's heads with it, too. You heard little Ullie last week, Marthe."

Her mother sighed.

"What did he say?"

"He called his sister a *drecksjude* when she knocked his block castle over. That doesn't come from nowhere."

"He could get it in school, Karl," her mother said.

"You always make excuses for them, Marthe. If Willy came home and said that, Eva, what would you do?"

"I'd explain it to him, that that's an insult, that the Jews . . . ."

"You see?" her father said triumphantly. "And do you know what that cow said?"

"Karl!" her mother said.

"I don't care, Marthe. She *is* a cow. She said," and his voice took on a falsetto, "'Your sister isn't a Jew, Ullie. We've exterminated the Jews.'"

Eva shook her head. "I guess Willy won't be playing with his cousins much. I'd hoped things were better here."

"The school is all right. Hack says his grandsons don't have any problems. No one seems to be pushing them into Hitler Youth uniforms."

"Well that's a relief. I talk to Willy, I make sure he reads books that aren't just propaganda, but at that age they want to be like their peers."

"It's amazing how he's developed," her mother said. "He always seemed a bit . . . ." She stopped. "I mean, the last time we saw him he wasn't talking at all, or even walking. Compared to that other boy, you know the one I mean, Eva, that other doctor's son . . . the ones who were living with you after his wife and baby emigrated. What was his name?"

"Martin."

"Right. When we visited you just before the war started, I couldn't help comparing . . . ."

"Children develop differently."

"True, but it's amazing how he's caught up."

"Almost as if he was a different boy," her father said quietly.

Eva looked at her father. He looked away.

"Please don't ever say that," she said.

Her mother inhaled sharply. "Would anyone like some tea?" she asked.

CHAPTER 16

Wolfenbüttel, September 1963

On the train ride home Margot did not read. Her head was full of what, if anything, she'd learned. She had taken a taxi to the Rathaus, an imposing baroque structure with a terra-cotta roof and copper dome, topped by a miniature castle, topped by another copper dome with a gilt steeple. She had spent over an hour looking at documents there. She found not only her birth certificate, but also Peter's. There was also her parents' marriage certificate. When she'd needed her birth certificate when she'd applied for her medical license, she'd guarded it carefully, certain that if she let it out of her hands, it would be irreplaceable. She needn't have worried. The Germans were nothing if not efficient, she mused. She had asked the clerk whether they also had death certificates, and the clerk had assured her that they did, "But that's another department," he'd told her. "Two flights up."

So she'd made her way to that other department and explained what she was looking for.

"I don't have exact dates," she'd said. "I'm told my brother died sometime in 1940, and my father in '44. Does that help?"

"A little," the woman said. "We won't have to look through *all* the years. So many people died. It was a terrible time."

Since the woman was not more than a few years older than Margot, she did not feel the need to ask, if only to herself, "And where were you? And what were you doing?" those questions that popped into her head whenever she met a German of the appropriate age. So she only nodded, said, "If I could look at those books . . . ," and waited while the clerk brought out several large ledgers bound in black leather.

"It's getting on to closing time. If you like I could look at '44 while you look at '40. Or start, anyway. '44 was a bad year. There are so many names."

"Thanks, that would be helpful," Margot said. She took the first ledger, and began poring over the names. It was hard going, unused as she was to the German script. The names were arranged by date of death, starting in January. Each name was followed by the date of birth of the person, and then by the cause of death and the place of death. She was midway into April when the name jumped off the page: Brenner, Peter, date of birth: 16/8/37, date of death: 23/4/40, cause of death: pneumonia, place of death: Sonnenstein.

"Where is Sonnenstein?" Margot asked.

"I'm not sure," the clerk said. "Did you find something?"

"My brother. It says he died of pneumonia."

"That's what a lot of them died of."

"Late April's a funny time for pneumonia," Margot said. "And children don't usually die of it."

She continued to look through the book, not at names, now, but at place and cause of death. She found a lot of Sonnenstein deaths. The ages of the deceased varied, from the very young to the very old, but the cause of death was unvarying: pneumonia. *Hmm*, she said to herself. And aloud she said, "I can look at some of the '44 now."

There were three volumes. The clerk was still in the first. Margot took the second of the ledgers, and began to slog through the long list of names. There were, she noted, quite a few deaths in Hannover, due, no doubt to the air raids, although the cause of death there, as often as not, was malnutrition. There were also the deaths of increasingly younger men, and the places of death were scattered: Italy, Belgium, France, London. *London?* she wondered, then decided they must have been shot down in air raids. The cause of their deaths was listed, simply, as "died in battle." And then there was the last category. Here the places of death read like a catalog of the camps: Auschwitz, Treblinka, Teresienstadt, Dachau,

Bergen-Belsen, Buchenwald, Ahlem. And the cause of death was depressingly similar: gassed, gassed, gassed. An occasional "shot trying to escape" or "typhus" appeared. After a while she concentrated on the names, speed-reading to the extent her unfamiliarity with the script allowed. She was grateful to her medical schooling, which had taught her to skim.

"Was your father's first name 'Martin'?" the clerk asked.

"You found him?"

"It's possible. Do you know his birth date?"

"November 10, 1905."

"I found him. He died at Auschwitz."

"That's what we were told. What was the cause?"

"It says shot trying to escape."

Margot thanked the clerk. She gathered her briefcase, walked down the four flights of marble stairs in a daze, and made her way out of the building, hardly noticing now the golden stones that shone in the late afternoon sun. Another taxi took her to the railroad station, and she sat in the waiting room, oblivious to the hustle of people running to catch trains or queuing up the stairs from the various platforms. Public address announcements droned continually, announcing tracks of trains going to various places. She had plenty of time; her train didn't leave until 6:45, and she knew the track, so she paid no attention to the disembodied voice.

She sat, head in her hands. *Sonnenstein . . . shot trying to escape . . . Sonnenstein . . . Sonnenstein . . . trying to escape . . . trying to escape.* The words kept running through her head. Would her father have tried to escape? Nothing her mother had ever told her had indicated that kind of heroism. On the other hand, who knew what people did under extreme conditions? She wished, for the thousandth time, that her mother were still alive.

On the train she chose a window seat. Once out of the terminal she could watch the country go by. It was starting to get dark. The days were getting noticeably shorter again. As they left the city the houses were farther apart. Lights were coming on in their windows.

She sat quietly, just letting the countryside flash by, trying not to think. Her stomach rumbled. She had eaten nothing since lunchtime. She could go to the dining car, get an inedible sandwich, or at least a cup of coffee. But she continued to sit.

She began to think of her interviews. She had liked Dr. Speer, in spite of herself. What's more, she'd believed him. Unlike Dr. Hermann, who'd done nothing but rationalize and make excuses, Dr. Speer had admitted his less-than-heroic behavior. But Dr. Meinhoff had said he'd been a Nazi, that he might have been the one who betrayed her father. Was it possible? Sure, but then why had he been willing to see her? Guilty conscience? Sure, but he'd been quite open about his cowardice, had admitted he was ashamed. So maybe Dr. Meinhoff was wrong, maybe he'd just put two and two together and gotten five. Wouldn't be the first time. Dr. Hermann, now: She could see him goose-stepping. But would he have known that her father was still at the Meinhoff's? She had no doubt he would have been happy to denounce both her father and Dr. Meinhoff, but she was sure that Dr. Meinhoff hadn't put up an announcement saying he was sheltering her father. But people talked. If someone knew, he might have told someone else, and it could have gotten back to Dr. Hermann. Or to anyone else for that matter. Who knew? She'd probably been on a wild goose chase.

On the other hand, it was good to hear, from yet another source, that her father had not only been a good doctor but a good person. Her mother hadn't been seeing him through the prism of nostalgia.

Something was bothering her. She shook her head. Something Dr. Speer had said, and then Dr. Hermann, too. The more she tried to call it up the less she could remember. She looked out the window again, trying to clear her mind so whatever it was would surface. It was dark now, and the lights of the occasional houses winked as the train sped by.

She thought again about her brother. Why would a healthy three-year-old die of pneumonia? Why did so many people die of pneumonia, and where was Sonnenstein? She'd never heard of the town. She'd look it up when she got back to Wolfenbüttel. But why was her brother sent to that town when her father was sent to Auschwitz? Of course she didn't know when her father had ended up in Auschwitz. Maybe he'd been at Sonnenstein, too. How terrible it must have been for him, a doctor, not to be able to save his son. She knew, as a doctor, that any patient's death was hard, but your own baby! He'd been a beautiful little boy, with curly blond hair and blue eyes, and the last picture her mother had of him, in a sailor suit, had shown a chunky little guy, pink cheeks, an impish smile, glowing with life. Of course, with the war maybe food had become scarce, and once they were taken, maybe his good health hadn't lasted. Children were more vulnerable.

Her father, she was sure, would have tried to see that Peter got what little there was to eat, but who knew? She'd read how the Nazis separated families, so maybe her father hadn't even been there when Peter died. She wondered whether there was a way to track her father's road to Auschwitz. With the meticulous records the Nazis had kept, there had to be a way. They were so bureaucratic, she had read somewhere, that when they sent the Jews off to the camps they'd kept track, and charged each one the fare, payable by the money confiscated from the Jews themselves. The rationale, she remembered, had been that the railroad was a separate entity, and of course its books had to balance. If they had still been following the rules under which Margot and her mother had left, it would have been a first-class ticket. Margot had always found that particularly galling, that the Nazis had made emigrants buy round-trip first-class tickets when they were leaving Germany. She wondered whether she should apply for a refund for the return tickets they'd never used. *Maybe I can get them to pay for my trip home,* she mused.

Back at Frau L.'s, where supper was long over, her landlady asked, "So how was your trip to the big city?"

"Interesting."

"I haven't been in Hannover in years. It's gotten too busy for an old lady like me."

"There's a lot of traffic," she said, "but I'm used to it. New York is even busier." She started for the stairs.

"Have you had supper?" her landlady asked.

"I had a big lunch. I looked up one of my father's old friends."

"Would you like a cup of tea? And a piece of bread and butter."

"I don't want to be a bother."

"It's no trouble. I was just going to make myself some tea. Sometimes, when I can't sleep . . ."

"In that case, sure. Let me just put my things away, and get into something more comfortable."

When she came back downstairs she joined Frau Lindemann in the kitchen, where the kettle was just starting to whistle. The round table was covered by a red-and-white-checked oil cloth. Half a loaf of bread sat in the middle, next to a dish with a slab of butter and a jar of jam, clearly home preserved. Two plates and two knives had been laid out, as well as two white napkins, with the same napkin rings that Margot recognized from their suppers. Frau Lindemann poured the hot water into a teapot and brought two blue and white cups to the table.

"Do you take milk or sugar in your tea?"

"Neither, thanks. This is really very kind of you."

"It's nice to have company," her landlady said. She brought the teapot, made of the same blue-and-white china as the cups, to the table, and poured tea into each cup. Then she sat, placed her hands around the cup, and inhaled some of the steam before adding milk and sugar and taking a sip.

"Ahh," she inhaled.

Margot took a sip of her tea as well.

Frau L. sliced some bread and offered Margot a slice, before taking a slice for herself. As she buttered and put jam on her slice she asked, "So, was your trip useful?"

"I don't know about useful. I was just . . . . My father died when I was so young. My mother always talked about him as though he was perfect. I'm trying to get a more realistic picture."

"And?"

"And maybe my mother was right. He sounds as though he was one of the good guys."

"The good guys?"

"It's an expression, from American westerns. You know, there's the hero and the villain."

"Ah. John Wayne."

"Right. Anyway, this friend of my father's in Hannover, he worked at the same hospital, he said my father was a good doctor, a good man."

"How old were you when your father died?"

"About six."

"And you don't remember anything at all?"

"The last time I saw him was when I was less than a year old."

"You mean your parents were divorced? Then why does your mother . . . ?"

"No, they weren't divorced. They got separated. By the war. My father never got out."

"You're Jewish?" A look of . . . enlightenment? . . . broke over her face. "I didn't realize. Brenner is a German name."

"Does it matter?" Margot asked.

"Of course not. Not to me. I was never a Nazi." Margot, remembering her earlier comment about the dirty Italians, wasn't so sure, but she certainly wasn't about to dispute the fact. She knew what side her bread, literally as well as figuratively, was buttered on. She took a bite of said bread, before continuing.

"We were all supposed to go, but my brother got sick."

"A terrible time," Frau L. said. Margot thought she'd scream if she heard that one more time today. "So . . . your father ended up in one of the camps?"

"Auschwitz."

"And your brother, too?"

"No. He died of pneumonia, in a town called Sonnenstein. Do you know where that is?"

"I don't know of a town called Sonnenstein. But there was a hospital by that name, near Pirna. That's near Dresden. There were whispers about Sonnenstein."

"What kind of whispers?"

"That things were done there . . . that we weren't supposed to know about."

"What things?"

"There was a doctor when I was in Italy. He'd been at Sonnenstein. He asked to be reassigned. We were . . . friendly, so he talked to me sometimes. I asked him once why he'd wanted to leave a safe place for the front lines. This was before you Americans were bombing Dresden, of course."

Margot held her tongue.

"Turned out Dresden wasn't so safe either. But I guess maybe we deserved it. Anyway, Bertholdt said he'd rather be at the front. He didn't want any part of what was going on at Sonnenstein. He swore me to secrecy, and I've never said a word to anyone."

"What was he talking about?"

"The killings. Of undesirables?"

"Undesirables?"

"You know. The old, the terminal. Mental defectives. And of course Jews."

"At a hospital!"

"Yes. Have you ever read *Mein Kampf*?"

Margot shook her head.

"I hadn't either. Pity more of us didn't read it earlier, because Hitler laid it all out. The Master Race." She made a spitting sound. "And him a dark-haired runt. Some Master Race."

Margot took another swallow of her now-tepid tea.

"Anyway, Bertholdt showed it to me, the part where he talked about getting rid of the inferior specimens. It was there in black and white. And Bertholdt told me that's what they were doing at Sonnenstein. At first they were shooting them, the old people, the ones with tuberculosis, the imbeciles. Then they decided that was too slow . . ."

"The death certificate says my brother died of pneumonia," Margot said.

"Sure. That's what Bertholdt said they had written. When they sent the ashes home to the families. Or rather, when they sent some ashes . . . I don't think they cared whose ashes, or whether they were even human ashes."

"So my brother was shot? He was just a little boy, not even three years old."

"If he was lucky. After a while they put them in trucks, stuck the exhaust hose in, and gassed them. It saved time. I'm sorry. Maybe I shouldn't have told you."

"No, I'm glad you did. I wanted to know. It's why I came. I just can't believe . . . even after having heard all about Auschwitz and the other death camps. I just can't believe . . . but I knew something was funny when I was looking at the book and saw that all those people were dying of pneumonia. And pneumonia usually isn't a killer of children."

"We have a lot to answer for."

"Could I talk to your friend, this Doctor Bertholdt?"

"He was killed in '44."

"Do you know anyone else who was there? Or who knew about it?"

"No one. As to who knew about it, it's a funny thing. After the war no one knew about anything. Haven't you noticed," she said wryly, "no one knew about the camps? No one ever heard of Hitler. It's amazing, the amnesia that afflicts my countrymen."

Margot nodded. She'd noticed.

"Me. I don't talk about it either. There's no use, but if someone tells you he didn't know what was happening, don't believe him. We were there at *Krystallnacht*. We saw them burn the synagogues, round up the Jews. Here in Wolfenbüttel they beat up the rabbi of the synagogue before they took him to Buchenwald. And after they deported him? You think the people who moved into his house didn't know he wasn't coming back? Or the people who took over Goldmann's department store? Or all the other Jewish property?"

She took a breath, then rushed on. "And the people who lived near the camps? All right, Auschwitz was in Poland, but Dachau wasn't. Buchenwald wasn't. And you could smell the smoke. You'd have to be deaf, dumb, blind, and incapable of smelling not to have known."

Margot didn't know quite what to say, so she said nothing, took another swallow of tea.

"People sent pictures home to their wives. Some of the wives, when things were still going our way, went to visit their husbands. They came back with photographs; you know, family pictures—the proud Papa with his wife and children. Only, instead of the white cottage in the background there were the barracks, and the emaciated inmates. Or the stacks of bodies. And the proud Papa was smiling broadly."

"They took pictures??"

"Oh yes, they took pictures. And the wives bragged about it. Told us how well their husbands were living. Showed us some of their 'souvenirs'—wedding rings, fur coats, picture frames with the pictures still in them. It was disgusting. I was glad when I was called up . . . because I was a nurse. My husband was already in the army. We had no children to give to the Fatherland. My husband never came back. He was killed in France, at Normandy. So don't believe it if someone tells you they didn't know. They knew."

Margot drank her tea. The ticking of the grandfather clock in the living room seemed very loud.

"So what do you think of our Germany now?" Frau Lindemann asked after a while.

"It's a beautiful country, from what I've seen of it. And in Hannover, the rebuilding is remarkable."

"Yes, we're an industrious, hard-working people. Pity we didn't put it to better use."

They finished their tea and the bread and butter. Margot got up to clear the cups.

"Leave it, I'll do it," Frau Lindemann said. "I have my own way of doing things."

"If you're sure . . ."

"I'm sure," she smiled. "And you should get to sleep. I imagine you have a full day tomorrow."

"Every day is a full day," she said. "Thank you. And for telling me about Sonnenstein, too."

But once in bed it took her a long time to get to sleep. Images of Peter, in his sailor suit, crammed into a truck of screaming people, kept playing before her eyes.

CHAPTER 17

Wolfenbüttel, November 1963

She'd had a letter from John yesterday. He was, he wrote, incredibly busy. His internship was going well; he was even getting to do some surgery, had done part of a scoliosis repair the day before. But he was always tired. *Tell me about it,* she thought. Her own days were long, starting before the sun rose and sometimes going on until well past sunset. Now that the days were shorter that was no surprise, but often by the time she got home, dinner at Frau L.'s was long over. She'd have been just as glad to fall into bed, but on those days when she dragged herself in at nine or ten at night, her landlady often greeted her with a bowl of soup or a plate of meat, vegetables, and potatoes that she'd kept warm in the oven. Not wanting to be ungrateful Margot would force her eyes to stay open while she dragged her fork or spoon to her mouth. On her rare day off she'd sleep practically around the clock, putting in an appearance only at the evening meal before flopping back into bed.

And so the days passed. At the hospital she was settling into a routine. She now knew which doctors would not only teach her, but would actually let her do more than hold retractors or put in a final stitch, and she knew which ones to avoid. She didn't go around wearing her Jewishness, such as it was, on her sleeve, and, as Frau L. had said, Brenner wasn't an obviously Jewish name. But if someone asked her, she didn't deny it, and there were some doctors, especially among the older ones, who, Margot was sure, were not as cleansed of their past as their de-Nazification certificates proclaimed. Dr. Rausch was one. In addition to his other charms—his inability to keep his hands to himself, his shoddy work, and his habit of blaming others for his faults—he was also in the habit of telling ethnic jokes, never Jewish ones, of course, since those could get him into trouble. On the few occasions when Margot couldn't manipulate the rotation to avoid working with him, she was always gritting her teeth as he joked about the stupid Poles, the lazy Italians, the oversexed Negroes, the shiftless Arabs who were 'invading' the country. And he'd look at her to see her reaction. She always made a point of keeping a straight face, refusing to react, but she breathed a sigh of relief every time she was finished 'assisting' at one of his surgeries.

Over the past several months she'd gotten friendly with her fellow roomer, Hedwig Krantz, and when their schedules allowed they tried to have lunch together in the hospital cafeteria. Often, on those occasions, Willy Meinhoff joined them.

"I think he likes you," Hedwig had observed after one of their lunches.

"He has a girlfriend," Margot said, "and he knows I have a boyfriend."

"Even so. And he is cute."

"Maybe he likes you."

"Nah. He never takes his eyes off you. I might as well be a post."

"We're just friends. Our parents knew each other before the war, and he says if we hadn't had to leave we'd have grown up together."

"Right. And that's why, when you get up to get a cup of coffee, his eyes follow you like a lovesick puppy's."

"Oh, come on, Hedwig. I don't think it means anything. Some guys are just like that; it's an automatic response. You know, hormones."

"If you say so. But he doesn't look at me that way."

With her dark curly hair, her soft brown eyes, straight little nose, and full red lips, and with a figure that could have been on a pin-up picture, Hedwig caused stares when she entered the cafeteria or walked down the street. Even in the emergency room men momentarily forgot their troubles to ogle her. Was she correct? Margot wondered. Was Willy interested in her? He was cute, and fun to be with, but she wasn't interested. John was her guy, and she couldn't wait until his visit in just over six weeks. She was counting the days.

"What?" she said to Hedwig's "Margot?"

"You were a million miles away."

"Sorry. Not a million. I was thinking of John."

"He doesn't mind your being here?"

"He does, but it was a great opportunity. I just couldn't pass it up."

"Being a surgeon means that much to you?"

"It does. But it was also the wanting to know, to see what I could find out about my father."

"Are you making any progress on that?"

Margot had told her about her day in Hannover, but had said nothing about her conversation with Frau Lindemann about Sonnenstein. She had gotten the distinct impression that it wasn't something the landlady wanted to share with the world at large.

"Not really. Dr. Meinhoff, Willy's father, says that when they were arrested he was separated from my father. They took him, Dr. Meinhoff, to the Gestapo headquarters, and he thinks they took my father to Ahlem. That was a collection point, but Dr. Meinhoff isn't sure. And even though I've written to the British government to see whether they have any data, I haven't gotten an answer so far."

"Was Dr. Meinhoff in a camp too?"

"At Buchenwald, but only for a few weeks. Then they let him join the army."

"Lucky him."

"Better the army than a concentration camp."

"I suppose. But my father was in the army, and from what he says it wasn't much fun, either. He was at Stalingrad. He doesn't talk about it much, but aside from the fact that he's missing several toes, he was one of the lucky ones. At least he came back."

"Do your parents talk about those years at all?"

"Not much. And then only about how hard it was, how they had no food, how they were always ducking bombs. But that's an improvement over the early years after the war. Then no one even knew there'd been a war. In school somehow we went from Weimar to Adenauer without a pause."

"So what changed that?"

"I don't know. I think there was some vandalism in a Jewish cemetery, something like that. And the schools decided maybe silence wasn't such a good idea. Then suddenly we learned all about the Nazis. It made for some interesting conversations."

"I can imagine."

"Can you? At least you have good memories, images, of your parents. How would you feel if you learned that your father wasn't just a soldier, but that he'd been a guard at one of the camps?"

"Is that what happened to you?"

"Not to me. But one of my friends. When she found out she left. She lives in London now, and she still writes to me from time to time. But she hasn't spoken to her parents since. To know your father is a murderer . . . all right, that was extreme. Most people weren't so . . . uh . . . actively involved. But when we asked our parents and our grandparents why didn't they do something, say something, they didn't have any good answers. And there were a few bad years before we could get on with each other."

At least you could still talk to your father, Margot wanted to say, but she didn't. Hedwig was a good person, a good friend. She certainly harbored no feelings of anti-Semitism that Margot had ever sensed. She had nothing but feelings of contempt and horror for Nazism and what it had done. *But still*, she thought, there was that note of . . . something. *I suffered too. Yeah, maybe, but it wasn't the same*, Margot thought.

"Time to get back to work," she said aloud. She picked up her tray and took it over to the corner where other soiled dishes waited to be washed. Hedwig followed suit, and they walked out together, then separated as Hedwig headed back to the emergency room and Margot to scrub up for the next surgery, this one a routine tonsillectomy with Dr. Sauer.

"I haven't seen you in a while," Dr. Sauer said as they scrubbed. "Outside of the hospital, I mean."

"I don't have much time off."

"I remember. Are you on call this weekend?"

"Friday night and Saturday 'til noon."

"I'm having some people in Saturday night. If you're awake you'd be welcome."

"Can I make it a maybe? I'd hate to fall asleep in the middle of your party."

"Of course. And it's not exactly a party. Dr. Meinhoff is coming, and young Willy and his lady friend. And my friend Pauline. She owns the bookstore on Krummestrasse, and she spent the war years in America, so I know she'd like to meet you."

For a change she actually got off call on time Saturday and was able to take a nap. When she awakened it was already dark, but a look at her watch told her it was not yet six. She sat up, took her soap, shampoo, towels, and bathrobe, and headed for the bathroom. She was lucky to find it unoccupied, and that there was still enough hot water left for a bath. Although she was in a perpetual state of sleep deprivation—a condition, she had been warned, that would last as long as her internship—she was awake enough so she could be social.

Back in her room she debated her wardrobe, settling finally on a pair of black slacks and a beige sweater set. With her black pumps she looked sufficiently dressed up. She decided to wear her hair loose, with just a mother-of-pearl clip to keep it out of her eyes. She put on a light layer of lipstick, a dab of the Chanel perfume John had given her last Christmas, took her coat and purse, and turned off the light.

She stopped at a stall selling flowers, and selected a bouquet of button mums, yellow and orange and purple, then found Dr. Sauer's house without any trouble. Wolfenbüttel was not a hard city to get around in..

The house, like most, was the typical Tudor with dark wood beams contrasting with the beige stucco, the roof tiled in terracotta. Light shone out of several downstairs windows, and when Margot rang the bell and Dr. Sauer opened the door she heard the sound of laughter from a room to the right of the entrance foyer.

"I'm glad you could make it."

"I was able to nap, so I'm almost fit for human company." She handed Dr. Sauer the flowers.

"That wasn't necessary," she protested.

"It's nothing."

"Well, thanks. I'll just put these in a vase. You can hang your coat here," Dr. Sauer said, indicating a piece of mahogany furniture with a bench seat, a full-length mirror surrounded by more mahogany, and, at the top, five large brass hooks. Margot took off her raincoat and hung it on the one unoccupied hook, took a quick look in the mirror to see whether her hair needed attention, decided it would do, then made her way into the living room where, in addition to Willy and his father, there were two women. The younger of the two was a knockout, with blonde hair cut short and legs that could give Betty Grable a run for her money, legs that showed to full advantage under a short skirt. The rest of her figure didn't need to be hidden either, and wasn't, in a navy dress that clung at the waist and then flared. The dress had long sleeves, and the material draped across full breasts that were not quite exposed by the vee neckline. She wore pearl earrings and a single strand of pearls.

"I'm Brigitte," she said as Margot approached. Her blue eyes were intelligent as she looked Margot up and down, and Margot felt positively dowdy. "I've heard a lot about you."

"And I about you," Margot said. "Willy says you're a hot-shot lawyer."

"I think that's why he puts up with me. In case he ever gets into trouble." She laughed.

"This is my friend, Pauline Metzger," Dr. Sauer said, coming back into the room with the flowers in a vase, and leading the other woman in the room over. Tall and rail thin, her hair—black with a white streak—was combed in the kind of pageboy that Margot envied but had never been able to manage. She wore a pantsuit, a gray pin-stripe, and a pink silk blouse. Her fingers were long and tapered, and she wore a topaz ring and no other jewelry.

"Nice to meet you," Pauline said in only slightly accented English. "Sophie says you're from New York."

Margot nodded.

"I was only there twice. Once at Radio City, and once at the Metropolitan Opera. I lived in Boston."

"Boston's supposed to be a great city. Were you in school there?"

"Graduate school. I was only supposed to stay for a year. I was working on my doctorate in medieval literature, and was doing some research at Harvard when the war started. I was lucky."

Before Margot could ask how, Dr. Sauer, who had put the vase on the coffee table, came over. "Would you like a drink? I have wine and I have some whiskey."

"Just some water, I think. If I have a drink I'm not sure I'll stay awake."

Dinner was served in a formal dining room, around a long table covered by a damask cloth, and set with cream-colored china edged in gold. A pair of crystal candlesticks flanked a low crystal bowl filled with ivory chrysanthemums. Dr. Sauer was seated at one end of the table, Dr. Meinhoff at the other. Margot sat at his right, with Willy next to her. Brigitte sat opposite Willy, and Pauline across from Margot.

Conversation was lively. They spoke about the hospital, about the unreasonableness of some patients. Brigitte told them about one of her clients who thought that, because he'd engaged a lawyer, he was entitled to her full attention, seven days a week and twenty-four hours a day.

"One day he actually called and asked me to make a dental appointment for him."

"Would he ask a male lawyer that?" Margot asked.

"Probably not. Although who knows. He's been passed around at our firm. He was originally someone else's client. I'm the newest member of the firm, so now he's mine."

"I guess we all have our problems with customers," Pauline said. "My least favorite is the woman who buys a book, goes home and reads it, and then comes back and returns it. She says she realized she already had it, and wants her money back."

"And does she get it" Willy asked.

"I'm afraid so. She has the receipt. If it only happened once or twice, but with this woman it's a habit. I want to tell her I'm not the library."

"Why don't you?" Margot asked.

"What? And lose a good customer?" Everyone laughed.

Dinner was simple, but good. A young woman, red-cheeked and blonde-haired, had served, and after she had cleared the main course, Dr. Sauer said, "We'll have coffee and dessert in the living room, Klärschen."

They returned to the living room, with floor-to-ceiling dark oak book cases on two walls. The sofa was a dark brown, with several needlepoint pillows strewn along the back. There were, in addition, two armchairs, one covered in a rust-colored leather, the other a wingback covered in a taupe linen. On the floor was a large and well-worn *bokhara*. The wood floor that was not covered with the rug shone. An oak coffee table with a dark red marble inlay sat in front of the sofa, and held the vase with Margot's flowers, several art books, a heavy crystal ash tray, and a small copper statue of a prancing horse. Next to each armchair stood an oak side table, inlaid with the same marble as the coffee table. Each of these also held a lamp, the bases cream colored china, the shades ecru.

Margot was sitting in one of the armchairs. Pauline sat on the couch, at the end closest to Margot. Dr. Sauer and Dr. Meinhoff were also on the couch, and Brigitte sat in the other armchair, with Willy at her feet. They sipped at coffee, nibbled at the *sachertorte* that Dr. Sauer assured Margot she had **not** baked herself.

"Don't let her fool you," Dr. Meinhoff said. "Sophie is actually a very good cook."

"You think anyone who can boil an egg is a good cook," she teased.

"That veal roast this evening was more than an egg. And I know Klärschen didn't cook that."

"And how do you know that?"

"For one thing, she used to work for me."

"Right, I'd forgotten."

He turned to Margot.

"So, how are you liking it here?"

"Very much. I'm learning a lot."

"At the hospital?"

"Yes. About my father not so much."

"Let it go."

"It's not that easy. I'd just like some answers."

"Sometimes there are no answers. Or not after all this time."

"What is it you want to know?" Pauline asked.

"About my father. He was a good friend of Dr. Meinhoff's."

"Was he?"

"Yes. And he tried to protect my father and brother. Someone betrayed them."

"And you want to know who betrayed them?" Sophie asked.

"If I could. But it's not only that. I'd like to know . . . I mean, I know he ended up at Auschwitz, but I don't know where he was before. And whether he was with my brother when he died. Stuff like that."

"What would knowing do?" Pauline asked.

"Nothing. Just . . . I don't know. I've just always felt the need to finish things. When I start a book, even if I don't particularly like it, I have to finish it, see how it comes out."

"Life is too short," Dr. Meinhoff said.

"Maybe. But I think if I knew I could let it go."

"I can understand that," Brigitte said. "Maybe I could help. Sometimes a letter from a lawyer gets more attention . . ."

"Would you? I'd really appreciate that."

"You'll just have to give me some of the particulars." She reached down, opened her purse, and took out a business card, which she passed over to Margot.

"When you get a chance just send the information to me; you know, the names, dates of birth, whatever you have."

"When I said earlier that I was lucky I got caught in America," Pauline said now, "it was because I didn't have to make hard choices. I always wondered whether I'd have had the stomach . . ."

"Willie did," Dr. Sauer said.

"One does what one has to," he said mildly, seeming abashed.

"Most people didn't," Pauline said. "I don't know if I could have. I was glad I was in America."

"Did you have family here?" Margot asked.

"My mother. My father died in the First World War."

"And your mother survived?"

"Physically."

"Some more coffee?" Dr. Sauer asked.

"I'd love some, Sophie," Pauline said. Dr. Sauer poured from the china pot, and Pauline added two cubes of sugar.

"I'll have a bit more too." Dr. Meinhoff extended his cup.

"You won't sleep tonight."

"Is that a promise?" he smiled. She blushed.

"Anyone else?"

There were no other takers, and she put the pot down. Margot wondered whether that proffer of coffee had been strategic. She'd ask another time, wondering what Pauline didn't say about her mother.

"So how does Wolfenbüttel compare to New York?" Brigitte asked.

"It's not that different, really. Everyone thinks of New York as this big anonymous place, but it's really just a bunch of neighborhoods. And in your own neighborhood it's just like a small town. I grew up in a place called Washington Heights. In Manhattan. I knew all the neighbors. They all knew us. If I did something wrong my mother knew about it before I got home."

"Sounds just like here," Willy grinned. "Remember that time, Papa, when Hans and I decided to paint the statue of Herzog August." His father smiled ruefully. "Papa had the bucket and soap and water ready by the time I got home. And the strap."

"I never hit you," his father protested.

"True. But you threatened."

"Why were you painting the statue?" Margot asked.

"We were eleven," Willy said. There was general laughter.

"So it was just you and your mother in America?" Pauline asked.

"Right. I have some aunts and uncles. They lived in the neighborhood too, but basically it was just Mom and I."

"And how did you live? Or were you able to take your money?"

"My mother worked. By '39 we were lucky to be able to take our furniture. She had been taught dressmaking, but no one would hire her because she didn't have 'American experience.' She told one boss 'A Singer is a Singer,' but she couldn't convince him. 'How am I supposed to get American experience if you won't hire me?' she asked, but he didn't care. Wasn't his problem."

"So what did she do?"

"She cleaned houses. She took care of sick people, cleaned bedpans. One of my aunts who had a heart condition so she couldn't work took care of me. Eventually Mom got a job working for a seamstress. That gave her the American experience she needed, so after a while she could get a job in a factory. One of her proudest days was when she came home with her union card. I remember that. I must have been about five, but I still remember that."

"She must have been a remarkable woman," Brigitte said.

"She was. I miss her."

"She's not alive anymore?" Pauline asked.

"She died of cancer last January. She just missed seeing me graduate from medical school."

"She was a beautiful woman," Dr. Meinhoff said.

"Her daughter's not bad either," Willy said. Brigitte looked at him.

"Look at the time," Pauline said. "I'd better be going. I have to open the store tomorrow."

"So you can exchange that lady's book?" Willy laughed.

"I hope more than that. You really must come by the store one day, Margot. We really didn't get a chance to talk that much. Mondays and Tuesdays are usually slow, so if you have some time off . . . maybe we can even have lunch."

"I'd like that. I'd better get going, too," Margot said. "Thank you so much, Dr. Sauer."

"Sophie."

"Sophie. I had a wonderful evening. Good seeing you again, Dr. Meinhoff, Willy. Nice meeting you, Brigitte. And you, Pauline."

"We'll give you a lift home, Margot," Willy offered.

"And Pauline," Brigitte added.

"Of course," Willy said quickly.

"Not necessary," Pauline said. "I live just a few houses down."

"Well, we'll see you to your door then. Even this town isn't as safe as it used to be, since all the foreign workers have . . . ."

"Willy!" Brigitte said.

"Well it's true. I'm not saying it's their fault. They live in lousy housing, and get lousy pay, but still . . . we never used to have break-ins, or muggings."

"No, we had Nazis," Brigitte said.

The air had turned chilly. Margot shivered in her raincoat. They walked down the street, Willy with one arm around Brigitte's and one around Margot's shoulders, then waited until Pauline opened her door before turning back and heading to Willy's car.

He opened the back door for Margot and then the passenger door for Brigitte before going around to the driver's side.

"By the way, if you're interested in Willy . . . ," Brigitte said.

"I have a boyfriend," Margot said quickly.

"You wouldn't be stepping on my territory. I mean, we enjoy each other, but it's nothing serious."

Willy opened his door and got in.

"Don't forget to send me that information," Brigitte said. "And let's get together again, yes?"

"I'd like that."

"Even without Willy."

"Hey," he said.

"You know, girl talk," Brigitte smiled at him.

"Yeah, yeah," he grumbled.

Back in her room, Margot undressed quickly, went to the bathroom and washed up and brushed her teeth. She was sure she'd be asleep as soon as her head hit the pillow, but instead tossed for what seemed like hours.

Why, she wondered, was everyone throwing Willy at her? Did he really like her? How did she feel about that? She tried to summon John's image, tried to imagine them in bed together. Willy's smiling face kept intruding.

CHAPTER 18

Kassel, May 1945

The war ended on May 8, 1945. The only immediate difference it made in Kassel is that the American and British planes no longer flew over, the bombs no longer dropped. The swastikas, of course, disappeared from flagpoles and windows, and British flags miraculously appeared. Men who, just the previous day, had been strutting in uniform, suddenly wore ill-fitting suits.

Willy, a gangly seven and a half, his wrists sticking out of his sleeves, came home from school to report that his teacher had told them that the Hitler Youth Group had, all along, been only a soccer club. They knew that, didn't they? What's more, his teacher reported, while everyone was welcome to join, it had not, as someone had mistakenly thought, been obligatory. He just wanted everyone to be clear on that.

"But that's not what he used to say, Mama," Willy told her.

"Yes, well, things may be confusing for a while," she said mildly.

"Now that the war is over, will we have more to eat?" he asked.

"I hope so."

But they didn't, not for quite a while. They'd been lucky. Her parents had a garden behind the house, had been able to plant cabbage and potatoes, and in the summer some beans and peas, so that they'd never gone hungry. But Eva didn't remember the last time they'd had meat or eggs or milk. Still, she didn't complain. She knew others had it far worse. The last time she'd heard from her friend, Lore, she'd written that their house had been destroyed in an air raid, that there was nothing to eat in Hannover, and that she and Helga were going home to her parents in Heigerloch. And even at that, Eva knew, others had it worse. By then they'd heard about the camps, the gas chambers, the ovens.

"Will Papa come home now that the war is over?"

"I hope so," she said again. She hadn't heard from Willie in the last two months, didn't even know where he was or whether he was still alive. At night, in her solitary bed, she tried to remember what it had felt like to have his warm body next to hers. It all seemed so long ago since he'd come back from Buchenwald, his face grim. When she'd questioned him about what had happened, he hadn't wanted to talk about it.

"We're in for some bad times," was all he'd said. "Take the boy. Go home to your parents."

"But this is our home."

"Go home to your parents. Trust me. When things get better . . . if things get better . . . you can come back."

"My parents don't have room . . . ."

"They'll make room. Eva, trust me. It's better for the boy if you go somewhere else. Where people don't know, where no one will talk. You never know . . ."

That last night, before Willie left for the army, they'd clung together, made desperate love.

"Take care of Willy," he'd said before they'd fallen asleep. "He's our boy now."

"'Til after the war," she'd said. "Then maybe . . . ."

"He's our boy now," Willie had repeated.

"Do you know who betrayed you?" she'd asked.

"Does it matter?"

"Of course it matters. Every time I look at someone, one of our friends, I wonder . . . ."

"I don't know," he said brusquely. "Maybe it's for the best. You were driving yourself crazy, worrying. Remember, you said you didn't know how much longer you could take the uncertainty.

Every time the doorbell rang. Every time you looked at Willy. At least the uncertainty is over. Now go to sleep."

But she hadn't been able to sleep, not that night, not for many nights thereafter. It had taken her another two months, and the partial destruction of the building, before she could bring herself to make the move to Kassel.

Now that the war was over, she wondered whether Martin would come back. What would they do? She couldn't bear the thought of giving up Willy. She no longer thought of him as Peter, hadn't for years. And what if her Willy were still alive? It would be a miracle. She'd heard the whispers about what the Nazis had done to the '*Untermenschen*,' but what if? Would he even still remember her? Willy/Peter didn't seem to remember anything of his parents. How would he react, feel, when he found out? They had to prepare him.

And then one day, a weary and bedraggled Willie appeared on their doorstep. His shoes were tatters, his uniform rags. His hair reached almost to his shoulders; his beard was matted. He smelled. But she held him as if she never intended to let him go, and his arms so tight around her, felt like heaven. When her mother came to the door they were standing there, entwined, tears streaming down their cheeks, his making tracks in his dust-covered face.

Willy was still at school when his father arrived, and by the time he got home, Willie had had a bath and shaved with his father-in-law's straight razor. Eva had taken a pair of scissors and cut his hair, and in a pair of trousers and shirt of his father-in-law looked, if not well-dressed, at least no longer like a scarecrow. Still, when Willy arrived, flinging his knapsack on the hall table and crashing into the kitchen, he came to an abrupt standstill.

"Say hello to your papa," Eva said. Willy stood mute.

"You don't remember me?" Willie asked. Willy shook his head.

"That's all right, son. Five years is a long time in a boy's life. You've gotten tall." Willy hung his head, looked down at the wooden shoes they were all wearing now that leather had become non-existent.

"How was school?" Eva asked, trying to inject a bit of normality.

"Fine," he said.

"Anything exciting happen?"

"I got a one on my mathematics test."

"A one," Willie said, impressed.

Willy hung his head shyly. "Can I go play with Konrad?" he finally asked.

"Change your clothes first."

Wordlessly he headed for the room he shared with Eva. That would have to change now, she realized. The sofa in the living room, until they could go back to Hannover?

"It'll take some time," Willie said, "but he'll be all right."

"Of course. He's never done well with strangers. At least not since you left."

"It hasn't been easy for him. For you." He paused. "For any of us."

She came over and poured him a cup of what passed for coffee, mostly chicory and assorted weeds they'd gathered. Her father was at work. Her mother had withdrawn discreetly, wanting to give them some time alone.

"We don't have much . . . but would you like a piece of bread? We still have a little jam from last summer's gooseberries."

"A bit of bread would be good. If it can be spared."

"It hasn't been that bad. We haven't gone hungry. With Papa's salary, and the garden . . . ."

"Then you've been luckier than the army. For the last few months it hasn't been good."

"But they said . . . the shortages . . . . We were sacrificing for the soldiers."

"Yeah, they said a lot of things. They told us we were sacrificing for another offensive, to drive out the Amis and the Brits."

"Where were you?"

"Where wasn't I? In North Africa, then in Italy. In Belgium. And then here, defending the Fatherland. Hah! Inch by inch, we moved backwards. Then one day our captain told us it was over. We were near Düsseldorff by then. We thought, okay, it's over. We'll be transported back to our homes."

"And?"

"And first we were interrogated by British intelligence. It wasn't as bad as the Gestapo, but it wasn't fun. Once we were cleared, they said, 'Thank you. You can go home now.' When we asked how, they shrugged. So we walked."

"You walked? From Düsseldorff?"

"Mostly. Five of us started out together. We slept in barns. We foraged for food. Not that there was much. Once we got lucky and found a hen that was still laying eggs. Once we got a ride with some American soldiers in a jeep. There were only two of us by then."

"What happened to the others?"

"Nothing bad. When they got to forks in the road leading to their homes . . . . The Americans were generous. They gave us a couple of chocolate bars. That lasted us for a day. Anyway, here I am, and yes, I'd love a piece of bread."

She cut a thick slab of coarse bread—part barley, part wheat, part potato. She brought him the jar of gooseberry jam and a knife, and he spread a thin layer onto the bread, took a bite, and chewed slowly. He swallowed and smiled.

She sat next to him, holding his hand while he ate. Willy came back. He had changed out of his threadbare school uniform into a pair of equally threadbare, and barely fitting, shorts. The sleeves of his shirt came to just below his elbows. He rolled them up as he came into the kitchen.

"I'm going now,"

"To Konrad's?"

"Yes. We may go play some football. If we can find a ball."

"Be home by six."

"I will, Mama."

"Say goodbye to your papa, Willy."

"Goodbye, Papa," he mumbled. And he was off.

"We'll have to tell him, now that the war is over," she said when the door had slammed.

"Why?"

"Why? Because we have to prepare him. When Martin comes back . . . ."

"You don't really think Martin will come back, Eva. You heard what they did . . . ."

"Yes. But not everyone died. Martin was a doctor. I heard that some of them were liberated. Last week Gustav Kahn—you remember, he was a neighbor—he came back. He'd been in a camp in Czechoslovakia, Teresienstadt. And he came back. And he was older than Martin. He said it was hard. Terrible. But some people survived."

"We can cross that bridge when we come to it. *If* Martin survived."

"But even if he didn't, Willie. He has a mother."

"You're his mother. You're the only mother he knows. Look how he was with me. And you say he's shy with strangers. What would it do to him, if suddenly he had to go to America? A whole other language, a whole other world?"

"That's why we have to prepare him."

"Eva. He's our son. We gave up our Willy . . . ."

"What if our Willy survived?"

"He didn't."

"How do you know that?"

"I heard what they did at Sonnenstein."

"What's Sonnenstein?"

"It's . . . it was a hospital. Near Dresden. It's where they sent Willy. And it's where they killed all of them."

"Them?"

"The ones they considered *Untermenschen*. The old, the sick, the ones like Willy."

"How do you know?"

"When I was in Italy, one of the doctors had been there. He told me."

"About Willy specifically?"

"Of course not. But he said they 'cleaned out' the place. Those were his words. Only he said he couldn't take it and asked to be sent to the front."

"They didn't send Martin there?"

"No. From what I heard they sent him to Dachau. After that, I don't know. To Auschwitz, someone said."

"How do you know so much?"

"I asked questions. Discreetly, understand. But people talk. Some because they felt guilty, others because they didn't."

"And what did they say?"

"You don't have to know. Just . . . it was bad, believe me. But the point is Martin isn't coming back, and Willy is our son."

"It's not right, Willie. He has a mother in America."

"And she has a daughter. And do you think she can give him what we can? She's in a new country, probably doesn't have much. They're probably just squeaking by."

"You don't know that."

"What? You think they came to America and suddenly they're rich? The streets are paved with gold?"

"Of course not, but . . . ."

"And the President, Roosevelt, he was waiting for them, and he said, 'Why don't you move into the White House with us?'"

"Don't be sarcastic, Willie. Of course I don't think that. But if it were I, even if I didn't have anything, to get my boy back . . . . I'd work around the clock, scrub floors, whatever . . . ."

"That's you, Eva. You're a special woman. But that's not the point. Even if Claire is like you, think of the girl. She'd suddenly be deprived. Half of not very much is even less."

"Money isn't everything, Willie."

"No. But think of Willy. Here he has two parents, grandparents, a future. Now that the war is over, I can start a new practice.

He'll be able to go to good schools, to university. And in America? Who knows? And not only that. We're the only parents he knows. Do you really want to uproot him?"

So she had given in, with the understanding that, of course, if Martin did come back, or if they heard from Claire . . . but they never did. They moved to Wolfenbüttel soon after Willie returned.

CHAPTER 19

Wolfenbüttel, November 1963

After they dropped Margot off at her house Brigitte said, "You really like her, don't you?"

"She's nice," he said.

"Come on, Willy. I saw the way you were looking at her."

"What? All right. She's a good-looking woman, and I'm a man. I'm not immune to good-looking women. You're a good-looking woman, too."

"Thanks. Look, it's okay. What you and I have, it's convenient."

"That's all?"

"No, of course not. It's fun. And I like you. But we both know it's not going to be forever. So what I'm saying is, if you really like her, go for it."

"She's going back to America when she finishes her internship."

"Maybe not if she had a better offer."

"Anyway she has a boyfriend. He's coming to see her next month, for the holidays. I don't know why we're even talking about this. She and I are just friends."

"Right. If you say so."

They had gotten to her house, and he parked the car, got out and walked with her to the door.

"Can I come in?" he asked.

"I'd be angry if you didn't," she said. They spoke no more of Margot that night.

In the morning he got up before Brigitte. He found his boxers on the floor, put them and his slacks on, and, after washing up, went into her kitchen, recently remodeled, with a new stove, sink, and refrigerator, and new cabinets with glass fronts. He took the new electric coffeepot off the counter, filled it with water, and spooned in coffee from the tin she kept in the refrigerator. He went to the front door, took in the bottle of milk, and poured the cream off the top into a creamer. Then he took out eggs, bacon, and butter from the refrigerator, and after frying the bacon to the crispness he wanted, went about scrambling the eggs. While the eggs cooked he found a tray and put cutlery and napkins and plates and cups on it. He spooned the eggs onto the plates, put the creamer on the tray, and took it into the bedroom, where Brigitte still slept. One bare leg stuck out from under the quilt.

Quietly he put the tray down on her dresser, and tiptoed out to get the coffee maker. Then he walked over to the bed, and kissed her at the base of her neck. She stirred, stretched, sat up. The quilt fell off.

"Breakfast," he said, smiling. "Although . . . ," he looked at her exposed breasts, ". . . I'm not sure there aren't distractions."

She reached under the pillow, pulled out a tee shirt she'd never gotten around to putting on the night before, and drew it over her head and down to cover her nudity.

"That coffee smells too good for distractions," she grinned. "Let me just pee and wash my face and hands." She left for the bathroom while Willy poured them each a cup of coffee. When she returned, she climbed back into bed next to him, and they ate, chatting about his work, hers. When they'd finished he put the dishes on the tray, took off his slacks and got back into bed, saying, "Now, about those distractions."

It was past noon by the time they resurfaced.

"I'm on call this evening," he said.

"You told me. That's all right. I have to go in to the office later anyway. Do you want to give me a ride?"

"Sure. But I should stop at home first. We don't want people wondering why I'm wearing the same clothes."

"I'm sure no one would notice under your doctor's coat. But that's all right. I'm in no rush."

They showered together, which delayed their departure somewhat, but finally, dressed and presentable, the dishes washed and dried and put away, they left the house.

When they came out, Brigitte's next-door neighbor was coming up her stairs.

"There goes my reputation," she murmured to Willy.

"Good afternoon, Fräulein Hegel," the neighbor said. "Did you hear the news?"

"What news?" Brigitte asked.

"About the American president. Kennedy?"

"What about him?"

"They shot him."

"What?" Brigitte and Willy said.

"Yes. Dead. The Communists." She smiled triumphantly, as though this validated the Nazi past of which Brigitte had long suspected her. Having delivered her news she brushed past Brigitte and Willy and went into the house, leaving them standing, stunned, on the steps. Finally,

"Let's find a newspaper," Willy said.

They walked down the street together until they reached the news agent on the corner. A cluster of people stood outside. Several held newspapers. All looked solemn.

"He was a good friend," one of the women said.

"I wonder what it will mean for us," an old man said.

Willy went inside, paid for a copy of the *Staats-Zeitung*, and they walked back to his car. The sun shone. The air was crisp and cool, a beautiful November day. They sat in the car and read the story: The young president in the car, his lovely wife next to him. There was the photo of Mrs. Kennedy on the back of the limousine, another of the new president, Johnson, being sworn in, Mrs. Kennedy, in her pillbox hat and bloodstained suit next to him.

"What a world," Brigitte said.

"Sounds like the guy who killed him was a crazy man."

"Not the Communists after all," she said. "Sorry, Frau Nudelmann."

"I wonder what the Russians will do," Willy said.

"Why should they do anything?"

"Well . . . they're always exploiting weakness. If there's insta-bility in America . . . ."

"Didn't you see the picture. They already have a new president, and . . . he was an important Senator, I think, before he became vice-president. The way these things work in America, nothing much will change. Do you remember when Roosevelt died?"

"Not really. I wasn't even eight."

"I wasn't even eight, either but I remember. My mother thought it meant the war would be over, and that Hitler had won. She was very depressed."

"And she was wrong."

"Right. Nothing changed. Truman became president and nothing changed. You'll see, the same thing will happen now."

"Still . . . ."

"Yes. It's sad. He was a great man, the way he stood up to the Russians, but you'll see . . . ."

"I hope you're right."

"I'm always right." He grinned impishly.

At the hospital that evening he was unusually busy. There'd been an accident on the autobahn, five cars piling up in the rain and fog, and there were casualties. All hands were needed, even general medicine residents like Willy. Margot was there too, and when there was a momentary lull for Willy, he watched her, liking not only her blonde good looks, but also her cool and efficient manner. *You'd never know,* he thought, *that this is her first year here.* Finally, at sometime after two, things quieted down. The patients who'd needed surgery had been cut up and put back together, the ones who only needed bandaging and watching were in rooms, and the two who no longer needed anything had been wheeled down to the morgue.

Willy dragged himself down to the cafeteria, thinking that last night's activities had, perhaps, left him more tired than, on call, he ought to be. He grabbed a cup of stale coffee and a tired looking piece of pound cake, and sank gratefully into a chair. He stirred in some milk and a lot of sugar to disguise the boiled-coffee taste, took a swallow, and leaned back and closed his eyes.

"May I join you?"

He opened his eyes, and Margot Brenner, holding a companion cup of coffee, stood there. Her hair was pulled back into a ponytail, but wisps had escaped and curled around her ears. She still wore scrubs, although, since they were not bloodied, she must have changed out of her OR gear. He nodded, and she lowered herself into the chair across from him. She took a swallow of her coffee, made a face.

"Lots of sugar helps . . . a little," he said. "So does this." He indicated the cake.

"I don't think anything can help this." She smiled. "But it may keep me awake." She took another sip.

"Would you like some cake? There's more than enough for us both."

"No thanks. I don't usually eat in the middle of the night."

They sat in silence for a few minutes. Then, "She's nice, your girlfriend."

"Yes, she said the same about you. She's not really my girl-friend." He stopped. *Why am I telling her that?* he wondered. She raised a quizzical brow.

"I mean . . . she is, sort of. But we're not serious. We're just . . . very good friends. She, uh, we enjoy each other's company, and we really are good friends . . . ."

"And that's all?"

He blushed. "Well," he said.

"Sorry, that was an indelicate question, and . . . ."

"No. It's . . . . I don't know. In America maybe women in the professions are more willing to get married, but here . . ."

"I don't think it's so different in America. We still have to choose, our profession or a family. It's one of the reasons they give for not wanting to let women into med school or into the prestigious internships. The old-line doctors say it's a waste of training, that we no sooner get trained than we go off to have babies."

"Is that true for you?"

"I'm not having any babies right now."

"I mean, do you want to get married?"

"Yes, but he'd have to know that I intend to keep working."

"So what about your boyfriend? Is he agreeable to that?"

"He says he is."

"Well then, you won't have to choose. Brigitte, on the other hand, says that at her firm as soon as a woman gets pregnant—or at least as soon as the firm knows it—they call her in for a little chat. And then she's gone."

"That's terrible."

"I suppose. Anyway, Brigitte says she's in no hurry to settle down, and when she does she wants to marry someone who has enough money so they won't miss her income."

"And that's not you?"

"That's not me. A general practitioner, like my father, makes a decent living. I've never wanted for anything. But we're not rich. And when I take over the practice I won't be rich either."

"Does that bother you?"

"What? That I won't be rich?"

"That too. But I meant that Brigitte would trade you in for someone with more money."

"Trade me in?"

"You know, like a car. Get a better model. It's what people do in America as soon as they can afford it."

"Ah, I like that, 'trade me in.'" He grinned. "No, it doesn't bother me. We've never pretended, Brigitte and I, that this was undying love. But the arrangement suits us for the moment. I can't

afford to get serious right now, and if she met that someone, well
. . . ." He shrugged.

"What about your father and Dr. Sauer?"

"I keep telling him to make an honest woman of Sophie. Even
though I don't know whether that's what *she* wants. I wish he'd
remarry, so he'd have someone when I move out. My mother died
too young. I think the war took a lot out of her. She was never that
strong after the war."

"Were you in Hannover the whole time?"

"No, we moved to Kassel, shortly after my father went into the
army. We lived with my mother's parents."

"Are they still alive?"

"No. Opa died not too long after my father got home. And
Oma died less than a year later. We stayed in Kassel 'til she died,
and then Papa took a job here. He took over the practice from old
Dr. Frank, and was on the staff at Georg-August."

"Do you remember anything from before the war? Do you
remember us?"

"Not a thing. It's funny. I think I told you last time, I remember
the air raids in Hannover, but otherwise I don't remember much
before my father came back from the army."

"Do you still have family in Kassel?"

"An aunt and uncle and a bunch of cousins. My mother's
brother's family. But we're not close. My uncle still belongs to
some right-wing veteran's group. I think they close the curtains,
pull out the photo of Der Führer, click their heels and salute. And
my cousins are just as bad. The oldest one is named Horst, which
should give you some idea."

"Horst?"

"You know, for Horst Wessel. Anyway, he got arrested for
painting swastikas on the Jewish cemetery in Kassel, and Uncle
Ullie thought it was no big deal. The younger kids aren't quite as
bad. They didn't get quite as much indoctrination, but . . . we don't
see them much."

They both drank some coffee. Then, "Have you heard any news today?" he asked her.

"No. I slept straight through 'til it was time to come on, and since then we've been so busy that . . . why?"

"So you haven't heard about Kennedy."

"Is he coming here again? '*Ich bin ein Berliner*,'" she mimicked.

"He was shot," he blurted.

"Shot? Omigosh, is it serious?"

"Fatal," he said. "I'm sorry. Sorry to be giving you the bad news, and sorry it happened." Impulsively he took her hand.

"Who? How? Was it the right wing? The Southerners who were mad about his civil rights position? Do you know anything?"

"There was an article in the *Staats-Zeitung*. They say it was some crazy loner, with ties to Fidel Castro."

"Oh, that poor man, that poor woman. And those two little kids." She shook her head. "Do you still have the paper?"

"In my car. When I go off call, I'll leave it in your box."

"What a world. Goes to show no one is safe. A crazy loner, huh? I wouldn't be surprised if Johnson had something to do with it."

"Your vice-president? I mean, now your president?"

"Or his wife. You know, like Shakespeare's play, *Macbeth*. Did you read Shakespeare in school?"

"Absolutely. In English, even."

"No wonder your English is so good. I don't think I could read Goethe in German."

"Of course you could."

"So Johnson is president now. Oh, poor Jackie."

She finished her coffee, now cold as well as bitter, and stood.

"Back to the salt mines," she said, and, still shaking her head in disbelief, bussed her cup at the station and left.

CHAPTER 20

Wolfenbüttel, November 1963

When she got off call the following afternoon the *Staats-Zeitung* was in her mailbox. She read the article quickly, surprised that she was crying as she read it. She'd been busy after leaving the cafeteria and hadn't had a chance to absorb the news. Now she stood, feeling devastated. She wished her mother were here. She wished John were here. She wished she could talk to someone who would feel what she was feeling, as if the world had shifted. She put the paper into her briefcase and walked home in a fog. People stood on street corners, talking. She heard snatches, *"Auch erschossen," "Grauenhaft," "Ein guter Mann."* When she got back to the house Frau Lindemann greeted her.

"Ah, Dr. Brenner, I'm so sorry."

"It's unbelievable," she said.

"And now they shot him, too."

"What? Who?"

"The man who killed the president. They shot him."

"I don't understand."

"I don't understand, either. I was listening to the radio and they just announced that the police were bringing him, the killer, into the police station, and some other man came up and shot him."

Margot stood, speechless.

"Would you like something? A cup of coffee? Tea?" Frau Lindemann put her arm around Margot's waist and steered her toward the kitchen where a large pot steamed on the cast iron stove. The smell of some sort of meat and onions filled the room.

Margot sank into one of the chairs. She was exhausted from being on call, but her head was spinning with this latest news, and she knew she'd never sleep. She might as well accept the offer of tea and make it through dinner before crashing. Frau L. filled the teakettle before coming to stand behind her. She patted Margot's shoulder, muttering, "It's terrible. What a world! You have my sympathy." The phrases were punctuated with heavy sighs, and when Margot turned, her landlady had tears streaming down her ruddy cheeks.

The teakettle whistled, and Frau L. busied herself with the teapot before coming back to the table with two cups of tea. She seated herself in the chair next to Margot, instead of in her customary one at the head of the table, and continued patting Margot's shoulder. Margot felt weird. She was being treated like a mourner, or an invalid. What she really needed, aside from sleep, was to talk to someone who shared her feelings. She was sure Frau L. was truly sad, too, but she wasn't American; it wasn't her tragedy. And besides she felt uncomfortable sharing her suspicions, her anger, with a . . . stranger? Outsider? German? Again she wished John were here.

She wondered how much it would cost to call New Haven. She looked at her watch. It was six hours earlier in Connecticut, so it was only eleven in the morning there. John wouldn't even be home, and she could never reach him at the hospital, even if she tried. And if she called his house she'd have to speak to his mother. Aside from the fact that Mrs. Watts was a lifelong Republican and sputtered at the mention of the Kennedy name, talking to her was not what Margot wanted. So . . . she sipped her tea and agreed with her landlady that it was, indeed, terrible; that yes, there were too many guns in America; and no, she didn't think the Russians would take advantage of the situation.

"They'll be too busy trying to show they had nothing to do with it."

At dinner an hour later the other boarders treated Margot with the kind of solicitude reserved for the frail. They passed her the dishes first. They spoke in whispers. When one started to laugh the others glared reproachfully and the guilty one turned the laugh into a quick cough. Margot couldn't wait to finish dinner and get to bed. She passed on the stewed fruit that was dessert, pleaded fatigue, and escaped as quickly as was decent.

She was in her pajamas and brushing her teeth when Hedwig knocked on the bathroom door.

"Telephone for you, Margot. America."

Margot spit out the toothpaste, rinsed her mouth hastily, and followed Hedwig down the stairs. The telephone was on the wall in the front hall, the receiver lying on a small table. Margot said "Hello?" while Hedwig returned to the dining room.

"Is this Dr. Brenner?" an operator asked. When she declared that she was, the operator said, "Your party is on the line, sir."

"Margot," John said. "God, it's good to hear your voice."

She looked around for a chair, and finding none slid down the wall and sat on the threadbare carpet.

"I miss you," she said. "I'm so glad you called. I wanted . . . needed . . . ."

"I know. Look, I don't have long, but I figured you could use a touch of home."

"You can't imagine. Everyone here is tip-toeing around me, as though I'll break. And the news is sparse, and a couple of beats behind. What's happening? Is it true that . . . ."

"What have you heard?"

"That some loner killed Kennedy and that somebody shot the loner in the police station in Texas. Is that true?"

"Yeah, you have the basics."

"How could someone get into a police station with a gun?"

"That's the $64 question, isn't it?"

"So what are people saying? Do they think Johnson had something to do with it?"

"People are saying all sorts of things. It's the Mafia. It's the Cubans. It's the CIA. Pick your theory."

"What do you think?"

"I don't know, Babe. I feel numb. Most people do. I was off this weekend, and I spent the whole time in front of the TV. Much to my mother's annoyance, I must add."

"I wish I were there."

"I know. It's weird. Everyone is going around in a daze, asking, 'Where were you when you heard?' It's like the whole country has stopped. Only it hasn't, of course. At the hospital it's business as usual. Mother said only a parvenu would wear a pink suit, and Father is muttering about chickens coming home to roost. But most of the country is in shock. What's it like there?"

"Everyone is shocked too, but it's sort of once removed. You know, as if someone else's father had died. It's sad, but it's not their tragedy. It makes me feel very alone."

"I wish I could hold you," he said.

"Soon. It's less than four weeks now."

"Gotta run," he said. "We're doing a discectomy and the surgeon said I could actually *use* the scalpel rather than hand it to him."

"Great. I'm glad you called, John."

"Me too. Love you."

"I love you too," she said, and held the phone even after the connection had been broken.

Tired though she was, sleep eluded her. She tossed, she turned, she fluffed the pillow, she reversed the quilt. "Too many guns in America," Frau L. had said. It was true, but was there a hint of condescension there? Or was Margot being hypersensitive? She didn't really want to hear criticism of America as a cowboy culture from a German. No, that wasn't fair. Frau L. had been nothing but kind to her. She shouldn't lump all Germans . . . but still. She wondered whether she'd made a mistake in coming here. What was she proving? Even if she found out anything more about her father, so what? Well, at least she was getting surgical training out of it. But she wished she were home. She closed her eyes and thought of John, of lying with him on some sunny beach with the

Mediterranean blue in front of them. She thought of them in bed together. She wished he were here now, his long body next to hers.

In the morning, before she went to work, she wrote a note to Brigitte, giving her the specifics about her father and Peter. She took out Brigitte's card, addressed and stamped an envelope, and mailed it on her way to the hospital.

So the days passed. She went from the hospital to the rooming house, from sleep deprivation to round-the-clock stupor. She began to feel more comfortable in the OR. Her German, good to begin with, was fluent by now. Often she found herself thinking in German. Sometimes she met Willy in the cafeteria, and they had coffee or a sandwich together. She began to look forward to these meetings. He was funny; he was warm. His politics were liberal. And he was good-looking. If it weren't for John . . . .

One Sunday afternoon when she was free she went to the movies with Hedwig. They saw a mindless comedy of manners, and afterwards had supper at a Rathaus. It was noisy, the bar packed with young people laughing, smoking, raising their glass to make a point. Several guys offered to buy them drinks, which they politely declined. Hedwig had confided to Margot that she was just recovering from a relationship with a doctor—married, it turned out.

"I didn't know it when it started. He 'forgot' to wear his wedding ring, 'forgot' to mention the fact. By the time I found out I was already involved."

"A doctor at Georg-August?"

"Yeah."

"Do I know him?"

"I don't know. He's not on staff, but he has admitting privileges. I met him when we were treating a little boy who'd fallen out of a tree. Johann actually came to the ER to be with the little boy's mother. I was impressed by his dedication."

"That is impressive."

"Not really. Turns out it was his kid."

"Oh? He forgot to tell you that, too?"

"Yes. You know how it is, a busy man. He 'assumed' I knew, that I realized."

"Sounds like a prize."

"Well, he is gorgeous. And good in bed. But I make it a rule not to go out with married men. So I broke it off. He still calls from time to time, says he's leaving his wife."

"And of course she doesn't understand him."

"Of course not. Anyway, that's history. But I haven't met anyone since who makes me tingle. If you know what I mean."

"I'm sure you will. That's one of the good things about a hospital. There are lots of guys."

"Right, and the good ones are usually married. Or they're . . ." she wiggled her hand. "Or all they want is to go to bed with you. So when is your boyfriend coming?"

"In seventeen days and . . . ," she looked at her watch, "four hours and twenty-two minutes."

They laughed.

"That guy over there," Margot said, "the tall blond one with the leather jacket. He's been staring at you."

Hedwig turned. The man raised his beer stein at her in a salute, smiled.

"He's cute," Hedwig said.

"So invite him over."

Hedwig smiled. "You don't mind?"

"Why should I mind?"

The young man shrugged a question. Hedwig nodded. He picked up his glass, threaded his way through the crowd, and folded himself into the empty chair at their table.

"Ladies," he said. "Can I buy you a drink?"

They assured him they were fine.

"I'm Günther Straus."

They introduced themselves. He was, he told them, an architect. He was new to Wolfenbüttel, having just finished a project in Bonn, and having been recently recruited by a firm of architects here.

"It's a smaller firm, but I'll have a chance to be creative. In Bonn I did mainly the details for the bosses. And took the blame when things went wrong. Here I'll actually get a chance to do some of my own work."

"That must be exciting," Hedwig smiled. "Maybe some day you can build a house for me."

"Any time you're ready," he said. His eyes crinkled when he smiled. "And what do you do?"

They told him, and he seemed impressed. After a bit Margot looked at her watch.

"Time for me to get home," she said. Hedwig started to rise.

"Must you?" he asked. Hedwig looked at Margot.

"I can get myself home," she said.

"You're sure you don't mind?"

"Really not."

Hedwig sat back down. Margot put down money for her meal and left. As she made her way through the crowd she heard someone call her name. She turned and found Willy and Brigitte sitting at the bar.

"I was going to call you," Brigitte said. "I thought we could have lunch."

"I'd like that," Margot said.

"Am I invited too?" Willy asked.

"No. I think this will be girls only." Willy pouted. "Actually, it's business, Willy. We promise not to talk about you."

"Do you have any news for me?" Margot asked.

"Not yet. But I found a good contact. I should be hearing any day now."

"Would you like to join us?" Willy asked.

"Thanks. I'm on my way home. I saw a movie and had dinner with a friend, but I have a long day tomorrow."

"Your friend, is he still here?" Willy asked.

"It's Hedwig, from the ER, and yes. She met someone, and I said I could get myself home."

"Would you like us to take you home?" he asked gallantly.

"Not necessary. Thanks." She turned to Brigitte. "When would be good for you?"

"I'm rather busy this week. We have a trial that's getting to the interesting stage. Maybe next Saturday, for lunch?"

Margot did a quick mental scan of her schedule.

"I think that works. Let me check when I get home, and I'll call your office tomorrow and leave a message. Is that all right?"

Outside she buttoned her coat against the chill December night. The stars shone here in a way they didn't in New York. As she walked down the dark streets, past houses where lights still shone through the drawn curtains, she enjoyed the quiet. An occasional car drove by, its lights shining as it approached and gradually fading as it continued down the road. A group of teenagers approached, their boisterous voices shattering the quiet. They smiled at her as they passed. Although the streets were mostly empty, she felt no sense of danger. Maybe, she thought, that was foolhardy. She knew that in New York she would have been uneasy walking down deserted streets.

She let herself into the house, made her way quietly up the stairs, and, after washing up, sat down and wrote a letter to John before getting into bed. She hoped Hedwig and Günther were hitting it off.

CHAPTER 21

Wolfenbüttel, December 1963

Brigitte was waiting at one of the small tables near the entrance, sipping a glass of white wine. She waved to Margot, who slipped into the seat across from her. The restaurant was on the square, and in the summer had tables outside where a diner could watch the passing scene while enjoying a beer and a sandwich. Now the square was nearly deserted as people hurried along, their heads down against the cold rain that also drove into the windows. But inside it was cozy.

The wood beams were dark, and the cheerful fire in the stone fireplace reflected off their shiny surfaces. The white stucco walls were filled with photos of groups of men in lederhosen and tyrol hats, and of women in peasant blouses and full skirts. The tables had white cloths and checked blue-and-white napkins. The flatware looked heavy. A waitress, her plump arms giving the appearance of a stuffed sausage, hovered.

"Something for the lady to drink?"

"I'll have some coffee, please," Margot said.

"You don't want a glass of wine? They have a nice Piesporter . . . ."

"I have to go to work later. I'd better stick to coffee."

The waitress put down heavy menus and waddled off, returning shortly with a silver pot from which she poured steaming, aromatic coffee into a thick ceramic mug with the restaurant logo, two rampant lions facing each other on either side of what looked like, but couldn't possibly be, a golden pretzel.

Having poured the coffee she waited expectantly.

"We're not ready to order just yet," Brigitte told her. "But you might bring us a plate of cheese and bread to nibble on."

Margot took a sip of her coffee and gave a contented sigh. "Good," she said. "They don't make it like this in the hospital."

"So what do you think of Willy?" Brigitte asked. Margot looked up, startled. Brigitte grinned. "He's a sweet boy," she continued. "But you know we're not a serious item, and I think he likes you."

"I like him, too."

"No, I mean *really* likes you." She took another sip of her wine, and cut a piece of cheese from the wedge the waitress had brought. She tasted, said, "Ahh," and cut off another piece that she offered to Margot. "Try this with the black bread. You can't get anything like this in America."

"It is good," Margot agreed after taking a bite.

"It's a local cheese. I've never gotten it anywhere else in Germany either. But in America all you get is . . . ."

"You've been to America?"

"Yes, last year. My company sent me. They had a case with an American . . . complication. So they sent me. My English is better than that of anyone else at the firm."

"Where were you?"

"Detroit. But I spent a day in New York. There's a city where I could live. In fact, one day I might." She smiled. "I met a man there . . . if things work out."

"Is that why you asked me about Willy?"

"Maybe. Partly. They're sending me back right after Christmas, to New York this time."

"Poor Willy," Margot said.

"You don't have to worry about him. Women are after him like ducks on a bug. But if you're interested . . . I just wanted to tell you not to worry on my account. And he does like you."

"I have a . . . boyfriend? Fiancé? He's coming for the holidays."

"Okay. Just thought I'd tell you. So tell me about your friend."

"We've known each other since we started medical school. He's tall, handsome. Sexy." She blushed. "He's thoughtful and generous, and doesn't mind that I have a working brain."

"He sounds wonderful. Why in the world did you let him out of your sight?"

"I really needed to come here. And I couldn't pass up the opportunity for the surgical residency. In New York I would have been forced into pediatrics."

"That doesn't sound so terrible to me."

"It's not, except that I really wanted surgery."

"So. Is he good in bed, your . . . what's his name?"

Margot blushed again.

"Sorry. Willy always says I lack tact. Forget I asked. So . . . what's his name, your fellow?"

"John. John Watts." She smiled, thinking of him. She was really counting the days until he came.

"Ah, your whole face lights up when you say his name. He sounds like . . . how do you say it in English? 'A good catch.' And he didn't mind your coming here?"

"I think he minded, but he understood. His parents were happy. They hope it'll end the relationship. You know. Out of sight, out of mind."

"His parents aren't happy with you?"

"Oh, it's nothing personal. They just think he should marry someone from their social circle."

"So, even in America?"

"Even in America. But enough about that. Have you found out anything?"

Their waitress had returned. "More wine? More coffee?" she asked.

They both nodded, and while the waitress went off they looked at the menus. Their drinks refreshed, they ordered—Brigitte goulash and noodles, Margot the trout.

"I spoke to this man, one of our clients. He was pretty high up in the government during the war. Of course," she sneered, "he never knew what was really going on. And of course he was never a Nazi."

"Of course not," Margot said.

"Anyway, he's been rehabilitated. He's pretty high up in Bonn now. He likes me, and I called him. He said he'd see what he could find out."

"And?"

"He sent me this. It came last Thursday." She reached into her purse and pulled out a legal-sized envelope, from which she pulled two sheets of onionskin paper. She handed the papers to Margot. On the top was the seal of the German Republic, and a letter, addressed to Brigitte at her firm. The letter was typed, double-spaced, and several of the letters were somewhat blurred, as though the typewriter needed cleaning.

Dear Rechtsanvalt Hüber:

I'm sorry I haven't responded sooner, but it's taken some time to get the information you wanted. The events that occurred at Sonnenstein, near Pirna, are not generally talked about, and I had some difficulty, but I finally found the assistant to the former director, a man who is now ashamed of his part in the unfortunate events. His name doesn't matter, so I'm not including it. He did have access to records, and with a little encouragement from me was willing to look for the information you asked for.

He found no record of a Martin Brenner ever having been at Sonnenstein, either as a doctor or as a patient. He did, however, find a Peter Brenner, a male child aged not quite three. The child was an imbecile, and was euthanized on April 23, 1940. My source says they were using gas by then, but the official cause of death was given, in all cases, as pneumonia.

Since you told me that Dr. Brenner died at Auschwitz I'm still looking into things there. I still know a few people who may have specific records. As you know, we're a good people for keeping accurate records. I'll be in touch as soon as I have something.

If I can be of any further use, please don't hesitate to ask me.

Yours truly,
Siegfried Wolff

Margot dropped the sheets on the table, and wiped at the tears streaming down her cheeks. Brigitte reached across the table and took one of her hands.

"I'm sorry," she said.

"I mean, I knew this, but seeing it in black on white! And the ordinary tone, 'my source says they were using gas by then.' My God, it's as if he's talking about, I don't know, as if they stopped using quills and were up to fountain pens! But what I don't understand . . . he says Peter was an imbecile. From what my mother said he was a bright little boy."

"Mothers don't always see their children clearly," Brigitte suggested.

"I know, but an imbecile! Mom always told the story of when we were leaving, and my father said we'd just go on ahead and they'd follow. That Mom would have dinner on the table when they arrived. Oh, God." She sobbed, took a swallow of water, composed herself. "He asked Peter what he wanted my mother to cook for him when they got to New York, and, according to my mother he answered 'Ice cream.' Does that sound like an imbecile to you?"

"I don't know. I guess not. Maybe the illness? Sometimes, I'm told, high fevers can damage a child's brain. Maybe . . . ."

"I suppose that's possible. Meningitis. I'll ask Dr. Meinhoff . He should know."

"That's right. They were staying with Willy's parents, weren't they?"

"Right. And this Mr. Wolff. Do you think he'll be able to find out what really happened to my father?"

"If anyone can, he can. He has good sources, knows all the old Nazis who were, of course, never really Nazis. Personally I think he's despicable, but I saved his neck on a case not too long ago, and he feels he owes me. And whatever else he is, he's reliable. If he says he'll get back to me, he will. I just hope it's before I go to New York."

"How long will you be there?"

"Two months. But if things go the way I hope . . . who knows?"

Their food came. Brigitte dug in. Margot picked.

"Not any good?" Brigitte asked.

"I seem to have lost my appetite. I keep thinking of that poor little boy, those poor people."

"Yes. That makes me a clod, doesn't it?"

"Sorry. Of course not. I'll be all right." She took another sip of her water. She felt as though there was a log lying across her esophagus. Brigitte had put her fork down.

"Please," Margot said, "I don't want to ruin your lunch." She took a deep breath, took another swallow of water. This one went down. The trout on her plate, golden and crisp, was surrounded by fried little potatoes and green beans with almonds. She picked up a green bean, brought the fork to her mouth, chewed, swallowed.

"There," she forced a smile. "Please, eat."

Outside, the rain beat against the windows. She picked up the letter.

"Do you mind if I keep this?" she asked.

"It's yours. But you can't make this public. I mean, much as I loathe Herr Wolff, I don't think this is common knowledge; and while, personally, I don't care how much trouble he gets into, he did do me a favor. And my firm wouldn't like it if he got into trouble. We don't want scandal."

"Whom would I tell? I tell you what, why don't we take off the letterhead and the signature. I don't need those anyway. I just want the facts for . . . I don't know. History. My grandchildren."

She took the first page, folded it just below the letterhead, and took her knife to slice through the paper. She did the same with the bottom of the second page. She handed the identifying parts to Brigitte, then folded the letter and put it into her handbag. That done, she took another swallow of water and took a bite of trout. It was actually excellent, and she found that she could, after all, eat.

They talked, for the rest of the meal, about the man Brigitte hoped would become Mr. Right. She had met him at a party when she'd been in New York. There had been an instant chemistry, a spark. "You know, like the line from *South Pacific*: 'Some enchanted evening you may see a stranger across a crowded room.' We've been in touch since then. He was here earlier this year, and the spark . . . how should I put it? . . . It flamed." She smiled. "We'll see."

"What does he do?" Margot asked.

"He's an attorney too. But he comes from old money. Lives on Park Avenue. Has a summer house in a place called Martha's Vineyard. Does that mean anything to you?"

"I hear it's beautiful. I don't think he's on welfare."

"I don't think so either. I don't want you to think I'm after him for his money, Margot. But my mother always said it's as easy to love a rich man as a poor man."

"I suppose that's true. Except it's probably easier to meet a poor man. There are definitely more of those. But you have a good career."

"I do. But if I want to have children, and I do, then I won't be able to work, at least not for a while. So I need a husband who can support us."

"Willy could support you."

"We're just friends. I told you that."

"No spark?"

"Well, I wouldn't exactly say that." She smiled impishly, soaked up the last of her gravy with a piece of roll. "But . . . it's never been serious. Men aren't the only ones who can enjoy a good bed partner without its having to lead to the altar."

"I suppose."

"Anyway, we'll see where this goes. Porter hasn't asked me to marry him either."

Margot looked at her watch.

"Do you have time for dessert?" Brigitte asked. "They have wonderful pastry here. Their creampuffs . . . ."

"I'll just have some more coffee, and then I've got to go."

"I'll have some coffee, too," Brigitte told their waitress. "And a *Mohrenkopf.*"

A busboy cleared their dishes and brought Brigitte a cup. The waitress refilled Margot's cup as well and set down a perfect cream puff—whipped cream oozing out of the center and covered with a rich, dark chocolate glaze. Brigitte took a bite, sighed.

"Would you like a taste? It's sinfully rich."

"No, I'm fine, thanks. I don't know how you keep your figure."

"Metabolism. I burn it off worrying." She grinned.

"Do you? Worry?"

"Really? No. But I've never had a weight problem. I eat what I want, and I can't gain an ounce."

"I can. But with my schedule that hasn't been a problem. Look, I'd better go. Thanks for getting that information for me."

"I'm sorry it upset you."

"It didn't. I knew it. Well, it did, but I wanted to know. And please, as soon as you hear from Mr. Wolff . . . ."

"Of course. This was fun. Let's do it again before I leave for your city. And maybe when your John comes we can all go out, you two and Willy and I."

It was agreed. Brigitte refused to let Margot pay.

"I'll put it on my expense account. After all, we were discussing a client. In fact, I'll find some way to put it on Mr. Wolff's account. It's the least he can do." She smiled her impish smile again. Margot left her finishing her coffee and pastry, and went home to change before heading for another thirty-six hours at the hospital.

CHAPTER 22

Wolfenbüttel, December 1963

By the time she came off call she was past exhaustion. This close to the holidays, people were finding all sorts of ingenious ways of injuring themselves and others. Whether it was an increase in drinking; whether it was the fact that there were fewer hours of daylight; whether appendixes burst more often in winter months; whether gallstones, stirred awake by rich holiday food, made their presence known; or whether it is none of the above, the fact remained that lots of cutting and stitching was required. Every time one surgery was over and she put her head on the pillow in the on-call room for a catnap, someone else appeared, needing surgery. She doubted that she'd gotten an hour's uninterrupted sleep in the past thirty-six. She dragged herself home and fell into her bed.

She dreamed that the Nazis were after her and she was hiding in her closet. Her mother was there, too, and they were clutching each other, trying to still their breathing so as not to reveal their hiding place. The knocks grew louder.

"Margot. Telephone."

It took her a minute to come awake. She shook her head.

"Margot, telephone. From America." It was a man's voice. She sat up, swung her feet over the side of the bed and pushed them into her slippers.

"Coming," she mumbled. She looked outside the window. It was dark, but since it was getting dark a little past four that didn't mean anything. She looked at her watch. It was almost ten, or four o'clock in the states. She grabbed her bathrobe and shrugged into it, tying the belt around her waist before she opened the door.

Alex Weerbel stood outside.

"Sorry to wake you, but . . ."

"No. That's all right. Thanks." She smoothed down her hair, and stumbled down the steps to the phone, the receiver of which lay on the table.

"This is Margot Brenner," she said.

"We have a call for you from New Haven. Please hold."

She held, wondering.

"Margot, it's John."

"Is everything all right?" she asked.

"Actually no. It's Father. He had a stroke this morning."

"Oh, John. I'm so sorry. Is he . . . ?"

"No. He's alive. But he's not responding, and his left side seems to be affected. The doctors say the next forty-eight hours should tell us more, but . . . ."

"How are you coping?"

"I'm a little numb right now. I found him. He was in his office, and he wasn't answering his phone."

"Where was his secretary?"

The office wasn't open. He'd just gone in to catch up on some stuff. It's lucky I called. If I hadn't who knows what . . ."

"Poor John. How's your mother?"

"Stiff upper-lipping. You know Mother. She's at his bedside, doing her duty. She's *even* canceled her tennis game."

"John!"

"I know, I'm being unfair. I'm sure she's upset. You'd just never know."

"I'm sorry. Do you want me to come home?"

"I'd love it. But not because of this. There's nothing you could do. But I can't come over there now. I'm sorry."

"It's not your fault."

"No, but I'm sorry. Not apologizing sorry. Regretting sorry."

"Me, too. I was so looking forward to it."

"Me too. I'd say come here instead, but I think you should save your time off. I still want us to go somewhere together. I'll reschedule when things are resolved. Can you do that, too?"

"I'm sure I can. They're always glad to have an extra pair of hands over the holidays."

"Just like here. Some things are universal, I guess."

"Poor John. I wish I could give you a hug."

"That's not all I want to give you."

"Careful, the operator may be listening."

"I've got to go. I love you, I'll call you again as soon as I know anything."

"Okay. I love you, too. Tell your mother . . . oh, never mind. She probably doesn't care what . . . . But tell her I'm thinking good thoughts."

"I will. And I'm sure she'll appreciate it. Anyway, I do. It's hard to believe. He's never been sick a day in his life. He wasn't overweight, only smoked the occasional cigar. Okay, maybe he liked his scotch a little too much, but still. And he's only sixty-two. It's hard to believe."

"I know. I love you," she said again, and they hung up.

When she got back upstairs, Alex Weerbel was coming out of the bathroom.

"Bad news?" he asked.

"Sort of. My fiancé's father had a stroke."

"That's too bad. A serious one?"

"Seems to be, but it's too soon to tell. Thanks for getting me."
She went back into her room, and after shedding her robe and slippers, she got back into bed. She pulled the quilt up to her chin, burrowed into her pillow. *Poor John*, she thought. She wondered whether, if his father died, he'd be expected to take over the practice. It wasn't what he had in mind, she knew, but . . . his father did have a partner, so maybe that would get John off that hook. She wasn't a particular fan of the senior John Watts. And it wasn't only that he thought her unsuitable. His whole outlook was not

her cup of tea, from his belief that women should stay home and mind the house to his oft-stated opinion that Blacks should stay in their place (and, although never overtly stated, at least in her presence, that Jews should do the same). He thought the New Deal had been a terrible blot in America's history. The name Roosevelt engendered, practically, hisses and boos at the Watts' dinner table, and the Kennedy name wasn't much more beloved. John's mother, as befit a woman of her circumstance, nodded acquiescence and voted as he did. How, she wondered, not for the first time, had they managed to raise John? She supposed they often wondered the same. Still, though she wasn't, obviously, overly fond of either of John's parents, she was sorry they were suffering. She was sorry, too, that the much-looked-forward-to trip to the Costa del Sol was off. Well, she'd tell them at Georg-August tomorrow. She hoped it wouldn't be too long before they could reschedule. And here she'd started taking birth control pills last month. Ah well.

She burrowed down into the pillow and tried to lull herself to sleep by thinking of John's hands on her breasts, on her belly, on . . . .

As expected, her announcement that she was available for holiday duty was enthusiastically greeted not only by Dr. Prange, who was in charge of scheduling, but by Klaus Shüler, a fellow intern who had been too late to put in his request for the Christmas/New Year week off, and who now would be able to go to Bavaria to see his parents after all. Klaus was a bear of a man, over six-five, with the hands and feet to go with it. While Margot was, at five-eight, tall for a woman, next to Klaus she felt absolutely petite, and when, after getting the good news, he enveloped her in a hug, she almost disappeared.

"I'll bring you back some beer," he promised. "We have the best local beer in the world."

She extricated herself from his embrace. "That's not necessary," she said. "And I'm not much of a beer drinker. I know, I know, it's one of my few faults."

At lunch she bumped into Willy.

"So, how was your girls' lunch?"

"It was fun. And instructive."

"Sit." He indicated the empty chair at his table. The cafeteria was busy, and most of the tables were filled. There were two other doctors she vaguely knew sitting with Willy, and she nodded hello. They continued eating, while nodding back.

"When is your boyfriend coming?" Willy asked when she was seated.

"Don't know. His father had a stroke yesterday."

"That wouldn't keep me away from you," he said. He grinned to show he was joking. "So," he went on, "does that mean you're not taking the week off?"

"I'll save it until he can get away."

"Then you have to come and have Christmas dinner with us. Papa always roasts a goose. It'll be fun. Sophie will be there . . . and I'll ask Brigitte."

"I may be on call on Christmas.

"Well, if you're not?"

"Then sure. Thanks. If it's all right with your father."

"Of course it'll be all right with him. The more the merrier. When Mama was alive we always had a crowd. Uncle Ullie and his family." He made a face. "I don't miss them, but I miss Mama."

He took a bite of his sandwich, made another face. "I don't know why I always expect this will be edible. You wouldn't think they could mess up a salami sandwich."

Margot had opted for two hard-boiled eggs and a roll. She put butter on the roll, unpeeled the eggs, and took a bite.

"That's why I stick to this," she said. "One summer when I was in high school I worked at the food counter of Woolworth's, a big department store in the U.S. The girl who was training me taught me how to make egg salad and tuna salad. You put white bread in the egg salad, and whole wheat in the tuna."

"Bread?"

"Sure. It's cheaper than eggs or tuna fish. But what convinced me to eat only what I can identify was when I was making fresh-squeezed orange juice."

"What can they do to orange juice? Water?"

"That wouldn't have been so bad. That would only be dishonest. No. One day we were taking the oranges out of the crate, and there were a couple of really rotten ones, mushy and moldy. I showed them to Rita, and she said 'Put them aside.' I did, figuring we'd return them to the shipper, you know, for credit. The next time I was making a fresh orange juice I suddenly heard a shriek behind me. I turned around, and Rita yelled, 'What are you doing?' 'Making juice,' I said. 'You have to use those first,' she said, pointing to the rotten oranges I'd put aside. I said, 'But they're rotten.' She answered, 'That's why you have to use them first.' So now in places like this I try to eat things no one can adulterate."

"I don't think hospitals would use rotten food. At least I hope not." He took another bite of his sandwich, looked at the salami. "Of course who knows what they put into the salami."

"There used to be a saying about Armour, one of the sausage companies in America, that they use everything of the pig except the squeak."

Willie took another dubious look at his sandwich, then took a resolute bite.

"There's a book that was written about the meat industry in the US early in the century." She continued. "It's called *The Jungle*. It's enough to make one a vegetarian. That book helped to pass the Food and Drug Act, but obviously it doesn't keep places like Woolworth's from being creative."

"So what other jobs did you have?"

"Mostly baby-sitting. I didn't stay at Woolworth's long. I also worked in a factory. For a while I worked after school and Saturdays at a department store on Fifth Avenue. That was all right. And summers I worked as a counselor in camps."

"Camps?"

"For children. Places their parents can send them in the summer to get them out of the city. You don't have that here?"

He shook his head no.

"I went to camp every summer after I turned six. The first few years, when I was little, I minded. I missed my mother, but she had to work, and this way I was safe. When I was a bit older I loved it. Until I got too old. Then I worked for three summers as a mother's helper, out at the beach. That was good, too. But during the school year, I mostly earned money baby-sitting, or tutoring."

"I was lucky. I never had to work. But I'm making up for it now."

"And speaking of work," she said, "I have to get back. I'm scrubbing with Dr. Prange."

"The big man himself? I didn't know he still did surgery."

"He doesn't, usually. But this is the wife of one of the trustees, and she wants only the top. I probably won't do more than hand him instruments, but that's okay. I hear he's good, so it'll be fun watching."

"You think watching someone's insides cut up is fun?"

"You don't?"

"You want to hear a secret? I'm not that crazy about the sight of blood."

"Psychiatry, then."

"No. I've had enough studying. I'll join Papa's practice after this year."

She was on call Christmas Eve, but miraculously it was quiet. She managed four hours of uninterrupted sleep in the on-call room, and when her shift ended at noon on Christmas Day she felt almost human. She went home to change and to pick up the bottle of good cognac and the box of chocolates she'd bought for Dr. Meinhoff. The house was quiet. Most of her fellow boarders had gone off to family or friends. Frau Lindemann had said that after church she was going to spend the day with a cousin, and that her boarders would, in any event, be on their own.

She had told Margot that she could make herself a sandwich if she so chose, but Margot had assured her it wouldn't be necessary.

She took a leisurely bath, enjoying the unaccustomed luxury of not having to hurry to make the bathroom available for the next customer. She washed her hair, and after drying off put her robe back on and returned to her room where she worried for a bit about what to wear. A skirt? A dress? Slacks? She should have asked Brigitte or Hedwig what the custom was on Christmas.

She knew she wouldn't go to her relatives on one of the Jewish holidays in pants. Did that hold true here for Christmas as well? Better to play it safe, although a dress meant stockings and a garter belt and a slip. What a pain. No wonder men got further than women in the world. They didn't have to worry about girdles or garter belts. She'd given up girdles after one memorable time when she'd been snookered into buying a Playtex that, when worn, felt as though she'd been forced into a sausage casing. Or an iron maiden. But even garter belts were a nuisance, and while nylon stockings and heels did make her legs look good, she'd as soon slip on a pair of jeans.

She settled for her black wool dress, a simple top with a flared skirt, and the single strand of pearls her mother had bought her when she graduated from Vassar. She put on matching pearl stud earrings, and after applying a bit of lipstick, put a dab of Muguet de Bois perfume behind her ears. Satisfied that she'd pass muster, she took her coat and purse and locked the door behind her.

Willy had offered to pick her up, but she had declined, and she walked down the desolate streets, looking at the houses she passed. Unlike America, where every Christian door boasted not only a wreath but strings of green-and-red blinking lights, here the houses were unadorned.

But there were lights on in many of the houses, and, where the curtains weren't drawn, she saw groups of people moving about in the rooms. It was dusk, and she moved quickly. She wondered where John was. They had spoken yesterday. His father had come out of his coma but was still unable to move his left arm, and his speech, though recovered, was still somewhat slurred. They were moving him, shortly, to a rehabilitation center, and they hoped for further recovery.

"But I don't know whether he'll be able to resume his practice," John had reported.

"What does that mean for you?"

"It doesn't change anything. Father knew I wouldn't join his practice. If he can't go back I imagine his partner will buy him out. That was always their agreement."

"That's good, then. Any idea when you'll be able to get away?"

"Not yet. Once he's back home, and settled . . . . But I don't want to leave Mother until then."

"Of course not," she'd said, although she'd had the suspicion that Mother might not want to be left even after Dr. Watts' return, especially not if the departure was Margot-connected. She had not, of course, shared that suspicion with John. He had enough to worry about, and it was, in any case, probably an unworthy thought. True, maybe, but still unworthy.

Willy greeted her at the door with an enthusiastic hug. He had a glass of brandy in his hand, probably not the first judging by the ruddy cheeks and effusive greeting. He took her coat, brushing her throat—inadvertently?—as he helped her off with it.

"This is for your father," she said, handing him the package.

"You needn't have," he said.

"I wanted to."

He ushered her into the living room where a fire burned cheerfully. Although Margot had been at the Meinhoffs several times she had never been in this room before, and it had an unused look. The sofa, a dark blue with wooden arms, sat against the wall facing the fireplace. At either arm was a drum end table with leather inlay, on each of which rested a china-based lamp. Brigitte leaned back on the sofa, her legs curled under her, her shoes on the floor. She, too, held a brandy snifter in her hand, and she waved it at Margot. Her blond curls gleamed in the firelight. She was wearing a red dress with narrow long sleeves, cut low in front. Margot was glad she'd opted for her dress as well. Sophie rose from one of the armchairs and came over to greet Margot. She wore a long black skirt, with a white silk blouse. A slender gold chain adorned her neck and fell into the vee of her blouse.

"I'm glad you were able to make it," she said to Margot. "Willy tells us your young man couldn't get away."

"Right, his father is ill."

"Bad timing," Brigitte commented.

"Very," Margot agreed.

"You remember Pauline?" Willy nodded to the woman seated on the sofa next to Brigitte.

"Yes, hello. How are you?" Margot said.

"And this is Herbert Köhler, an old friend of my father's."

The gentleman rose from one of the armchairs. He was short, round, with a head as bald as a light bulb. He wore brown corduroy slacks, a maroon turtleneck shirt, and a beige cardigan with leather patches at the elbow. He bowed from the waist, said, "*Gnädiges, Fräulein,*" and sank back into the chair to continue the conversation he was having with Pauline.

"Nice to meet you," Margot said, although, absorbed as he was by something Pauline was saying, she was sure he neither heard nor cared. *So much for social niceties*, she thought.

Dr. Meinhoff, an apron covering his slacks and sweater, came out of the kitchen. He was wiping his hands on a towel, and extended one to Margot.

"Thank you for the cognac and chocolate," he said. "It wasn't necessary."

"You're welcome. Thank you for including me."

"Our pleasure. You've met everyone?"

"Yes, thank you."

"You like goose?" he asked.

"I've never had it. But I'm sure I will."

"It's Willie's specialty," Sophie said. "Otherwise he relies on the kindness of strangers, but he does cook a good goose."

"I can cook," Dr. Meinhoff said. "Tell her, Willy."

"He can cook," Willy said dutifully. "He just prefers not to."

"Well, you're hardly ever home . . . ."

"Boys, boys," Sophie laughed.

"Can I get you a drink, Dr. Brenner?" Willie asked.

"Margot, please. And yes, I'll have a little brandy."

"You have some catching up to do," Dr. Meinhoff said. He went to the sideboard where a crystal decanter stood open. He took a snifter from the shelf and poured a generous splash which he brought across the room and handed her. Margot sat on the sofa next to Brigitte while Willy sat on her other side. Pauline and Herbert continued their conversation. Dr. Meinhoff took the chair opposite Sophie. He picked up his snifter from the end table, and raised it

"To good holidays," he toasted.

"To good friends," Willy added.

Everyone sipped. On the coffee table in front of the sofa sat a silver dish with mixed nuts. A wooden tray held an assortment of cheese, with small slices of black bread as well as water crackers. Willy leaned forward, cut a piece of cheese from a triangle of brie and put it on a piece of bread. He handed it to Brigitte, then repeated the process for Margot.

"Sophie?" he asked.

"Why not?"

"Herbert? Pauline?"

They nodded, and Willy served them all.

"Papa?"

"Yes, thank you."

They sat and nibbled, talked of Christmases past, of the hospital, of Brigitte's upcoming trip to New York. Pauline said the store had been unusually busy this holiday season. Herbert said nothing, listened, smiled at the appropriate places, and sipped his brandy. Dr. Meinhoff got up periodically for an oversight trip to the kitchen. Odors of roasting goose mingled with the smell of burning pine.

"This is nice," Margot said.

After yet another trip to the kitchen Dr. Meinhoff announced that the goose was ready. They rose, and followed him into the dining room.

"Sophie, you sit there." Dr. Meinhoff indicated the foot of the table. Then, "Brigitte, you sit here on my right, and you, Dr . . . uh, Margot, on my left. Herbert, why don't you sit next to Margot here, and Pauline on the other side. Willy, we'll let you sit next to Brigitte. But first you can help me bring some things in."

They sat as indicated while Willy followed his father out. They returned with Dr. Meinhoff bearing a large platter on which rested an enormous goose, wonderfully brown and crisp and surrounded by a halo of roasted potatoes. Willy followed, carrying a covered tureen.

Willy put the tureen on the table, left, and came back with a bowl filled with small red berries in one hand and a large bowl of mashed turnips in the other. While Dr. Meinhoff carved the goose, Willy served what turned out to be red cabbage from the tureen, then the turnips. He passed the bowl with the berries first to Sophie.

"Ah, lingonberries," she said appreciatively.

"With goose, of course," Dr. Meinhoff said. He then passed the carved goose, holding the platter while each guest selected meat and potatoes. He went back to the kitchen and returned with a gravy boat, then sat and took a taste.

"Not bad," he said modestly.

"It's delicious," Margot said.

"Your mother never cooked goose?" Dr. Meinhoff asked. "She was a good cook, as I remember."

"There were just the two of us," she said. "It would have been like cooking a whole cow."

"That's true, I suppose. We used to have wonderful dinner parties when we were first married. Your mother made a delicious sauerbraten. And her cheesecake was a work of art."

"Yes, she was a good cook."

"And did her daughter inherit her talents?" Willy asked.

"I was too busy with school. Do you cook much, Brigitte?"

"Absolutely not."

"You mean they didn't tell you the way to a man's heart is through his stomach?" Margot asked.

"Oh, they told me all right. And I told them that he could get a maid." Everyone laughed.

When everyone was as stuffed as the goose had been, Dr. Meinhoff pushed back his chair. Sophie also rose and helped clear the table. Margot and Brigitte's offers of help were turned down, so the three young people, as well as Pauline and Herbert, remained at the table.

"So, Brigitte," Willy asked. "Did you get Margot any of the information she wanted?"

"Some. I'm still waiting to hear about the rest of it. I imagine with the holidays . . ."

"When are you leaving?" Margot asked.

"The day after tomorrow."

"And when will you be back?"

"At the end of February. At least that's the plan now."

"Where will you be staying?"

"Ah. The firm has an apartment. On, I think, Madison Avenue."

"Very nice," Margot said.

"Is it? Is that near where you lived?"

"Hardly. Neither geographically nor metaphorically."

To their puzzled looks she said, "It's a different world. Madison Avenue, at least the part below 86th Street, is one of the most exclusive parts of the city. It's not only expensive, but restricted."

"Restricted?" Willy asked.

"No Jews. No Blacks. No immigrants at all, I don't think, unless they come with their servants and their diamonds. And then they'd better be from English-speaking countries. It was by custom, of course, not by law; but custom is just as powerful. There are also wonderfully exclusive shops on Madison Avenue."

"Sounds as though you'll love it, Brigitte," Willy laughed.

"Sounds as though it's calling my name."

They were quiet for a minute. "Papa and Sophie are taking a long time in the kitchen. I thought they were bringing in dessert and coffee. Should I see what's keeping them?"

"Leave them alone," Brigitte said. "You can't be hungry again."

"I left room for dessert."

"I don't know where."

"I have a special dessert pocket in my stomach."

"That doesn't sound like any anatomy I ever heard of. How about you, Margot. Have you ever heard of a two-pouch stomach?"

"Sure. In cows." They all laughed.

Just then Sophie reappeared, looking somewhat flushed, and with her hair, which she'd had in a French twist, slightly disarrayed. She carried a plate holding a fruitcake. Dr. Meinhoff followed, carrying a plate of cookies in one hand and a bowl with whipped cream in the other. His face, too, was somewhat red. *It must still have been hot in the kitchen,* Margot thought. *Or they'd taken advantage of the privacy to wish each other a special happy holiday. Good for them!*

"Coffee is coming," Dr. Meinhoff said. "Or does anyone want tea?"

No one did. Meanwhile Sophie took cups and saucers from the sideboard and put them on the table.

"The cake and *lebkuchen* are compliments of Sophie," Dr. Meinhoff announced. "So ... I decided ... *we* decided ...." He smiled sheepishly. "Well, how can you let a recipe like that get away?"

"Papa! Congratulations!" Willy beamed. "You are saying what I think you are, right?"

Sophie and Dr. Meinhoff both smiled broadly, nodded.

"This calls for a toast," Willy said. He rose, went into the kitchen and came back with a bottle of Veuve Cliquot. "From a grateful patient," he said. He went to the sideboard and got champagne flutes, then came back and struggled with the cork until it popped satisfyingly. He poured champagne into each flute, passed them around, then raised his.

"To Sophie and Papa. I wish you many years of happiness. You deserve it."

"Hear, hear," Herbert said. Everyone echoed that, and they all drank.

They sat and talked about details.

"A simple wedding," Sophie said. "Just a few friends, and immediate family. We thought we'd do it soon."

"Are you going to sell your house?" Willy asked.

"Or rent it. We'll see."

"I could rent it," Willy offered. "That way you'd have a reliable tenant, and I wouldn't be under foot here."

"I don't know about reliable," his father joked.

"You don't have to move," Sophie said. "I don't want to displace you."

"Ah, honeymooners don't need anyone cramping their style."

Sophie blushed. "You wouldn't . . . ."

"I'm twenty-eight years old. I think it's time anyway. I just didn't want to leave Papa alone."

"All right, we'll talk about it," his father said.

"There's nothing more to talk about," Willy rejoined. "Anyway, Sophie, I'm delighted. I've been hoping . . ."

Shortly thereafter Margot said her goodbyes. She had wanted to ask Dr. Meinhoff about her brother's illness, but clearly this hadn't been the time or the place.

"We can drop you off," Herbert said. "I'm giving Pauline a ride home, and it would be no trouble . . ."

"We can do it," Willy said. "It's less out of our way. Right, Brigitte?"

In the car Margot said, "That's good news about your father and Dr. Sauer, Willy. I really like her."

"So do I. And I'm not only gaining a mother, I'm getting a place of my own."

When they got to Margot's house, she said, "I guess I won't see you before you leave, Brigitte. Have a wonderful time in New York."

"Thank you. Listen, I called Herr Wolff last week. I told him that since I'd be away for a while he should send whatever he finds out directly to you."

"I appreciate that," Margot said. "Would you like my friend Chris' phone number? He's living in my old apartment. I know he's busy, but it's always good to have the name of someone when you go to a new place."

"That's all right. I have contacts through the firm . . . . But if I change my mind I can always call you. It's one of the fringe benefits of an expense account."

CHAPTER 23

Wolfenbüttel, August 1945

They had taken over the house of Dr. Frank when Willie took over the practice. Because the old man was moving in with his son in Frankfurt, the family was eager to sell the house with the practice, and Willie had been able to arrange good terms, paying off both over time. With his salary from Georg-August in addition, Willie knew he would be able to swing it.

Eva, while she missed her parents, was happy to be in a home of her own again. Willy would be starting the new school year in yet another school, but he quickly made friends with several neighbor boys, and the transition went easily.

For weeks she worried each time the mail was delivered, jumped whenever the phone rang. As time went on, however, she settled in, pushed the worry to the back of her mind, and concentrated on finding food, still a problem after the War. It was made a bit easier by the fact that, money being hard to come by for most Germans, Willie was often paid in produce or a chicken or eggs or milk, sometimes even by a side of lamb or some beef. She cooked tempting meals, trying to get Willie fattened up again.

At night when Willy was asleep and they sat in the kitchen drinking a cup of tea, sharing the tea bag because tea, too, was still hard to come by, they avoided the topic that still troubled her. They spoke, instead, about Willie's practice, about the politics at the hospital, about those of Willie's colleagues who were rewriting their histories.

"I know for a fact that Brunner was in the SS," Willie told her. "And not just the *Waffen* SS. But to hear him talk he was an early anti-Nazi."

"It's amazing how few Nazis there were," Eva said. "Do you challenge him?"

"What's the use? That's not my job. He was cleared. Heaven knows how, but he was cleared."

"With everyone afraid of the Russians, no one wants to hear about Hitler anymore. It's the same thing with our neighbors. When they talk about the War, they all didn't know anything, didn't *do* anything. Sometimes I have a hard time not saying something when they start in, but I don't want to make things hard for Willy, or for you. So I keep my mouth shut too."

"Poor Eva."

"Oh, it's all right. At least, when I hear them talking, I can think to myself that we did the right thing. We don't have to rewrite our history."

"At least we tried."

"We did more than try, Willie. How many people that you know sheltered Jews? And went to prison for it?"

"Not many. But I wasn't in prison for long. I didn't really suffer. And it was to our advantage."

"But that's not why we did it, Willie."

"But still."

"No. Don't minimize what you did. Of all your colleagues, who else was willing to employ Martin? Who was willing to take him and the boy in?"

"No one. But . . ."

"No buts. And you did go to prison. And you didn't know when you went in that it'd be for only a few weeks. You were heroic, Willie."

"You suffered too, Eva. If I was heroic then so were you. Those were bad times."

"Yes. I think the worst was before they took Martin away. Every time I looked at our Willy . . ."

"I know. I know." He took her hand. "I wanted to make it easier for you."

She looked at him hard.

"Are you saying . . . ?" She couldn't finish the sentence. He nodded, looked down.

"It was just a matter of time anyway. And one night you said the waiting was the worst part. I knew it was just a matter of time anyway . . . ."

CHAPTER 24

Wolfenbüttel, January 1964

The holidays were over. The hospital was back to normal staffing, so Margot's life was as routine again as the life of an intern ever is. Dr. Sauer—Sophie—was away. She and Dr. Meinhoff had, according to Willy, gotten married in a small civil ceremony the past weekend and were now off for a week's holiday on the Riviera. John's father was home from his rehab, and John had written that he thought he'd be able to get away in a month or so.

"So, have you moved into your new quarters?" she asked Willy when they were sharing a cup of coffee in the cafeteria.

"Not yet. I'm waiting for the honeymooners to return."

"When will they be back?"

"On Sunday. I'm making a welcome home lunch for them. Would you like to come? I'm asking Pauline and Herbert . . . and our neighbors, the Obermessers. And Frau Klebe."

"Thank you. Sure. What do you hear from Brigitte?"

He made a face. "Nothing. It's as if she disappeared into a black hole."

"I imagine she's busy."

"I imagine she's left me behind."

"Oh, Willy."

He smiled sheepishly. "That's all right. I'm only playing the wounded suitor to get your sympathy."

She laughed. "All right. You have my sympathy."

"Enough to go to a movie with me?"

"Sure."

"Are you free tomorrow evening?"

"Barring an emergency. I'm not on call again until Thursday."

"Good, tomorrow evening then. I'll meet you here at six. Maybe we can get a little supper before the movie, is that all right?"

"Sure. But Willy, you know I'm . . . ." She couldn't say 'engaged,' because she wasn't. In a relationship? Involved? Anything she said sounded lame, presumptuous. They were just going to a movie. He wasn't asking her to marry him.

"You're what?"

"Nothing. Oh . . . you know . . . about John."

"Ah, the mythical John."

"He's not mythical," she said hotly.

"I know. I'm teasing. But he's not here, and I am. How is his father, by the way?"

"Better. He's home again."

"So then where is your John?"

"We're trying for the Easter holiday." Why did she sound defensive? Was it because she'd been wondering herself? "He wants to make sure his father is all right before he makes such a long trip."

"Of course. A dutiful son. There is a mother?"

"Yes. There is a mother."

"But still, a dutiful son. Admirable."

She rose. "I'll see you tomorrow at six." She walked off feeling irritated, but she wasn't sure at whom? At John for not coming over? At Willy for questioning his reasons? At herself?

They went to see *Singin' in the Rain*, which she'd seen several times before, but never in German.

"It's funny that way,' she told Willy afterwards.

"The dancing transcends language," he said.

"True. But I like sub-titles better than dubbing."

"I do too. But apparently my compatriots don't want to read."

"It was fun, though," she said when he deposited her at her door. "Thanks."

"We'll have to do it again some time. See you on Sunday, say, about one?"

He pulled her to him, and kissed her lightly on the cheek.

"Around one," she said, slipping out of his embrace. "Goodnight, Willy."

Sunday came. She had wondered what she could bring for the newlyweds. Well brought up by her mother as she was, she didn't want to arrive empty-handed. On the other hand, she certainly wasn't a close friend, so a wedding gift would be inappropriate. She settled on a Christmas cactus, its delicate fuschia flowers like ballet dancers. Willy answered the door, and gathered her into a quick embrace before she had a chance to take off her coat. She set the plant, in its foil-wrapped pot, on the hall table, and then hung her coat on one of the pegs on the wall before picking up the plant again and following Willy into the living room.

Sophie greeted her warmly. She looked glowing, Margot thought. Her hair, in its French braid, shone in the light from the fireplace; she was tanned, her cheeks almost as pink as the cactus flowers. Margot said, "Congratulations," and handed her the plant. Sophie went to the windowsill where several other plants, looking dry and neglected, sat.

"Willie isn't much good with plants," she said, stating the obvious. "I'll have to take charge of that, I think."

"Can I get you a drink?" the plant neglector asked, coming into the living room.

"Nothing alcoholic, thanks," Margot said.

"Some coffee, then?"

"If you have it made."

"I'll get it," Sophie offered.

"No," Willy said, "I'm the host today." He left and returned shortly with the coffee, while Margot said hello to the other guests.

It was a pleasant afternoon. The guests of honor recounted their week away, including a memorable evening spent at the Casino in Monte Carlo.

"Willie put a coin into a slot machine," Sophie said. "He pulled a lever, and coins started pouring out." She laughed. "He looked at me and said, 'I think the machine is broken.'" Dr. Meinhoff smiled sheepishly.

"Well, I'd never been in a casino before."

"That's all right, Willie. You made up for it at the blackjack tables."

"Did you win?" Herbert Köhler asked.

"No, he gave it all back. Everything he won from the slot machine."

"Ah, we had fun though, didn't we?" he said.

Her eyes sparkled. "Yes, we did."

Margot wanted to ask Dr. Meinhoff (she still couldn't get herself to call him by his Christian name) about her brother's illness, but again didn't think the time was right. Finally, when she was saying her goodbyes, she said to him, "I'd like to talk to you some time about my brother."

"I don't know anything I haven't already told you," he said, with more coolness than Margot thought was warranted. *I shouldn't have brought it up today*, she thought as she walked home.

Willy was clearing away the dishes he'd washed. The last of the guests had left, and he had refused to let Sophie or his father help him.

"Go, sit in the living room. Have another brandy," he'd told them.

So they sat, sipping their brandy.

"That was nice," Willie said.

"Yes, it was. I think Pauline and Herbert have really hit it off. She told me that she's gone to dinner with him several times since our Christmas dinner."

"That's nice. He's a good man, and she deserves a little happiness."

"She's been gun-shy ever since that bastard . . . ."

"I've never heard you curse."

"There are still a few things you don't know about me, Dr. Meinhoff. But I don't usually curse. It's a failure of vocabulary.

However," she continued, "I could think of worse things to call him."

"I knew she was divorced, but I've never heard the details."

"The details," she said, "are too numerous to mention. Anything in skirts, anything young—preferably under-aged. It started shortly after they got married, when she came to his office to pick him up for lunch and found him with his secretary—on his desk! He was contrite. It would never happen again, he told her."

"And?"

"And it didn't. That is, she never actually caught him at it again. But women were always calling the house, and hanging up when Pauline said Klaus was out. And then she got syphillis. Since they'd been tested before they were married, and since she'd been monogamous, she knew it was Klaus. She left him immediately. And then he tried to get the bookstore."

"All right. That wasn't a curse. It was a description." He took her hand. "Herbert is a good man. As far as I know he was faithful to Trude even when she was an invalid and no longer even knew where she was."

"I wish Willy would find a nice girl. Do you think he and Margot . . . ?"

"What's wrong with Brigitte?"

"You haven't noticed? She's not here."

"That's temporary. She'll be back at the end of February."

"Maybe. She told me, at Christmas, that she might stay longer. Anyway, that was always only a convenient relationship. At least that's what she said."

"Yes" he agreed reluctantly. "That's what Willy always said, too. I just hoped . . . ."

"I like Margot. She's well respected at the hospital . . ."

"Ach. She's going back to America. And she has a young man anyway."

"As far as the young man goes," she smiled, "I haven't seen him. Out of sight, out of mind."

"Absence makes the heart grow fonder," he rejoined.

"Except that Willy is here. And he's good-looking, and nice, and definitely available."

"But she'll be going back to America."

"I don't see why, necessarily. She says she has no family there, and if she were to find someone here . . . and she'll have her training here, so that wouldn't be a problem."

He said nothing further, stared moodily into the fire.

"Why don't you like her?" she asked.

"Who says I don't like her?"

"I know you."

"It's not that I don't like her. She's a perfectly nice girl."

"Woman," Sophie corrected.

"Girl. Woman. She's perfectly nice. I just don't think she's right for Willy."

"Who's not right for me?" Willy asked, coming into the room with a brandy snifter and seating himself in one of the armchairs.

"Sophie and I were just talking . . ."

"I noticed that. Who's not right for me?"

"Margot Brenner," Sophie said.

"And why is she not right for me, Papa?"

"I just don't think she is."

"Why not," he persisted.

"Your backgrounds are too different."

"What does that mean?" Willy asked. "We're both doctors. Our fathers were both doctors. Actually I think we have a lot in common."

"Well, there's the religious thing."

"The religious thing!! What, because she's Jewish?"

"Yes," his father said.

"Willie!" Sophie said. "Where did that come from? You've never given a hoot about religion."

"Papa. You of all people!"

"I don't care. It's not that I care about religion, *per se*, but when people marry . . . the children . . . ." He ended lamely.

Willy laughed. "First of all, no one said anything about marriage. You're getting ahead of things. Second, even if we got married, I wasn't raised as anything. When's the last time I was in a church? When's the last time *you* were in a church? And as far as I know Margot doesn't care about religion either."

"Yes, but with Jews it's not just about religion."

"What!" both Sophie and Willy exclaimed. "I can't believe that you, of all people . . ."

"What I mean," his father said, "is that, especially after everything that's happened . . . I mean, I can't imagine that someone with her background, who lost her father and brother the way she did, I mean, the Germans . . . I can't imagine she'd want to marry a German."

"I'm not a German, Papa. I'm me."

"True, but you are German. And I'm sure that has to influence her. And she's . . . what's the word—monomaniacal is too strong, but . . . dogged? persistent? She just can't let go. I've told her everything I know, and she still keeps on. Even today, as she was leaving, she asked me about her brother again. I just don't want you to get hurt."

"I can't believe I'm hearing this from you," Willy said.

"I just don't want you to get hurt," he repeated stubbornly. Then, "Let's talk about something else. How has the practice gone? Any problems while I was away?"

So they talked of other things. Willy told them he planned to move out the following week; he'd arranged with a friend to help him move his things. Sophie was having a mover on Tuesday to move the items she wanted, but, "You won't be coming into an empty house, Willy."

"I wasn't worried," he said. "So . . . I'm going up to my room. I have an early start tomorrow."

When he was gone Sophie asked, "What was that all about?"

"What?"

"That business with Margot?"

"I don't want Willy being hurt."

"You said that. But why should he get hurt? Granted I don't know her that well, but from what I've seen of her she's a decent, ethical woman. If she's not interested in him she won't lead him on."

"She has a boyfriend."

"Then you don't have a problem. But something else is bothering you, Willie. I've never seen you like this. It's not really the religion thing, is it?"

"Yes and no. Willy's right, I don't care about religion, but if I were Jewish, and my family had been killed by the Germans I'd have some hard feelings."

"She's never given any indication of that, Willie. I don't think she sees you and Willy as typical Germans. I see the way she works with people at the hospital."

"Still, that's not marrying . . ."

"If the last thirty years have taught us anything it should have taught us to look at people as people, not as labels."

"You're right, of course."

"But?"

"I don't want Willy to get hurt."

She shook her head and dropped the subject, sipping at the last of her brandy.

"Shall we go to bed, Dr. Meinhoff?" she asked, getting up and taking the glass to the kitchen.

"Shameless woman," he smiled. "I was thinking something of the sort myself."

CHAPTER 25

Wolfenbüttel, January 1964

It was one of those raw gray days, with a dampness that threatened snow. Margot turned up the collar of her coat, pulled her scarf securely around her neck, and considered rethinking her adamant stand against hats. She unlocked the door of Frau Lindemann's house and was grateful for the blast of warm air and the smell of something baking that greeted her. She wiped her feet carefully on the mat before going further into the entry hall. Frau L. came out of the kitchen, her cheeks flushed, wisps of hair standing out from her head.

"A letter came for you, Dr. Brenner. It looks official." She reached into her apron pocket and withdrew a legal-sized envelope. Margot looked at the return address, saw it was from Herr Wolff.

"Ah, it's not really so official," she assured her landlady. "It's about my father. A friend put me in touch with this man"—she waved the envelope—"who works for the government."

"That's good, then. I was afraid . . ."

"What. That they were going to revoke my license and send me back to the states?" She grinned.

"Well," Frau L. said sheepishly, "after twelve years of the Third Reich, I get nervous around official letters."

"I can understand that," Margot said. "Thank you for worrying. I'll go upstairs and change, and then I'll tell you what he says. Okay?"

"Of course. I wasn't trying to be nosey."

"I know that. And you've been very helpful. I'll tell you what he says."

She went up to her room, changed into jeans and a tee shirt, and went to wash up. Then she sat on her bed and opened the letter. When she finished reading, she sat for a few minutes, wiped her eyes, and went back downstairs and into the kitchen, where she sank into one of the chairs. Frau L. held a potholder and the lid of a cast iron pot in her left hand while with her right hand she stirred the contents of the pot with a wooden spoon. She turned as Margot came in.

"So? Is everything okay?" she asked.

"It's not much. The man—I guess I can say his name, Mr. Wolff—said that he was able to find out that my father, after being held in Dachau for two years, was sent to Auschwitz. He worked as a doctor at Dachau, and at Auschwitz as well. According to what Mr. Wolff found out he was such a good doctor that he was even treating some of the guards and their families. Then, it seems he was caught using some of the medicine to treat the Jewish prisoners. So they shot him."

"He must have been a good man."

"A lot of good it did him," she said.

"God took him."

"It would have been nice if God had waited awhile."

"Ah . . . we don't know God's plan."

Margot said nothing. She had no answer for those people who explained evil by saying humans just couldn't understand the Big Picture. Maybe so, but any plan that included the Nazis, not to mention children starving or dying of cancer or in earthquakes, was a plan she didn't want to understand. But there was no point in saying so to Frau L. She was trying to comfort Margot, and while she wasn't succeeding, it would be cruel to say so.

"So you have your answers now," her landlady said after a few minutes of silence.

"Most of them. What I still don't understand . . . . Everyone says my brother was slow, an imbecile. That's why they killed him at Sonnenstein. And by the way, Frau Lindemann, Mr. Wolff confirmed what your doctor friend told you. They gassed Peter, but put down the cause of death as pneumonia."

Frau L. nodded, shook her head in disgust.

"But what I don't understand," she went on, "is that my mother never said anything about Peter's being slow. In fact she said he was a bright little boy."

"Maybe she was ashamed. Being a doctor's son . . ."

"I suppose. But from the stories she told, he was walking and he was talking. When we were leaving, my father asked what my mother should cook for them when they joined us in New York, and Peter said, 'Ice cream.'"

"Sometimes even people who are slow . . . . I worked with a patient once who was in a coma. He came out of the coma after several months, but his brain was severely damaged. His wife wouldn't believe it, and sat at his bedside all day every day, waiting for him to recover. He could talk. He just didn't make any sense. One day, while his wife was sitting there, she asked him what he wanted for his birthday, and he said, 'Sauerbraten.' She was sure this meant he was cured. Of course when the doctor came in— the wife called him, all excited—and when the doctor asked him 'Who's the chancellor?' the man said, 'Sauerbraten.' You see what I mean?"

"I do. And I guess it's possible, except my mother was pretty realistic about me. I mean, she was very proud of me and my accomplishments, but when something wasn't good or right, she had no trouble saying so. She wasn't like some parents I know who say, 'That's wonderful!' if their child draws a dog and it looks like a camel."

"Yes, but you were there. Your brother wasn't. Memory plays tricks. I know. My husband certainly wasn't perfect while he was alive, but as the years have gone by," she smiled, "he's practically ready for canonization."

"You may be right. The other possibility is that maybe the sickness, a high fever, left him brain-damaged."

"That's certainly possible. Or maybe he was just a little . . . off. And your mother didn't notice."

"It's something I'm going to ask Dr. Meinhoff. If anyone knows he would."

Suddenly she remembered what both Dr. Speer and Dr. Hermann had said. When she'd told Dr. Hermann that Dr. Meinhoff's son had followed in his father's medical footsteps, Dr. Hermann had asked, "The imbecile?" Now she wondered. And Dr. Speer had also said that Peter was a bright little boy, while little Willie had been slow. And that people at the hospital had whispered that Dr. Meinhoff had better hide his son. Had the Meinhoffs had a second son, one who had been retarded? She could understand that Dr. Meinhoff wouldn't have talked to her about that, especially if that son had, in fact, been taken away. But the time frame didn't fit, and two retarded boys, both killed at Sonnenstein, was too much of a coincidence.

She shook her head to clear it.

"Something wrong?" Frau Lindemann asked.

"No. I just thought of something. Could I make a telephone call?"

"To America?"

"Of course not. Just to Dr. Meinhoff."

"Certainly. Are you going to ask him about your brother?"

"I'm going to ask whether I can come over. I don't think I want to do this on the telephone."

"You'll have dinner first?"

"Let's see when he can see me."

She came back into the kitchen after making her call.

"They can't see me tonight. They have concert tickets."

"I don't suppose another day or two will make a difference. Good, I've made stuffed veal for dinner. And I've baked an apple pie."

"So fancy? Is there an occasion?"

"No. I had some apples that needed using, and the butcher had a special on the veal. Anyhow, I enjoy cooking. I never had the time when I was young. I was busy at the hospital. When we were first married my husband laughed at my efforts. Poor Gregor. He should be around now, he wouldn't believe it's the same woman." She sobered. "I'm *not* the same woman."

When she had a few minutes between procedures the next day, she called Dr. Meinhoff.

"I'm really quite busy right now," he said testily. "We're just getting settled in, Willy's moving out. And I really don't know what else I can tell you."

"I just have a few more questions about my brother."

"Well ask them then. That doesn't require a visit."

Margot was taken aback. Dr. Meinhoff had been nothing but nice, but suddenly the frost in his voice chilled her.

"Do you know what was wrong with my brother?"

"You mean was he . . . ? What *do* you mean?"

"I mean, what was the diagnosis? Strep throat? Meningitis?"

"It could have been meningitis. We weren't sure."

"Did he have a high fever?"

"Of course. Otherwise your father would have left."

"Very high? High enough to cause convulsions? Did he have convulsions?"

"Yes. Yes, he did. Very bad ones. Afterwards he wasn't the same boy. Not the same child at all."

"You mean it left him brain-damaged."

"Ah? We didn't want to think so. Martin, your father, thought it would pass. He'd been such a bright boy. Yes. Maybe it would have passed, but then they were rounded up."

"Have you ever heard of Sonnenstein?" she asked.

"What's Sonnenstein?"

"It's a place where they carried out the euthanasia program. It's where my brother died."

"That's terrible. I guess then he hadn't gotten better."

"I guess not," she said.

"Once your father was taken, and I was arrested, as I said, I never saw them again. That's terrible," he repeated. "Poor Peter. So, does that answer your question?"

"I guess so. Just one more thing, Dr. Meinhoff. Did you ever have another son?"

"Another son? Of course not. Why would you ask that?"

"I just wondered. Something Dr. Speer said."

"Speer. I wouldn't believe a word he said. Not if he told me it was raining and the water was pouring down my collar. I told you, I think he's the one who betrayed your father."

"Yes, you did. Well, thank you for your time. I think you've answered my questions, but if I have any others I hope I can call again."

"Of course, of course. I'm sorry if I was abrupt, but we're so busy right now. When things settle down I'm sure Sophie will want you to come and have dinner with us."

"That would be nice. Thank you."

"Maybe when your young man is here. When is he coming?"

"I think at the beginning of April. But we're planning to go someplace warm, maybe the Riviera."

"Well, we'll see. Anyway, I hope now that you have answers you can put all this behind you and concentrate on the future. We can't change the past, you know."

"Yes, thank you."

She hung up, thinking that was one of the stranger conversations she'd had lately. First the coldness, and then, suddenly, invitations to dinner and inquiries about John. What had just happened there, she wondered. As she scrubbed for a splenectomy at which she had to assist, she replayed the conversation. At what point had the tone changed? It was when she'd asked about Peter's illness. It was almost as though he welcomed the chance to tell her how sick Peter had been. Weird. Who had mentioned the convulsions? She couldn't be sure, but she thought she'd been the one, and that Dr. Meinhoff had jumped at it eagerly.

"Ready, Dr. Brenner?" Dr. Fränzdorff asked.

"Ready," she said, snapping on a pair of rubber gloves, and grabbing a gown from the sterile pile in the basket. After that she had no time to think of anything until several hours later when she tied off the last vein and sutured the incision.

"Good work, Dr. Brenner," Dr. Fränzdorff said as they were washing up. "You've got the makings of a fine surgeon."

"Thank you, sir. I really appreciate that."

"I mean it. I'm going to ask Prange to make you my regular backup. Would that be all right with you?"

"That would be wonderful."

"That doesn't mean you wouldn't be able to work with other doctors. It's good to get experience, and I don't want you to miss out. But as my assistant you wouldn't have to work with . . . uh, how shall I put this diplomatically?"

"I understand. Thank you.

"Yes, well. Tomorrow I'm doing a bowel resection. Interested?"

"Absolutely. Thank you."

"No thanks necessary. I know talent when I see it, and I figured I'd get my bid in before any of the other surgeons do. I've heard talk, you know."

"Talk?"

"Yes. I overheard Dr. Speisser and Dr. Frölich talking about this year's crop."

"Crop?"

"You know. Of doctors. Interns. They both said you were the best of the bunch. That's when I decided to make you an offer before they did." He grinned. "You think some of the surgical staff aren't so—how shall I say it? —up on their skills? Well, young lady, some of the interns aren't so wonderful either. Truth to tell, we don't get the first-rate doctors here. Present company excepted, of course." He smiled again. "Why should we, when the top people can go to Frankfurt or Bonn, or Cologne or Hannover? So I wanted to get my offer in first."

"I'm flattered."

"It's the truth. Why did you come here, if I may ask?"

"You mean this isn't Paris? I must have gotten on the wrong plane," she quipped. "Seriously? In New York I couldn't get a surgical residency. Not because I lacked the qualifications, except for one."

"And that was?"

"A Y-chromosome."

"Ah."

"Yes, and I just happened to call Dr. Prange at the right time. One of the interns was killed in an auto accident, and . . . ."

"Well, I'm glad. Not that the boy was killed, but glad it worked out." He extended his hand. "See you tomorrow."

After he left Margot let out a whoop. She wanted to tell John, someone. She couldn't call John. Not only would he be at the hospital, but she couldn't make long-distance calls from the phones here. She'd write him a letter tonight, airmail, but it wasn't the same thing.

She combed her hair, and headed for the cafeteria. Maybe she'd be lucky and Hedwig would be there, or Willy.

She got herself a cup of coffee and, it being close to lunch time, a roll with Swiss cheese. She headed for the tables, and spotted not only Hedwig, but Willy as well. She sank into one of the vacant chairs.

"You look happy," Hedwig commented.

"Dr. Fränzdorff just asked me to be his backup."

"That's wonderful," Hedwig said.

"Super," Willy agreed. "How did that happen?"

So she told them, and they pumped her hand (Hedwig) and patted her on the back (Willy).

"This calls for a celebration," Willy said.

"You know what that means?" Hedwig asked.

"What?"

"No more Rausch!"

"Yes," Margot agreed. "That was one of Dr. Fränzdorff's selling points."

"He mentioned Rausch?"

"Well, not by name, and not in so many words. He just said that if I were backing him up I wouldn't have to work with, and then he paused, and asked how he could say it diplomatically. I said I understood."

"That's wonderful," Hedwig said again.

"Can I take you out to dinner tonight?" Willy asked. "To celebrate?"

She hesitated.

"Problem?"

"No. I was going to write John, but I can do that when I get back. Sure. I'll have dinner with you."

"You want to come too, Hedwig?" Willy asked.

"I'd love to," she said. "But I have a date."

"With Günther?" Margot asked.

"Yes."

"Is it getting serious?"

Hedwig nodded, smiled. "I think so. He wants me to come home with him at Easter and meet his mother."

"That's very serious," Willy said. "Why don't the two of you join us?"

"Sure. Let me check with Günther, and I'll let Margot know. All right?"

"Fine. Well, ladies, I have to get back to work. Some of us aren't teacher's pets. Shall we meet here, or shall I pick you up, Margot?"

"I'd like to go home and change. It's been a long day, and I could use a bath."

"Around seven then?"

The afternoon passed uneventfully, except that Dr. Prange stopped her after she'd assisted Dr. Schumacher and told her he'd talked to Dr. Fränzdorff and that if it was all right with her, she'd be his back-up. Margot said it was more than all right.

"I've been hearing good things about you, Dr. Brenner. Even Hans Rausch says you're not bad for a woman. That's high praise, you know. Your father would be proud of you."

"Yes, sir. Thank you sir."

"He was a good man, you know. I didn't know him that well; I was a few years behind him, but he had a good reputation."

"That's good to hear," she said. He paused, seemed to be about to say something else, then turned and walked off.

Margot, Hedwig, and Günther were seated in the rarely used living room when Willy rang the bell. Margot answered the door and Willy looked her up and down, taking in her tight-fitting jeans and yellow sweater set. Her hair was tied back by a yellow scarf into a ponytail.

"You look nice," he said.

"You look nice, too. When did you have time to get a haircut?" He wore chinos and, under his unzipped leather bomber jacket, a fisherman sweater over a blue turtleneck that brought out the color of his eyes, and he smelled faintly of a spicy after-shave.

"I stopped in on the way home. Are Hedwig and her friend joining us?"

"They're in the living room. Want to come in?"

"No, let's go before there's no more food left. I thought we'd go back to *Der Weisse Hase*. This time maybe you'll have a real meal there."

Margot went back into the living room and returned with Hedwig and Günther, whom she introduced to Willy. They put on their coats.

"Shall we take my car?" Günther asked.

"You just want to show it off," Hedwig teased.

"If it's bigger than my car, and almost anything is . . . ," Willy said.

"Or we could walk," Margot suggested.

"In this weather?" Willy scoffed.

They took Günther's car, a dark green Citroën.

"Very nice," Willy said, and they climbed in, Margot and Willy in the back, and Hedwig in the front passenger seat. "And very comfortable," he added.

"I like it," Günther said. "I hadn't planned on getting a car, but when I have to go from job to job it saves time."

At the restaurant they were greeted by Frau Lempke, who took them to a table near the fireplace, where a fire burned cheerfully.

"Is this all right, Dr. Willy?"

"It's fine. We're celebrating, so maybe a nice bottle of wine?"

"Certainly. Red or white?"

Willy looked the question at the others. They settled on white, and their hostess returned shortly with a bottle of *Kellerschwartzekatze*. She showed Willy the label.

"Unless you want something fancier," she said, "this is a nice wine."

"Something fancier will have to wait until I get a promotion— and a raise," he said. "This is fine."

"Nice," Günther said, after tasting his wine. "So what, exactly, are we celebrating?"

Hedwig told him, explaining why being made a back-up was cause.

"You make me want to stay out of surgery," Günther said when she was finished. "In fact, out of hospitals."

"Yes, hospitals are no place . . . ," Margot started

"For sick people," Willy finished.

"I think that's a joke only doctors find funny," Günther observed.

"I think it's pretty funny, too," Hedwig said.

"Well, you would. You're in the same business."

They all laughed, then looked at the menus.

"I think I'll have the chicken," Margot decided.

When their food came, they attacked it with gusto. Willy offered Margot a taste of his stew, which she declined.

"It's funny," he said. "I've always eaten everything. Maybe it's because during the war food was so scarce."

"I don't know," Hedwig said. "We didn't have much either, and there were times when we ate flower bulbs, yuck! But there are things I don't eat . . . even besides bunnies."

"Yeah, I can't stand asparagus," Günther said.

"How about *shwartzwurtzel*?" Margot asked, wrinkling her nose in distaste.

"I love it," Willy said.

"My mother did, too," Margot said. "She'd make it every winter, and couldn't understand why I thought it was vile. She thought I was just being stubborn."

"I don't like it either," Hedwig said. "How about rhubarb?"

"Yum," Willy and Günther said together.

"I can take it or leave it," Margot said.

The talk turned to politics.

"The Americans are getting into a mess in Vietnam," Günther opined.

"They should have learned something from the French," Margot agreed, "but there are people who say if we don't stop the Communists there all of Asia will fall."

"Are you one of those people?" Willy asked.

"Not at all. But John's parents . . . John is my boyfriend," she explained to Günther, "and all their friends do."

"If Kennedy had lived," Hedwig said.

"I don't know that anything would have been different. Although he was a smart politician, and what's happening in Vietnam isn't very smart."

"He did send 'advisors,'" Willy pointed out.

"Yes, but that's different from troops. I don't know what Johnson thinks he's doing. I'm really not up on what's happening, though, because as you know I've been here since last summer."

"Kennedy stood up to the Russians in Berlin and Cuba," Willy said. "So he probably would have wanted to stand up to them in Vietnam, too."

"Are the Russians in Vietnam?" Margot asked.

"Of course not," Günther said.

"Then . . . ?"

"You know, the Domino Theory. That's what the Americans say to justify it."

"It seems to me there are better ways of fighting the Communists," Margot said. "We did it with the Marshall Plan. I don't see why we couldn't do something similar in Southeast Asia."

"Tell it to your politicians," Günther said.

"Sure. And they'll listen to me. If I were home I'd join one of the peace groups, but from here . . ."

"Well," Hedwig said, "I think countries should mind their own business, not worry about what's happening thousands of miles away."

"You don't think the British should have done something about Hitler while there was time?" Willy asked.

"That was different. Hitler was a threat to world peace."

"And Ho Chi Minh isn't?" Margot asked.

"Who knows? At least he hasn't annexed his neighbors, like Hitler did with Czechoslovakia," Günther rose to Hedwig's defense.

"I think world disarmament is the way to go," Willy said.

"That's not going to happen in our lifetimes," Günther countered.

"You're probably right," Margot said, "but it would be nice."

When they had finished their meals, Frau Lempke brought the menus back.

"Dessert?" she asked. "We have some nice apple strudel with *shlagzahne*. I just made it this afternoon."

"Fine," Willy said. "Anyone else?"

When their desserts were finished and the bill paid—Willy wouldn't let her contribute, "It's your celebration," he said—they went back to the car.

"That was nice," Günther said, "thanks for including me."

Back at Frau L.'s, Willy and Margot got out.

"I'm going over to Günther's for a while," Hedwig said. "He wants to show me some of his drawings."

Margot smiled. Willy gave her a puzzled look. "In America," she explained as they went up the walk, "when a guy says to a girl 'Do you want to see my etchings?' it means 'Let's go to bed'"

"I think Hedwig and Günther are past that stage," Willy said. "They'll be married within the year."

"You think so?"

"I'd bet on it."

"You may be right. I'm happy for her. He seems like a really nice guy."

They were at the front door. Margot took out her key. Willy pulled her to him, and kissed her enthusiastically on the mouth. She pulled back.

"I'm sorry, Willy," she said. "I'm . . . ."

"Yes, I know. The elusive John. Don't worry about it," he grinned. "That was just friendly."

"Okay. And thanks. I had a lovely evening. Really."

"Good. I did, too. But tell your John that he'd better buy those tickets soon."

He waved, turned, and left, still grinning. Margot went inside, and walked slowly up the stairs, thinking that the kiss had been nice, that it had been a long time since she'd been kissed, and that, indeed, John had better buy those tickets soon.

It's not as though his father is still at death's door.

CHAPTER 26

Wolfenbüttel, February 1964

It had been a hectic day. Dr. Fränzdorff had had two scheduled surgeries, a routine hernia repair, and a tricky thyroidectomy, at each of which Margot had assisted. As they were changing after the last procedure, Dr. F was paged: a nineteen-year-old with a burst appendix was on his way upstairs. So they'd scrubbed again, put on sterile gowns, and gone to work. By the time the boy was on his way to the recovery room, Margot was a zombie. Dr. F shed his gown and gloves, washed his hands, and sank onto a chair. He sat there for a good five minutes, legs stretched straight out, eyes closed, just breathing in and out.

"Are you all right?" Margot asked.

"Just exhausted. That was a scary one. I hope he makes it."

Margot nodded, too tired to answer. He opened his eyes, looked at her.

"Get some rest," he said.

"I'm on call tonight."

"You could lie down in the on-call room. Things are quiet right now."

"I'm too jumpy to sleep. I think I'll go down to the cafeteria and get some milk."

"Maybe they'll warm it for you."

"Maybe they won't. But at least it's not coffee. Good night, Dr. Fränzdorff."

"Good night, Margot. Thanks. Having you assist really makes my job easier."

Buoyed by that praise, she made her way toward the cafeteria where Willy sat at a table with a cup of coffee and a sandwich. She joined him.

"You on call too?" she asked. Then, "Silly question. You're not here for the gourmet food."

"Sure I am. And for the chance you'd drop in." He stood and pulled out her chair. "You look beat. Hard day?"

"And a long one, too." She told him about the surgeries. "Dr. F is really good," she said. "I don't think that boy would have made it with another surgeon. He should get down on his knees and thank God it wasn't Rausch in the OR."

"But he'll never know how lucky he was. You're not going to tell him."

"Of course not, at least not about Rausch. But if I see him I will tell him that he's lucky he had such a good surgeon."

"He had you, too."

"Me. I just do the routine stuff."

"That's not what I hear."

"What do you hear? From whom?"

"Oh, word gets around. That you're really gifted with a scalpel."

She smiled, pleased. "Dr. F is generous. He gives people credit. He teaches. He makes me proud of the profession."

"You sound as though you're in love."

"With Dr. F?" She paused, smiled. "Well, maybe, like a father."

"You really like surgery, don't you?"

"I love it. To be able to go into a person's body and fix it . . . . It's like nothing else."

"Me, I don't think I'd want to do that."

"You didn't want to specialize?"

"With my grades? I was lucky I got an internship."

"Can I ask you something . . . delicate?"

"You want to marry me?" He grinned.

"No, seriously. Can I?"

"Of course."

"Your grades . . . ." She stopped. "Why . . . er . . . did you always have trouble in school?"

"Trouble in school? No. As a matter of fact, I studied hard, was a good boy, got all ones through Gymnasium and University. But after I got into med school I decided it was time to have some fun. What did your Benjamin Franklin say? 'All work and no play makes Willy a boring guy'?"

"Something like that. So, you weren't slow in school?"

"Slow? Why would you think that? Okay, my grades were mediocre, but I figured out that all I needed to get through med school was to pass. And it wasn't as though I wanted to go to some big city hospital. I wanted to come back here to be close to Papa."

"I just thought . . . . Well, to be honest . . . . You know I've been talking to some of the people who knew my father, in Hannover. And they said . . . ."

"What?"

"Well, they implied that you weren't so . . . sharp."

"Me?? I think you must have heard them wrong. It was your brother who was retarded. He couldn't even walk or talk, my Papa told me."

"That's not what they said. They said there were jokes in the hospital about it, that your father had better keep you hidden . . . but, obviously, it was just a developmental thing. There's certainly nothing wrong with you now."

"Why would they say that, those doctors?"

"I don't know. Maybe because your dad did the right thing and they didn't. One of them was a real Nazi. The other one was just a coward. He said that himself, apologetically. So maybe that was why. To get even with your father, somehow."

"That makes sense. But next time my father makes a remark about my medical school record I'll tell him that I did pretty well for an idiot." He smiled, patted her hand. "Are you free Saturday night? They're having a Gary Cooper festival at the theater, and on Saturday it's *High Noon*. I love that movie."

"So do I. I'm working Saturday, but I'm not on call, so it should be fine, unless there's an emergency."

They agreed that he'd pick her up at seven, and he bussed his tray and cup while she lingered over her milk and the lonely piece of pound cake she'd found on the shelf.

Strange, she thought. *Maybe it was just that Dr. Speer and Dr. Hermann were trying, somehow, to put Dr. Meinhoff down, but it didn't really make sense. And her brother had been killed at Sonnenstein where they killed mental defectives. Normally . . . God, how can I use the term 'normally' about those awful crimes . . . but normally Jewish children were taken to the extermination centers with their parents, where the mothers and children were gassed while the fathers, if they could work, were spared to be worked to death. But her father had been a doctor, and they'd used him. So maybe that's why they'd sent Peter to Sonnenstein.* It was less clear now than before she'd started looking into it all. Maybe she should just have left it alone. Whatever the reason, her father and Peter were dead. Still . . . her mother had never said Peter was slow, that he couldn't walk or talk. Okay, maybe he had had meningitis and that had left him damaged, but that still didn't explain why Dr. Speer and Dr. Hermann said that the Meinhoff boy had been an imbecile. "Very strange," she said aloud.

"Talking to yourself, Doctor?" Klaus Shüler asked. He carried a cup of coffee, and sank into one of the chairs next to Margot. "That's a bad sign."

"Long day," she said. "Two scheduled surgeries, and one emergency."

"That'll do it. And you're obviously on call tonight."

"Sometimes it works out that way."

"So why aren't you crashing?"

"Too wound up. But I'm going to go and lie down for a bit and hope there are no more emergencies tonight."

"I'll try to cover for you. I just came on at six, and I'm still reasonably alert. Unless it gets too crazy . . ."

"Thanks, Klaus."

"It's nothing. After you let me go home over Christmas, I owe you."

The next evening Willy was having supper with his father and Sophie.

"You're a stranger these days," his father said.

"I'm busy at the hospital." He speared a piece of potato, dunked it in some of the pot roast gravy, and put it in his mouth. "This is good," he said to Sophie.

"Yes, it is," she answered. "I didn't cook it, of course. Frau Hamburger did."

"Well, it's good. That's the one problem of living on my own."

"You're always welcome here, Willy."

"I know. And I appreciate it, but I'm a big boy. Anyway, usually I have my main meal at the cafeteria, and then just have a sandwich or something for supper. Unless I go out."

"Is Brigitte back?" his father asked.

"No. I had a postcard from her last week. With a picture of the Empire State Building. She's staying another month, at least."

"That's too bad."

"I think she's found someone else."

"Oh, poor Willy," Sophie said.

"That's all right. I'm not going to throw myself into the Oker. I've got consolations here in Wolfenbüttel."

"Margot?"

"Yes."

"I wish you wouldn't," his father said.

"We went through this, Papa. I'm a grown man."

"But you don't know everything."

"I never said I did, but what's that got to do with anything. I know who I like. And she likes me."

"She's got a boyfriend, Willy."

"Have you seen him? No? Neither have I."

"She's going to break your heart, Willy."

"Why do you say that, Willie?" Sophie asked. "She's a perfectly nice, decent young woman."

Willie chewed on a piece of meat, and said nothing, his mouth set in a straight line. After a few minutes, while both Willy and Sophie regarded him quizzically, he continued. "She called me again the other week, you know asking me all sorts of impertinent questions."

"Impertinent?" Sophie asked.

"Yes. About whether Willy had been slow, about whether we, Eva and I, had had another son."

"Those are strange questions," Sophie said, "but *impertinent?* That's a pretty strong word."

"Do you go around asking people questions like that?"

"Of course not, but she's trying to find out what happened to her father and brother."

"And what do these kinds of questions have to do with that?"

"I'm sure she had a reason, Willie. I know the woman. She's . . ."

"She did have a reason, Papa. She told me. She said that a couple of your old colleagues told her I was retarded, or something. But then she also said that it was probably because they still resented the fact that you were a hero and they weren't."

"You obviously aren't retarded. And no, Willy. Your mother and I only ever had one son."

"But Papa, you said that Margot's brother was slow. And she says her mother says he wasn't, that he was walking and talking early and . . ."

"She probably didn't want his sister to worry that she had bad genes or something. Or maybe she was just doing what people often do after someone dies, you know, remembering just the good things."

"You'd think she'd know whether her son could walk and talk."

"What do I know? But see, Willy, that's why I think you shouldn't start anything with her."

"Huh? What's the one thing got to do with the other?"

"I just have a bad feeling about it. Look at the dissension she's causing between us."

"*She* isn't causing any dissension. You're the one who's telling me . . . and anyway, there's no dissension. Just because I don't agree with you . . . ."

"I just don't think it's a good idea."

"Give me one good reason, Papa. A *good* reason."

"I don't want you to get hurt."

"I don't want to get hurt either, but that's not a good reason. And don't tell me she's from America, or that she's Jewish, or other garbage like that. If you can't give me a good reason . . . ."

"I think those are all good reasons."

"What do you think, Sophie?" Willy asked.

"I think I'm staying out of this one. In fact, I think I'll put on the coffee." She rose, but not before giving her husband another long look.

After Willy left, and he had helped Sophie dry and put away the dishes, Willie said, "I'm not tired. I'm going to stay up awhile and read."

"You could read in bed."

"I'm restless. You go on. Don't wait up for me."

"Ah, how soon marriage kills romance."

He gave her a hug. "That's not it. I'm just . . . ."

"I know. I'm teasing. Are you upset about the argument with Willy?"

"No. Maybe. I just have a bad feeling about this, Sophie."

"Want to talk about it?"

"There's nothing to talk about. It's just a feeling, and clearly Willy isn't going to listen to me."

"Did you listen to your parents when you were his age?"

"All the time."

"Really?"

"No. By the time I was Willy's age, my father was dead. And my mother loved Eva."

"And if she hadn't? Would you have listened?"

"Probably not. I don't know. We were taught to respect our parents."

"Right. But would you not have married her? My parents didn't approve of Alex . . . ."

"Why not?"

"He was a poor boy. His father was a laborer, his mother a maid. His two older sisters worked to help pay for his schooling."

"And your parents objected?"

"Oh, not to him. They couldn't object to Alex. He was bright and witty and . . . but he wasn't of our class."

"So you were a rebel."

"Obviously. Or I would have never have gone to medical school. I would have married the boy my parents had chosen for me and led a conventional, miserable life."

"And whom had they chosen?"

"Gustave Shumacher. His father owned steel mills, and his mother's family had a title."

"And what was wrong with Gustave?"

"Other than that he had a body odor, and was a head shorter than I?"

"Yes. Other than that."

"His politics smelled worse than he did."

"And still your parents thought he'd be a good match."

"My father said he could stand on his money."

"What did they say when you said you wanted to marry Alex?"

"I didn't tell them. We eloped."

"How romantic. And were your parents reconciled after the fact?"

"They disowned me. And then the war started. They were killed in Dresden, and after the war I inherited what was left of their estate. Ironic."

"Poor Sophie," he said. He hugged her again.

"Sure you don't want to come to bed?"

"I'll be up in a while."

After Sophie went upstairs, Willie poured himself a shot of cognac. He took it into his study and sat staring into space, thinking. He couldn't let the thing with Willy and Margot go on. It was a disaster waiting to happen. But if he told Willy why . . . impossible. Never mind that he'd only had Willy's best interest at heart. He'd—maybe—agree that that had been so about the switch of children. It had, after all, saved his life. But after the war? He'd want to know why they hadn't told him the truth then. And what could he say? There were good reasons. Eva had agreed that Willy was better off with them, but would Willy? And he'd say he had a right to know. Young people only saw things in black and white.

Maybe he should tell Sophie. But then she'd know he hadn't been the man everyone thought he was. Not that he'd ever bragged. In fact, every time someone called him a hero he'd tried to minimize it . . . but still. Sophie was a thoroughly decent woman. How would she react to what they—he—had done? Would she understand? Where was that confounded boyfriend? If there even was a boyfriend. Maybe she had made up the whole boyfriend thing because women that age didn't want to look as though they'd been left on the vine. A woman with a boyfriend was always more attractive than an old maid. Not that she was an old maid, of course; she was only twenty-five. But still. Maybe he could get Willy to realize she'd made up the boyfriend. Then he'd see she wasn't the woman he thought she was. No. What was he thinking? He had no reason to think the boyfriend wasn't real. Still, that might be a useful tactic

The thing was, what good would telling Willy now do? That was the thing. It would just upset him. Sure, there was a whole philosophy now of telling adopted children they were adopted. And then what? Then they suddenly wanted to go and find their 'real' parents. There was such a thing as too much honesty. He and Eva had been Willy's real parents. Willy always said he had the best father a man could have. That had to count for something. But if he told him the truth? Would he still think so?

He drained his cognac, got up, and refilled the glass. What to do? He wished he could tell Sophie, talk to her. She was not only intelligent; she was wise. Maybe she'd know what to do, how to proceed. But he didn't want to risk losing her good opinion.

There was no rush. Willy wasn't going to run off and marry Margot. It would be Easter soon, and the boyfriend was supposed to come for Easter. That might settle the whole thing. No point rushing into something that, once started, couldn't be undone. As he used to tell Willy when he was a little fellow, 'What you don't say you don't have to apologize for.'

He drained his glass, washed it out, and went upstairs. Sophie was still awake, looking beautiful with her blonde hair loose and touching the thin straps of her silk nightgown.

"Is that offer still good?" he asked, and when she smiled he went to her.

CHAPTER 27

Wolfenbüttel, March 1964

The days were getting longer again. On some days, when she came home from the hospital it was still light out, and there were the beginnings of swelling on the branches that, with a little imagination, might be baby leaves. On some days she could walk home with her coat unbuttoned.

Then, of course, would come a week of cold and rain and she would wonder whether spring would ever come. But that was March, and it was no different here than it was in New York. In like a lion and, she hoped, out like a lamb. Easter was less than three weeks away. Passover too, although there was no one here who celebrated, or even talked of, Passover. If she were in New York she'd be invited to one of her aunts for the Seder. If she were in New York she'd be invited to the Watts' for Easter Sunday dinner, and Annie would cook a ham, and Margot would push it around on her plate while Mrs. Watt said, "Oh, that's right, dear. You people don't eat pork."

John had written that he'd fly over on April 9th. She'd meet him in Hannover, and from there they'd fly to Nice, rent a car, and drive to a hotel on the beach. She couldn't wait.

In the meantime work was going really well. She was feeling more and more comfortable doing surgery. Dr. Fränzdorff was letting her do simple procedures by herself, just being there to back her up. She couldn't wait to tell John. Letters were fine, but it wasn't the same thing as being together. It was nice that Willy was around. He was a real friend, a good listener. They had fun together, too. When they were free at the same time they'd go to a movie or grab a bite.

He had finally taken her to a jazz club, and they'd heard The Modern Jazz Quartet, a terrific group who were touring Germany and, miracle of miracles, had actually made a stop in Wolfenbüttel. She'd loved watching Percy Heath on bass. He looked like a prince, tall and lean, his face intelligent and serene while he played.

Willy was a real jazz nut. He had records of groups she'd never heard of before, and many that she had. With some of his first earnings, he'd bought himself a good phonograph, and whatever money he could spare, he said, he poured into LPs. Sometimes, when they were not working, she'd go over to his place and they'd listen to records for hours: Armstrong and Gillespie, Artie Shaw, Billie Holliday, Bessie Smith, Miles Davis, Ella Fitzgerald, Benny Goodman, Ray Charles. Sometimes she'd bring food and cook it. Other times they'd just snack on salami and cheese and a good bottle of wine.

While he'd kiss her goodnight, chastely, at the end of an evening together, he never pushed, clearly accepting the fact that she was committed elsewhere. So they were just friends. Except that he kidded her about John, saying he'd have to see him before he believed in him, and that if he didn't show up this time then he, Willy, was taking over. He was giving her fair warning. She'd shown him a picture of John, of the two of them together at their graduation, both in their gowns and hoods. Dr. Watt, as was customary for doctors who had sons or daughters getting their MDs, had hooded John at the ceremony. So had the other fathers (and the one mother) who were also doctors. Margot had told Willy about that, and about how sad she'd felt that her father wasn't there to hood her. The fact that her mother hadn't lived to see her graduate only exacerbated the sadness.

Seeing the picture Willy had said, "A good-looking fellow, your John. Of course, that could be anybody."

"Why would I make that up?" she asked.

"I'm joking. It's just that we've all heard so much about John, and I've never seen him."

"Well, I'm showing him to you."

"Will I get to meet him when he comes?"

"If you want to come to the airport in Hannover. He's not coming here."

"Ashamed of your Wolfenbüttel friends?"

"Of course not. But time is limited, and we want to get to the Riviera."

"Well, I can understand that. Still, I hope I get to meet him some time."

"I hope you do, too. I think you'll like each other."

"Except that he's got my girl."

"I'm not your girl."

"Not yet. But, as I said, if John doesn't show up, I'll move in."

"Okay, I've been warned. I'll tell him."

When she asked whether he'd heard from Brigitte, he shrugged. "A postcard or two with a couple of lines: 'Having a wonderful time. Staying another month.' Stuff like that."

"You'll find someone else, Willy. You said yourself it was never serious."

"True. But a guy doesn't like to be thrown over."

"Poor Willy. You'll find someone. At the hospital half the women are in love with you."

"Sure, but not the right women."

"One of them will be, just wait."

"I know the one I want. And I am waiting. I'm a patient fellow."

When he drove her home he kissed her on the lips, hard. "That's just to stake a claim," he said. "In case."

"Good night, Willy," she said, and then worried, as she went upstairs, whether maybe, in spite of his protestations, Willy was beginning to take their friendship to the next level. She liked him a lot, she really did. He was attractive and, let's face it, sexy, and if she weren't attached . . . but she was. And she didn't want Willy to get hurt. He was too good a guy. On the other hand, she'd never made any promises, and to refuse the friendship would be to doubt his . . .

what? To doubt that a man and a woman could just be friends. If she said she didn't want to be friends, that would really be hurtful. He wasn't asking for anything. To rebuff his friendship would be to say she didn't trust him, his honesty, his decency. And she did want to be friends. Truth to tell, if it weren't for John . . . .

And then she got home from the hospital one night, exhausted from a particularly hectic on call, and Frau Lindemann told her there'd been a person-to-person call for her from America.

"They said it was important, and you should call the operator. Here's the number."

Margot took off her coat and kicked off her shoes before dialing. After assuring the operator that she was, indeed, Margot Brenner, she waited through a page at the New Haven Hospital before being connected, finally, to John.

"My father had another stroke," he said without preamble.

Margot bit back the question of whether there was method in the elder Dr. Watt's malady. Instead she asked, "How bad?"

"They don't think he'll make it this time."

"Oh, John. I'm so sorry."

"Yeah. You know that blows our plans out of the water. I feel terrible. If he pulls through again, they'll need me here, and if he doesn't . . . . Well, I'll have to be here for my mother for a bit."

"You have to do what you have to do."

"I know, but I feel terrible. I want to come over. I want to be with you. I almost feel as though he's doing this on purpose . . . my father. I know that's not so, but . . . ."

"Should I fly over? I've got the week off."

"I'd love it. But I don't know. I've got to be there for my mother, and . . ."

"And she wouldn't appreciate my being there?"

"You know how she is. In time of crisis we circle the wagons. The family hunkers down."

"And she doesn't think I'm family? If we marry will that still be the case?"

"*When* we marry she won't have a choice. Told you we should have eloped."

"Well, we *didn't*." Pause. "Okay, I'm sorry, John. I hope your father pulls through."

"Not if he's going to be a vegetable. He hasn't been a very good patient up 'til this point, and if he's not going to be all right, I'd rather he didn't make it at all."

"Well . . . whatever. I'll think good thoughts."

"Thanks. I love you, Margot."

"I love you," she replied. They both held on for a moment longer, neither wanting to break the connection. Finally he said, "I've got to get back to work. I'll call you again as soon as I know anything more."

She hung up, picked up her shoes and coat, and slowly went to her room where she sat on the bed and let the anger she'd suppressed while she was talking to John come out. Damn. If at least he'd said to hold off, that maybe they could still salvage the trip. It was still three weeks 'til Easter. If Dr. Watt recovered, maybe . . . and if he didn't, and the end came mercifully quickly, then why couldn't he still come over? Because he wouldn't leave his dear mother alone at a time like this. *Be fair, Margot*, she told herself. *If it were your mother . . . If it were my mother,* she answered herself, *she'd tell me to go.* At any rate, it wasn't her mother and John wasn't coming. Well, she'd make some other intern happy again when she told the hospital she was, after all, available over the Easter weekend. And what about Willy? Maybe she shouldn't tell him. He'd said that if John defected again he was stepping in. Did she want that? She realized she was too angry to think rationally. Right now she was so pissed at John that she wasn't thinking straight. But she couldn't help wondering whether it wasn't just as well that she was finding out now where she stood as far as John's loyalties went. Between Mommy and her, Mommy . . . no, *Mother* . . . would always come first.

After a not so good night's sleep. she was somewhat calmer. She'd been so exhausted that she *had* slept, but the sleep had been restless, interrupted by anxiety dreams, none of which she remembered in the morning. She was awake earlier than usual. The only good part of that was that she was first in the bathroom, and was able to take a quick bath before the hot water ran out.

At breakfast Frau L. asked about the phone call. She'd tactfully retreated last night after giving Margot the message. When Margot told her about the again delayed trip Frau L.was sympathetic.

"He sounds like a good son," she said.

"Yes, but does he sound like a good husband?" Hedwig, who was eating a bowl of oatmeal at the kitchen table, asked. "It's why I always said I'm only marrying an orphan."

"Is Günther an orphan?" Margot asked.

"Who says I'm marrying him? But as a matter of fact, yes."

"Yes you're marrying him, or yes he's an orphan?" Margot asked.

"Yes, I'm marrying him" Hedwig smiled.

"Oh, Hedwig, I'm so happy for you," Margot said. "He's a really nice guy."

"Congratulations, Fräulein Krantz. When's the big day?"

"We haven't decided. Soon. We're not planning a big wedding, since neither of us has much family. Just a few good friends down at city hall, and then a little celebration at a restaurant."

"That's wonderful, Hedwig," Margot said.

They walked to the hospital together. It was a glorious spring day. The birds were out in full force, calling to each other. The budding leaves on the trees were a delicate green, and tulips were sprouting in the gardens they passed. Hedwig was bubbly. Margot, in spite of being happy for her, was not feeling happy for herself.

"I'm telling Dr. Prange that I don't need Easter week off," she told Hedwig, "but I'm not telling Willy yet."

"Why not?"

Margot explained.

"So go for it," Hedwig counseled. "A bird in the hand . . . ."

"I don't know. I'm not being fair to John. I mean, I'm disappointed, angry. But what kind of person would he be if he left his dying father to go off to get laid."

"A sensible one."

"No, really. One of the things I love about him is that he's responsible, caring."

"And a Mama's boy."

"He isn't. Really he's not. Come on, Hedwig. Objectively, if someone's father is dying shouldn't he be there?"

"If he could do something for him . . . . But he's in good hands, I'm sure."

"Right, but his mother . . . ."

"What can he do for his mother? He can't substitute for her husband. At least I'd hope not."

"Of course not. But . . . . Oh, I don't know why I'm defending him. I wish he'd just tell them, tell *her*, 'I'll be back in a week.' I'm so mad."

"So . . . go for it with Willy. If you and John are meant to be there's no harm done. And if not, then no harm done."

"I'll think about it. In the meantime, do me a favor and don't tell Willy. Okay?"

"Sure. But you know, once you tell Prange . . . and selfishly I'm glad you'll be around, because we're thinking of the week after Easter for the wedding, and I hope you'll come."

"Of course. I'd come even if John were here. Then you could have met him."

They had arrived at Georg-August, and Hedwig headed for the ER while Margot went off in search of Dr. Prange, who commiserated with Margot for the again-deferred vacation, but assured her that her presence would be welcome news to one of her fellow interns.

Later that day Dr. Fränzdorff expressed delight that he would not, after all, be without her services.

"I thought I'd have to use that dolt, Max Metzger."

"Oh, Max is all right."

"He still can't suture worth a damn. He's been an intern for almost a year; never mind that you're supposed to learn stitching in medical school. It's not that he doesn't have the knowledge; it's just that he's all thumbs. I wish he'd find another specialty. Dermatology or general practice."

It was true, and nothing that she and some of the other interns hadn't said among themselves, but Margot felt bad for Max. Someone should tell him, but she wasn't going to be the one. And clearly, Dr. F wasn't going to, either. So Max would become a surgeon. She just hoped he wouldn't turn into another Dr. Rausch. She doubted that, because Max was a sweet guy, and Rausch was a worm. But maybe Rausch had started off as a sweet guy too, before his inadequacies as a surgeon had turned him into what he was today. She shuddered.

"Maybe you should talk to him," she suggested to Dr. Fränzdorff.

"I'm not his father. Not even head of the program."

"Someone should, before it's too late. And you'd do it with kindness."

"All right. Maybe. I'll think about it. So . . . your boyfriend abandoned you again?"

She winced. "His father's had another stroke."

"Ah, bad timing, then. While I'm playing everyone's father, maybe I should talk to him, too. Tell him you're too pretty a woman to leave alone for so long . . . . You're blushing," he added.

When she left the hospital that evening Willy was waiting by the front door. He fell into step with her.

"So, I hear you're not going to the Riviera after all."

"News sure travels fast. Did Dr. Prange tell you?"

"No. I ran into Bernard in the cafeteria. He was practically dancing a jig that he was getting Easter off."

"Ah, yes. John's father had another stroke."

"How convenient."

"Willy!"

"Sorry. But if it were my father I'd come anyway. What can he do for him there?" She said nothing. "It's not as though he's his doctor. And even if he were, even doctors go on vacation."

"His mother . . . ," Margot said.

"His mother needs her hand held? How old is he, Margot? Seven?"

"Twenty-five, like me."

"Old enough to be a man."

"Would you leave your mother alone if your father were dying? Or," she amended, since it was possible that even as they spoke Dr. Watt was already dead, "had just died."

"It depends on the circumstances. Would I leave to go to football match? Of course not. But to see my fiancé? In a flash."

"I'm not, officially, his fiancé."

"As good as. Or so you keep telling me. Anyway, would you like to get something to eat? Drown your sorrows? Juta Hippe is playing in Hannover tonight. She's sensational. If we left now we could probably catch the last set."

"I'm not up for driving to Hannover. I had a restless night, and we have four surgeries slated for tomorrow."

"Supper then?"

"Sure, why not. But I need to stop and tell Frau Lindemann I won't be joining them."

"I have the car. We can drive by and then go on to . . . . Where would you like to go?"

"I don't care. I'm not even that hungry."

"Want to come to my place then? I've got some leftover corned beef that Sophie gave me, and we could pick up some fresh bread. And I have some cheese."

They stopped at Frau L.'s, and then at the bakery where they got the last Bauernbrot and a couple of pieces of pastry.

In his living room Margot settled into the couch.

"A glass of wine? Or a beer?" Willy asked.

"Wine, I think. Thanks."

He opened a bottle of cabernet and poured a generous amount, then went into the kitchen and came back with a plate of cheese, and some cornichons, crackers, and mustard.

"Should I bring in the corned beef and the bread, too?"

"Fine with me," she said. She kicked off her pumps, put her head back, and closed her eyes. Willy came back in, put the plate with the meat on the coffee table, and then left again, returning with a wooden board, the bread, and a knife. He sat down next to her on the couch.

"I'm sorry," he said after a while.

"What are you sorry for?" she asked without opening her eyes.

"Not for. About. I'm sorry you're disappointed again."

"Thanks," she said. "You're a good friend, Willy."

"I know I've been joking about John, and about stepping in. But you know I'm just joking. I don't want to put any pressure on you."

"I appreciate that, Willy. Right now I don't know what I want. All I know is that I'm angry."

"At John?"

"At John. At his father. His mother. I know it's not rational, but that's how I feel."

"I can understand that." He took her hand, sat quietly.

"Want to hear some music. I have a new LP. Have you ever heard of a group called the Jimmy Giuffre trio?"

"No."

"They're super. Excellent. They have this great guitarist, Jim Hall."

He got up, turned on the phonograph, and lovingly took the record out of its case. He brushed it off with a soft cloth before putting it on the turntable, then sat back down on the couch next to her while they listened.

When the record finished he cut off a piece of cheese, put it on a cracker, and handed it to Margot.

"That was food for the spirit," he said, "but the body needs something too." He took another cracker for himself, ate it, and followed it up with one of the pickles.

"Mmm."

They sat and ate and listened to other records, ending with a Toscanini recording of Beethoven's Fifth symphony. When it ended Margot got up.

"Think I'd better go home," she said, "before I get too comfortable here."

"You can stay," he said.

"Not a good idea," she answered. So he drove her home and kissed her chastely on the cheek before watching her let herself into the house.

"What a stupid man," he said aloud as the door closed.

CHAPTER 28

Wolfenbüttel, April 1964

It had been another long day, with an unexpected gall bladder operation on top of the two scheduled surgeries. Margot's feet hurt even though she'd been wearing sneakers all day and had not changed into her street shoes since she was planning to go straight home and to bed. Daylight Savings Time had begun, so even at almost eight there was still some light. The trees were in full leaf now, and the birds were twittering their evening songs before settling down for the night. Willy, waiting in his car when Margot came out of the hospital, honked the horn. She walked over.

"Hop in," he said. "I'll give you a lift."

She got in and he reached over and closed the door for her. She leaned her head against the headrest.

"Thanks."

"I heard you had a rough day."

"The grapevine really works at Georg-August."

"Only if you want it to. I asked."

"Why?"

"I wanted to know how you were doing. I haven't seen much of you lately."

"I've been busy."

"That all?"

"Confused, too."

"So confused you're avoiding me?"

"Yes. No. I don't know."

He started the car. "Want to get something to eat?"

"I don't think so. I'm beat."

"You have to eat. I haven't seen you in the cafeteria either. Are you eating?"

"Yes."

He took his eyes off the road momentarily. "You're looking thin. You've lost weight. What's the matter, Margot?"

Surprising herself she started to cry.

"Hey," he said. He took one hand off the wheel and took hers. Then, needing to downshift he let go again. He signaled, made a turn, shifted, and then reached for her hand again.

"Where are we going?" she asked.

"How about *Der Weisse Hase?*"

"I'm not up to it."

"There's a nice pub up the street from my house. Is that okay? Or we can go to my place."

"Your place," she said quietly. He looked at her, said nothing further until he pulled into a space in front of his house. He got out, came around to her side, and opened the door for her. He took her hand and pulled her up, hugged her for a moment before releasing her. They walked into the house and he headed for the kitchen.

"Make yourself comfortable," he said. "I'll see what I've got."

"I'll help."

"You're tired."

"You worked all day, too."

"Yeah, but you know it's not as intense as surgery. It's practically a paid vacation."

"Ha!," she said, following him into the kitchen. He opened the refrigerator.

"Not much," he said. "A piece of liverwurst that I'm not sure is so edible any more. I could make us some eggs. I make a mean omelet."

"I know, it's a man thing."

"Sit." He motioned with his head toward the round table and two chairs under the kitchen window. She sat, while he went to the breadbox, took out a half loaf of dark bread, and poked it.

"Not too bad," he announced. "I can toast it."

He rummaged some more in the refrigerator. Margot sat, her head in her hands, her eyes closed.

The smell of melting butter made her open her eyes again.

"I could set the table," she said.

"I've got it." He poured egg and cheese mixture into a pan, then went to the cabinet and took out plates, cups, and saucers. He took two napkins and cutlery out of a drawer and placed them on the table as well.

"I still have some coffee from this morning, but I wouldn't recommend it. And it would only keep you up. How about some wine?"

"I don't think anything will keep me up, but wine's fine."

He took out two wine glasses and opened a bottle of burgundy. By this time the omelet was ready to be turned, and he managed it with a professional flourish.

"Voila!" he said proudly two minutes later when he slid half the omelet onto her plate and the other half onto his. Bringing the toasted bread to the table, he pulled out the other chair and sat down next to her.

"Very good," she said after taking a bite.

"I told you," he smiled. "It's one of my many talents."

They ate in companionable silence. When they'd finished and Willy had filled a pan with soap and water and put the dishes in, they moved into the living room with their wine.

"Take off your shoes and put your feet up," he offered.

He sat next to her, putting her feet in his lap and taking her hand in his.

"Now tell Onkel Willy what's wrong."

"What makes you think something's wrong? I'm just beat."

"And you always avoid me . . . and cry . . . when you're beat?"

"I haven't been avoiding you. Not really. It's just that I'm confused."

"So tell me about it. Maybe I can help."

"I don't know. I miss John, but . . . ."

"He's still not coming?"

"His father died last week."

"I'm sorry, I guess. So then why isn't he coming?"

"He says he can't until he winds up his father's affairs."

"I thought lawyers did that. Is he a lawyer as well as a doctor?"

"No. Just a doctor. And a son. But . . . ."

"So when is he coming?"

"I don't know. He said he'd see. Right now his mother needs him."

"And how do you feel about that?"

"Angry. Guilty about feeling angry. Angry about feeling guilty."

He laughed. "As you said, confused."

"I think maybe he doesn't really love me, and he's just using this as a way . . . ."

"He's a fool!"

"And then I think I'm being unfair. He and his father didn't have such a good relationship, so maybe it's because he's feeling guilty that he wants to be there for his mother."

"You're a nice person, Margot," he said. He leaned over and kissed her on top of her head, then pulled her against his chest and held her.

"This is nice," she said after a bit. "I haven't been held in a long time."

He stroked her hair. She rested her head against his chest, feeling his heart beat, feeling his heat. After a while she felt him stir against her hip, harden. He tilted her head up, kissed her lips. His tongue moved against her teeth before she opened her mouth. His hands moved to her blouse, into her blouse.

"I shouldn't . . . ," she said.

"Why not? We're grown-ups. Single."

"But John . . . ."

". . . seems to have chosen. Look, I don't want to push, or force you into something you don't want . . . ."

His hand had found her nipple and was massaging it. She shivered, felt the heat between her legs, moved against him.

"Am I bad?"

He kissed her again before saying "No. Just human." He undid the buttons of her blouse and the clasp on her bra, pulling them both off, and then kissing each breast. He unfastened the snap on her jeans, and began pulling them down her hips. She reached under his shirt and undershirt, stroking the fine hair on his chest, down to his navel. He pulled his shirt and undershirt off in one motion, then unzipped his fly and peeled down his pants and underpants. He was erect and ready.

"Oops," he said. "Be right back."

While he was gone Margot pulled off her jeans and underpants, then hugged herself. 'What,' she asked herself, 'am I doing?' Forget John, but what had happened to her promise to her mother that she'd stay a virgin until she married. She and John had never gone all the way, and now here she was, still officially John's girl, and ready to lose her virginity to someone else. She started to put her underpants back on, when Willy came back into the room, still erect, a condom in his hand.

"We could go to the bedroom," he proposed.

"I shouldn't . . ."

"You don't want to?"

"I do, but . . ." She still lay on the couch, one arm across her naked breasts, the other hand trying to cover her pubic hair. She looked up at him—tall, blond, his legs, chest, and belly covered with silky blond hair. Suddenly she jumped up, said, "Peter?"

"Actually I call him Hans." Willy said with a chagrined smile, looking at his rapidly deflating penis.

"That mark," she said, pointing to his right thigh.

"It's nothing, a birthmark. It's not contagious or anything. But maybe this isn't such a good idea right now." He reached for his shorts and stepped into them.

"My brother . . . . My mother told me once that he had a birth-mark on his right leg. That looked like a mushroom."

He stood for a moment, silent, then sank onto the couch next to her. She retrieved her clothes and put them on, feeling dizzy, saying nothing. Finally, "Coincidence?" she asked.

He was dressed again, too, and still said nothing.

"But . . . ," she paused. "It's beginning to make sense. Everyone saying Dr. Meinhoff's son was retarded. Oh my God!"

"What? No! Are you saying what I think you're saying?"

She nodded.

"That they switched us?"

She nodded again.

"I can't believe it. My father wouldn't . . . my mother . . . . They would have told me. I mean obviously not during the war, but afterwards."

"They saved your life," she said.

"They doomed their own flesh and blood."

"They saved your life," she said again. "You're my brother. My God, you're alive. Peter, you're alive."

He said nothing.

"I wish Mom were alive. But you are. You're my brother," she babbled on.

He still sat, unmoving, saying nothing, staring into space, seemingly not even hearing her.

"Oh my God, Peter, we almost . . . ." She stopped, remembering. He nodded. He got up.

"I'll take you home," he said dully.

"Aren't you glad? You've got a sister. You've found me. We've found each other."

"I have to talk to my father," he said.

"I'll come with you."

"No."

"I want to hear what happened, how it really happened."

"Not now. Not yet. I'll take you home."

They said nothing in the car, and when they arrived at her house, he said, "I'll talk to you tomorrow." He watched 'til she closed the front door, and drove off.

His father's house was dark when he got there. He had a key, but he chose instead to ring the bell. He waited, picturing Sophie hearing the bell, rousing his father, his father putting on his robe before coming down the stairs and opening the door. He would think it was a patient with an emergency. Sophie would be behind him, pulling her robe closed, mumbling about inconsiderate people.

"Willy!" his father said when he opened the door. "Where's your key? What's wrong?"

"We've got to talk," Willy said.

"It's after eleven. Can't this wait 'til morning?"

"Let me in. I don't want to do this on the front step."

His father stepped aside, and Willy strode into the kitchen, the older man behind him.

"Willie, what's wrong?" Sophie had come down the stairs. Her blond hair was loose around her shoulders, her cream-colored silk robe pulled tight around her. Her feet were bare.

"I don't know," her husband said. "Willy . . . ." He motioned toward the kitchen, and she took his hand and followed him in. In the kitchen, Willy was pacing back and forth.

"You want some coffee or tea? Sophie asked.

"I want answers," Willy said. He pointed to the chairs, said, "Sit."

"Don't use that tone with me, Willy." But he sat. Sophie did as well.

"What tone should I use? You lied to me. All these years, you lied to me."

"What are you talking about, Willy? I've always tried to be truthful with you."

"So I thought. Except for one little thing . . . *Papa!*" this last, sarcastically. "No wonder Margot asked whether I was slow, or whether . . . ."

"Margot? She's poisoned you against me."

"You mean my *sister*?"

"What??" Sophie gasped.

"That's right. My sister. He didn't tell you either? I thought I was the only one who didn't know."

"What are you talking about?" Sophie asked.

"Tell her . . . *Papa*." Again the sarcasm.

Willie sat at the table, his head in his hands, saying nothing.

"Shall I tell her then"

He took a chair, straddled it, his arms hugging the back. "All right. Here's how it went, I suppose. You and Mama had a son, Willy, an imbecile. The war started. You were a doctor, you knew about Hitler's euthanasia program. Am I right so far?"

His father nodded. Sophie sat, mouth agape.

"Dr. Brenner and Peter . . . me, I . . . were living with you and Mama. When the Nazis came you gave them your son. What I don't get is how you got my father to go along with the charade. Or did he?"

"Of course he did. What do you think, that I drugged him or something? He wanted to save his son . . . you . . . and we knew poor Willy was doomed anyway."

"How neat," Willy said. "So you sent your own son off to be slaughtered. Didn't that bother you? Didn't that bother Mama?"

"Can you even ask that?"

"At this point I can ask anything. And believe nothing."

"We did it for you, you know. To save your life."

"And you got a healthy son. Not such a bad trade-off. And my father agreed?"

"He loved you, Willy."

"*Peter*," he corrected.

"He loved you. He wanted . . . we all wanted . . . what was best for you. You weren't living in that period, Willy. You can't imagine . . . ."

"You were, Sophie. Can you imagine?"

"Actually I can," she said softly. "If your fathers hadn't done what they did, it wouldn't have saved Willy. It would just have doomed you, too."

"And after the war? Didn't my real mother . . . ."

"Eva *was* your real mother!"

"Didn't my real mother ask what happened to me?"

"We never heard from her."

"Did you try to find her?"

"No," he said softly.

"What? I can't hear you. Did you try to find her?"

"No. Your mother wanted to, but I thought . . . we thought . . . we were the only parents you knew. We thought it would be too hard for you, a strange country, strange people, a foreign language."

"Bullshit! And Mama was satisfied with that?"

"She wanted what was best for you. You were our son. I could provide for you well. In America . . . even if we'd found her, what kind of life would it have been? Your mother understood."

"You mean Eva. I don't know whether my real mother would have understood."

"If she'd gotten in touch with us . . . ."

"Margot says she tried."

"Not very hard, apparently. Margot had no trouble finding us."

"I can't believe what I'm hearing. So now it's my mother's fault that you lied to me all these years?"

"I'm not saying that. All right, maybe we should have tried harder, but by then you were our son. It was easy to convince ourselves that . . . and we'd given up our son for you."

"You just said he wouldn't have survived in any case. Don't give me that crap now."

"You're twisting my words."

"Am I? Okay, maybe I can understand why you did what you did originally. But you never told me. Not even when Margot wrote. Don't you think I had a right to know?"

"That's why I didn't want her coming here."

"So the lies could continue? You don't think I had a right to know?"

"Right to know? What's so wonderful about knowing? Do you feel better now that you know?"

"Do I feel better knowing the man I respected, loved, thought of as a hero, is a liar? No, I don't feel better."

"Willy, Willy. I never said I was a hero. Whenever someone said I was I denied it."

"Yeah. You said you only did what was right. But you didn't. You saved your ass, got a healthy kid, and lived happily ever after. Sure, you even went to jail for a bit. Made you even more heroic, didn't it? You suffered for your decency. Tell me, did you take my father and me in because you'd planned the switch the whole time?"

"That's unfair."

"Is it? All right. So you weren't a total shit, and you really tried to protect us. Whose idea was it to pass me off as your son?"

"I could lie to you now, tell you it was your father's idea. But I won't do that."

"How noble of you."

"I suggested it. And I protected him as long as I could."

"And how long was that?"

"They were taken off in the spring of '40. The war started in September of . . ."

"I know when the war started. So what, seven, eight months?"

"Longer. It wasn't safe even before the war started. If you hadn't gotten sick . . . ."

"Yeah. I heard the story. So there we were, and you weren't getting food rations for us, were you? And it was dangerous harboring Jews. So what happened? How come the Nazis suddenly came calling?"

"Someone betrayed us."

"Us? Someone betrayed my father. Margot says . . ."

"Margot says, Margot says . . . . That woman has been nothing but trouble since . . . ."

"Because she wanted to know what happened to her father and brother?"

"I told her some things were better left to rest."

"Sure. Better for you."

"And for you, too. You were perfectly happy . . . ."

"Living a lie. Wonderful. Do you know how close we came to incest?"

"I tried to warn you."

"Sure. You told me she wasn't good for me, she was Jewish, she was American, she had a boyfriend. You just forgot one little detail."

"It was too late by then."

"Yeah, by about eighteen years."

"Suppose I'd told you when she first wrote? Would that have made it better?"

"A little. I still can't believe you didn't tell me when the war ended. I was almost eight. I was old enough."

"If your father had come back . . . or if your mother had written . . . ."

"Sure. Then you wouldn't have had a choice. But you had a choice. And you lied. Did you really persuade Mama that that was the right thing to do?"

"Otherwise I'd never have done it."

"How did you do that? Mama was the most honest . . . the most ethical . . . but then I thought you were, too. So maybe I was wrong about her, too."

"Don't even think that, Willy. Think what you want of me, but your mother was a saint."

"So how did you get her to agree to lie?"

"She thought it was her fault," he whispered.

"What was her fault?"

"That they took Martin away?"

"And why would she have thought that?"

"Because," he sobbed, "it was true. We had to prepare you. You were a bright little boy."

"So, not an imbecile?"

"No. You were smart, curious. We couldn't risk that you'd give the whole thing away, so your father persuaded you to play a game. He became Onkel Martin and your mother and I became Mama and Papa. You slept with us, and little Willy slept with Martin."

"And how did you persuade the imbecile to go along with this game?" he asked bitterly.

"That wasn't a problem. Willy was a sweet, lovable, loving little boy. And he didn't talk."

"Ah. So how did that make it Mama's fault?"

"It was hard on her. Seeing Willy, not being able to hug him, hold him. He was her flesh and blood. It was eating her up. The waiting."

"So   ," he breathed.

"She wasn't sleeping, wasn't eating. One night she was crying bitterly, saying she couldn't stand it anymore, the waiting was unbearable."

"And?"

"So I ended the waiting."

The chair on which Sophie had been sitting crashed to the floor. She rushed from the kitchen.

"Sophie," Willie called, "Wait." She never turned back.

"You made the call?" Willy said quietly.

"I made the call. It was only a matter of time anyway."

Willy turned without another word, slamming the house door on the way out. Willie continued to sit at the table, staring into space, shaking his head from time to time. A while later Sophie, suitcase in hand, stuck her head into the kitchen.

"I'll be at my house," she said.

When the door slammed he got up. He went into the living room, took out a glass and the bottle of cognac. He took both back to the kitchen table. He went upstairs, took a photo of Eva out of his underwear drawer. He went to his office and took a bottle of codeine out of the locked cabinet, then went back into the kitchen, set the picture of Eva on the table, and poured out a full glass of cognac. He downed it, poured another. After the third glass he went to the sink for a glass of water. Very carefully he carried it back to the table, set it down, and quickly swallowed pill after pill before downing the last of the cognac.

CHAPTER 29

Wolfenbüttel, April 1964

The sun shone through the leaves of the cemetery, dappling the stones. The grave had been dug next to the headstone that read

Eva Meinhoff, geb. Müller
August 8, 1906–October 4, 1948
Loving wife and mother
Rest in Peace

Sophie, Margot, and Willy stood to the side as the gravedigger began to fill the hole into which the plain coffin had been lowered. There had been no church service. Willie had given up religion years ago, and neither Sophie nor Willy was a believer either. They would have a memorial service at the hospital, Willy had told Margot. "We owe him that much, I guess."

Sophie wore a black silk suit. Her hair was pulled back into a severe bun. Her eyes were red, her cheeks blotched. When the coffin was covered they turned away, and walked slowly down the path and out of the iron gates.

"Come for coffee with us, Sophie?" Willy asked. She shook her head no. "I think I need to be by myself for a bit."

"Are you coming back to your house?"

"Not today."

Sophie was the one who'd found Willie. She'd gone to his house the following morning.

"We have to talk," she'd told Willy. "I can't just leave him like that."

She'd rung the bell, thinking she'd given up her right to use the key, but when there was no answer, she'd used it anyway. The moment she closed the front door she knew. She'd been a doctor too long not to recognize the smell of death.

"Oh, Willie," she'd cried. Then she'd called the police and then she'd called Willy. To his credit he got there before the police, and they'd stood there, hugging each other, both of them with tears running down their cheeks.

"It's not so black and white, is it?" she'd asked.

Willie had left no note.

"So why weren't you home, Dr. Sauer?" Detective Sergeant Pollner had asked.

"We'd had a . . . misunderstanding."

"Serious, I'd think," the detective had commented.

She'd nodded.

"And where were you?"

"With young Willy, Dr. Meinhoff's son. He's living in my house since we got married."

"Interesting. You didn't touch anything, did you?"

She hadn't, of course, and while her fingerprints were all over the house, and on the brandy glass ("Why wouldn't they be? I'm the one who put them away after I washed the glasses"), only Willie's prints were on the water glass, the pill container, and the cognac bottle. Willy had confirmed that Sophie had left the house shortly after he had, had confirmed, as well, that he and his father had had a fight, "about history," and the coroner had, eventually, ruled the death a suicide.

"Good thing he wasn't a Catholic," the detective had said, "or they wouldn't bury him in the cemetery."

Now Margot and Willy sat in the pub near the hospital, drinking coffee.

"Are you going to move back into your house?" she asked him.

"We haven't decided anything yet. Maybe Sophie will stay there and I'll stay in her house."

"What about the practice?"

"I don't know, Margot. It's funny. I want to hate him, and I can't."

"He betrayed Daddy."

"Yes. And he sent his own son off to be killed."

"But he raised you—and he did a terrific job."

"Why, thank you." He gave a self-deprecating smile. "But he betrayed our father."

"He probably wouldn't have survived the war."

"Some people did," her brother said. "Christians hid them and they survived."

"Well, they saved your life."

"Maybe. Or risked it when he betrayed our father. As Sophie said, things aren't so black and white."

"I wish Mom were still alive. She"d have loved you, too."

"I never thought I'd hear that."

"What?"

"That you love me."

"Well, I do. And John doesn't even have to worry."

"Oh, Is John still in the picture?"

"He called the other night. He's coming next week."

"Leaving Mommy?"

"Apparently."

"Will I get to meet him or is it still straight to the Riviera?"

"No. He's coming here. I want him to meet my big brother."

New Haven, July 4, 1974

John was in the backyard, putting charcoal on the grill. Margot, in khaki shorts, white tee, and sandals stuck her head out of the kitchen door.

"That was Peter. They're at a gas station off the Wilbur Cross. They should be here in about forty-five minutes."

"Then I guess I won't start the coals yet. Need any help?"

"No thanks. Claire is helping me."

A little girl of four, dressed like her mother in khaki shorts and white tee shirt, hers with a picture of Bert and Ernie silk-screened on the front, came to the door. She carried a stack of paper napkins.

"Here, Daddy," she said. "Mommy said I can set the table."

"I'd wait awhile, Honey. The wind will blow them away. But you can come and help me put the charcoal on the grill."

She thrust the napkins at her mother and burst out of the door.

"She'll get her hands all dirty," Margot's mother-in-law said from behind her.

"That's why they invented soap and water, Mother."

Mrs. Watt sighed. She sat down at the kitchen table, sipping a glass of white wine.

"It's nice you could get the day off," she said.

"I've got enough seniority . . . unless there's an emergency. Let's hope all those holiday drivers don't start drinking early."

"So your brother is coming with the new baby."

"Yes. I haven't seen her since just after she was born. Between Peter's schedule and ours . . . ."

"Is his wife working?"

"Brigitte? No, she's decided to take some time off."

"How quaint. I thought young professional women today . . . you never did."

Margot bit back a testy retort, said "No. I didn't want to interrupt my training program again. I was lucky enough to have gotten the spot at Yale-New Haven, and I wasn't going to jeopardize it. You know that. Eloise has been wonderful with Claire, and John and I were able to work it out. I don't think Claire has missed out."

"I wasn't criticizing," said her mother-in-law.

Could have fooled me, Margot thought, but didn't say. She added mayonnaise to the potato salad, and put it into the refrigerator. She took out the London broil she'd been marinating and turned it before putting that, too, back into the refrigerator.

It was a beautiful day. The lilacs in the backyard were past their prime, but the grass was a bright green, the roses her mother-in-law had planted were in riotous bloom. Claire was chattering to John, asking, no doubt, when the fireworks would start. Their cat, an orange tabby, lay on the cobbled patio, basking in the sun.

"Won't Brigitte's taking time off ruin her chances of making partner," Mrs. Watt asked, breaking into Margot's reverie.

"Probably. But I don't think she cares. Corporate law has lost some of its charm. She wants to try Legal Aid or MFY Legal Services when Eva is a little bigger."

"That doesn't pay as well, does it?"

"No, but Peter's doing all right."

Claire came banging into the kitchen.

"Is the baby here yet, Mommy?"

"They should be here soon."

"Can we have a baby, too, Mommy? I want a sister."

"We'll see," said Margot. "Meanwhile, let's go wash your hands. And your face," she added, seeing the charcoal smudge on her daughter's nose.

John came into the kitchen, went to the sink and washed his hands, drying them on the towel hanging on the refrigerator handle. He looked at his mother sipping her wine.

"Getting a head start, Mother?"

"Don't go there, John. I'm a grown woman."

"Just looking out for your health, Mother."

"Wine is good for the circulation."

"Yes, Mother."

Margot took Claire into the bathroom and helped the little girl wash her hands. She sighed.

"Are you sad, Mommy?" she asked.

"No, I'm happy."

"Then why are you making sad noises?"

"That wasn't a sad noise, honey. It was a happy noise. I'm happy because we're all going to be together to celebrate: you, Daddy, Grandmother Watt, and Uncle Peter, Aunt Brigitte, and little Eva."

"But not your Mommy and Daddy. Is that why you're sad?"

"I'm not sad." *Well, maybe a little*, she thought.

It was almost five years now since Peter had left Wolfenbüttel. After Dr. Meinhoff's death, Margot had finished out the year, and then had followed John back to New Haven, where they'd married. Willy had officially changed his name back to Peter Brenner. He'd tried keeping up the practice, but somehow the patients dwindled. And there were too many memories. He'd explored a move to America. Margot and John had helped, and through a friend of theirs from medical school, Peter had been able to get into a residency program at New York Medical College. Once he was recertified, he'd joined a practice in Washington Heights.

He'd gotten back in touch with Brigitte who was working for one of the white-shoe law firms. She was involved with some bigshot lawyer who, it turned out, had forgotten to tell her about his wife and three children. Peter had come to her rescue.

"I just wish Aunt Sophie had come, too," she said to Claire.

"From Germany?" Claire asked.

"Right. Remember she came to visit last Christmas?"

"She brought me a stiff teddy bear."

"A Steiff. That's right."

"I like Aunt Sophie."

"I like her too, Honey. Maybe that's why I'm a little sad."

"Maybe she'll come again for Christmas," Claire consoled.

"Maybe she will," Margot said.

The End

About the Author

Born in Germany, **Hannah S. Hess** came to the United States via Ecuador. She was educated in the New York City public schools, and worked as a high school English teacher, assistant principal and principal there. The mother of three children, she lives in New York with her husband, Walter, a published poet and film-maker. She is the author of *The Third Side of the Desk; How Parents Can Change the Schools.*

Caravel Books, a mystery imprint of Pleasure Boat Studio:
A Literary Press.

The Cat Did Not Die ~ Inger Frimansson, trans. by Laura Wideburg ~
$18

The Other Romanian ~ Anne Argula ~ $16

Deadly Negatives ~ Russell Hill ~ $16

The Dog Sox ~ Russell Hill ~ $16 ~ Nominated for an Edgar Award

Music of the Spheres ~ Michael Burke ~ $16

Swan Dive ~ Michael Burke ~ $15

The Lord God Bird ~ Russell Hill ~ $15 ~ Nominated for an
Edgar Award

Island of the Naked Women ~ Inger Frimansson, trans. by Laura
Wideburg ~ $18

The Shadow in the Water ~ Inger Frimansson, trans. by Laura Wideburg
~ $18 ~ Winner of Best Swedish Mystery 2005

Good Night, My Darling ~ Inger Frimansson, trans. by Laura Wideburg
~ $16 ~ Winner of Best Swedish Mystery 1998 ~ Winner of Best
Translation Prize from ForeWord Magazine 2007

The Case of Emily V. ~ Keith Oatley ~ $18 ~ Commonwealth Writers
Prize for Best First Novel

Homicide My Own ~ Anne Argula ~ $16 ~ Nominated for an
Edgar Award

Orders: Pleasure Boat Studio books are available by order from your
bookstore, directly from our website, or through the following:
SPD (Small Press Distribution) Tel. 800-869-7553, Fax 510-524-0852
Partners/West Tel. 425-227-8486, Fax 425-204-2448
Baker & Taylor Tel. 800-775-1100, Fax 800-775-7480
Ingram Tel. 615-793-5000, Fax 615-287-5429
Amazon.com or **Barnesandnoble.com**

Pleasure Boat Studio: A Literary Press
201 West 89th Street
New York, NY 10024
Tel. / Fax: 888-810-5308
www.pleasureboatstudio.com / pleasboat@nyc.rr.com